F
M 696a

03-03-97

26.95/PA

ACCORDING TO
JAKE AND THE KID

ACCORDING TO
JAKE AND THE KID

A COLLECTION OF NEW STORIES

W. O. MITCHELL

⟦A DOUGLAS GIBSON BOOK⟧

M&S

Canadian Cataloguing in Publication Data

Mitchell, W.O. (William Ormond), 1914–
  According to Jake and the Kid

ISBN 0-7710-6073-4

I. Title.

PS8526.I88A72 1989   C813'.54   C89-094821-6
PR9199.3.M59A72 1989

Printed and bound in Canada

A Douglas Gibson Book

McClelland & Stewart Inc.
The Canadian Publishers
481 University Avenue
Toronto, Ontario M5G 2E9

To Geoffrey, Sara, Tiree,
Jaime, Brenna, and Kaley,
my grandchildren — so far

Contents

PREFACE

MOST THINGS NORTH AMERICAN DO NOT SEEM TO PERSIST much beyond five decades. Stooks no longer thimble prairie fields in the fall. Except on ranches, in the foothills, the saddle horse now belongs to the show ring, the parade, the trail ride. The great-rumped farm workhorse is gone forever, his departure accomplished by the tractor, the truck, and the combine. With the increase of farm mechanization came another casualty, and of them all it seems the most shocking disappearance from the western landscape. Like the top soil of the dirty Thirties, the hired man has drifted away.

When he flourished, he came from everywhere: Russia, Poland, Hungary, the British Isles, the Scandinavian countries; his blood lines roved the world. Whatever his genesis he always seemed to be long and lean. Perhaps this was an optical illusion, since I recall him mostly from the low vantage point of a boy. As well, he always seemed to slouch vaguely somewhere between the ages of forty and fifty. He was not to be confused with the seasonal and itinerant spikers, field pitchers, skinners, and stookers, who were hired for the harvest weeks. He was a man who had joined the farm. In the first two decades of this century he worked for forty to fifty dollars a month until the Depression, when his wages were room and board and five dollars a month, or simply room and board.

Like his employer, he was a jack-of-all-trades: blacksmith, mechanic, horse trainer, carpenter, concrete expert, and vet.

When the summer fallow steamed in spring and the gulls and killdeer swung low behind him, he seeded other men's crops, hayed other men's fields, milked other men's cows, ploughed other men's gardens, doctored other men's horses, and halter-broke other men's colts. Generally he slept in a bunk-house, but ate his meals with the family.

I can recall a number of hired men: Allan, a hard-drinking tobacco-chewing Peter Pan with a wild pale-blue eye, and his face turkey-red to the line of his hair. From there up it was mushroom white. There was Ben, a non-smoking, non-drinking, non-snookering Pentecostal with a passion for Maple Bud candies, and for working out endless problems at noon and suppertime: how many grains of wheat laid end to end would stretch from the corner of the chop-house to Spaffords' north granary – 8,683,251 – a surprisingly small number of wheat kernels to reach the corner of Spaffords' granary now I think back on it. And when I visited a farm near Manor, Saskatchewan, at the age of twelve, I met Jeff, from the north of England; he could pick a sweet mandolin for "Where Do the Flies Go in the Wintertime", "Marchita", and "Roses of Picardy".

The hired man was a sort of muscular yardstick; a boy measured his strength against his in the performance of chores. He was another sort of yardstick, too; if a man had an unusually large turnover of hired men, the community soon guessed that the farmer was (a) stingy, (b) bad-tempered, or (c) married to a wife who couldn't cook guts for a bear.

Generally it was the hired man who seated a .22 rifle properly against a boy's shoulder and showed him how to squeeze the trigger to touch off a gopher. Perhaps he was able to tap a willow stick with a jackknife handle to loosen the bark so it would slip free for a whistle, to make a minnow net from an onion sack, or a pike lure from a shoehorn. A hired man might teach a boy to play rummy or hearts or cribbage or Spit-in-the-Ocean, help him to fill out a form to send away for itching powder, sneezing powder, Ventrilo, or a Ten Thousand Dollar Contest. It was most likely his fine-cut that was smoked for the first time behind the barn. This extra fine rapport between hired man and farm boy did not mean that prairie fathers were remiss in their parental duties; it was simply that most hired men seemed to have one foot in the adult world and the other in the boy's world.

The hired man's contribution to colourful language, recognized in this story collection, would be hard to assess: "enough to give a gopher's ass the heartburn", "she could eat pumpkin through a wove wire fence", or "beef to the heels like a Mullingar heifer".

It may have been mechanization that killed him off. Certainly he is not around any more for the farmer who can afford to pay five hundred dollars a month and board and room – which is what most farmers can afford – and the job has no minimum wage, no pension or retirement fund plan, and no unemployment insurance.

The hired man must be busy somewhere making the tractors and the trucks and the machinery and the combines that killed the farmhorse – and him.

W. O. MITCHELL
CALGARY, ALBERTA
MAY 1989

ELBOW ROOM

THE FIRST TIME I SAW IT WAS IN THE SPRING IN MAC-Taggart's general store, the day I went to town with my mother. I always helped her take the eggs in and get groceries, ever since my father joined up and went to England. The gun was in the window, spang between the gopher poison and the harness sort of leaned up against a cream separator. The separator was pretty, all right, with the sun glinty on its sides, but it wasn't a patch on the BB gun. You can't touch off a gopher with a cream separator.

Trouble was, there isn't so much money hanging around a Saskatchewan farm about seeding time. So my mother said maybe I could have it, but not till after harvest. It was sure going to be a long wait, and Jake said not to hold my breath, and when I asked him why not, he said he didn't think she was too fussy about guns.

It happened way back when I was young. I mean *real* young, but it doesn't keep me from remembering just like it was yesterday: fall – harvest time – last year of the war and my dad was over there and Jake, our hired man, really running our farm down Government Road from Crocus, which is on the CNR line between Tiger Lily and Conception. My dad got killed just a week after we talked to him on the CBC, which was the best Christmas present Ma and me ever got. Jake's stayed on with us ever since. Maybe I haven't got a father any more, but I got Jake.

I keep remembering our stooker Jake hired that fall. Pretty hard to forget him the way the *Crocus Breeze* wrote it up. Got into all the city papers too, but they didn't tell everything; they didn't say a thing about my Little Daisy BB Gun, and I'm going to tell it right.

As soon as the snow melted and left the summer fallow bare naked and steamy under the sun, Jake got the tractor out and I rode behind him with the crows calling after us all over the south quarter. Jake's our hired man and not very big, but soople and and spry as anything. He's the only man ever threw Looie Riel three times in a row. And when Looie said Jake didn't wrassle fair, Jake didn't say a word, just tied his hand behind his back and took Looie on again. Made him say "Uncle" three times: once in English, once in French and once in Cree. It's a funny thing, but every time I tell Jake about somebody in Canadian history, he always knows a lot more than Miss Henchbaw told us. Miss Henchbaw says Jake doesn't stick to the facts. She says Looie Riel was hung about the time Jake was born, but I believe Jake before I believe her. She's a dick-tater, Jake says. Like Hitler. Jake says Hitler's a pretty bad potato.

Well, after we got the crop in, we watched the green sort of blush up – first in the slough spots. There's a pretty thing for you! All summer, we watched the sky, and whenever our wheat needed rain, the popcorn clouds got out of the way for the fat, grey-bellied ones that knew how to rain. Halfway through August she really got hot. Hot and still. So still the gophers squeaking sounded not right – like people whispering in church. Jake got out our binder and started cutting on the twenty-five-acre field. If only she didn't hail before we got her cut. My air rifle was in that crop!

The third day Jake was on the binder, I took his lunch out to him, and after he ate, he said he had time for just one game. This game we had was a good one Jake and I made up ourselves and called Night Patrol.

Jake gave me a hundred. I lit out over the stubble, ducked under the barb wire, got through the windbreak, and dived into the tall ditch-grass beside the road. I rolled over and lay there trying to get my wind back, listening to Jake counting far away hardly louder than the wind whispering in the grass around me.

A person feels very sort of peaceful lying on their back under a whole lot of sky. I could hear the wind going like when you blow on tissue paper. Somewhere a gopher squeaked. A meadowlark let go a few notes. But the gopher and the meadowlark sounded funny; they didn't sound real – not alongside all that quiet. She was kind of numb out there, like the prairie bumped its funny bone.

I couldn't hear Jake counting any more. I rolled over careful onto my stomach.

I up out of there like a scared jackrabbit. I wasn't fussy about lying near any dead man! There he was, lying awful still with his head on the crook of his arm. I guess I was so excited about our game I flopped in the ditch without seeing him. I might have lit on top of him! I yelled for Jake.

I met him the other side of the windbreak.

"What's wrong? You sound like you run across a grizzly!"

"There's a dead man in the ditch!" Jake, he didn't wait a minute – nothing scares Jake. He started for the road with me behind him.

"This ain't no corpus delicious," Jake said. The body had rolled over on one elbow and was getting sleep out of his eyes. "Some harvester takin' a nap. Save me goin' to town fer a stooker."

And that was how we got our stooker.

At first Jake figured he made a mistake hiring a stooker right off the bat out of a ditch. He was a greenhorn. He didn't have a roll with him; no blankets, or razor, or gloves, or anything – just the scuffed, brown jacket and black pants and other stuff he had on. He wasn't so husky either, but Jake said it wasn't tallow, it was knack that counted. Jake found that out when he had trouble with Chief Poundmaker; the chief had fifty pounds on Jake. And that's another thing Jake and Miss Henchbaw don't agree on. She says the history book doesn't say a thing about Jake capturing Poundmaker. How does she know? She wasn't there like Jake was. I can see easy how it happened, with Poundmaker not knowing joo jitsy the way Jake does.

I hate to think what Jake'd do if he ever got his hands on Hitler. He wants to, but they won't let him. Twenty-three times he's been in to Crocus to join up, but they keep right on telling him he's too old. Jake'd make a good soldier. He's been in two wars already and he's a dandy with a .22. Before he sold his so he could buy more war savings stamps, there wasn't a crow or a gopher or a tin can was safe with Jake around.

But like I say, our stooker sure didn't act like a harvester. We thought he was an Englishman, he talked so careful and polite. You should've seen his table manners. I used to think Jake was the neatest eater I'd ever seen, the way he hunches over his plate so he won't drop anything on the oilcloth, and instead of using a spoon on his pie, cuts it careful in pieces with his knife and fork. But our stooker had Jake skinned a mile at the dinner table.

If he was only half as good at stooking, he'd've been Canadian champion easy. But he wasn't; the whole first day all he set up was one skimpy corner. He went to bed right after supper.

It was my night to write my father and tell him how things were getting along, so I got out a pencil and paper. So did Jake. Ma was out in the shed; we could hear the click-a-ting of the cream separator and it purring to beat anything. I couldn't seem to get my letter started, the way my mind kept hopping like a frog from one thing to another, thinking things like: the coal-oil lamp flame was a butterfly's wing, the sticks in the stove were cracking their knuckles. You can't put that kind of stuff in a letter.

I took another try at her. Jake's nose was whistling – not loud, soft like through your teeth.

"How many pints in a quart?" he said.

"Two," I said.

"How many quarts in a gallon?"

"Four."

His head went down again.

Then was when I remembered about the egg I found in the manger Sunday morning. It was a white Wine-Dot egg and spang in the centre of the big end it had a "V". My father would sure be glad to know we had a "V for Victory" hen at home now. I wrote my head off.

"Twenty-seven five-hunnerd barrels!"

"What of?" I said.

"Tea."

"Tea!"

"Yep. I figgered her out. If yer Ma's thirty now, and she started up when she was fourteen, she's drunk twenty-seven five-hunnerd-gallon barrels of tea. 'Nough to fill the cow pasture slough."

Jake's smart. He's always figuring things. You'd think they'd let him fight.

While I was putting my father's name on the envelope, Jake said, "What you think of the stooker?"

"I don't know," I said.

"Awful quiet. When I stop the binder near him he ain't sociable at all. You'd think after a fellow's bin alone with all them stooks he'd want to talk to somebody. Does he act snooty with you?"

"I haven't been around him so much," I said.

"Except for bein' so close, he seems like a nice fellow. Guess it ain't so easy to be sociable when yer back's giving you hell."

"Going to keep him, Jake?"

"I dunno," Jake said. "See how he does tomorrow. I'll take some time off after morning chores and show him a few tricks."

After Jake showed him, the stooker didn't do so bad the next day. He wouldn't have made any contract stooker, but he sure was a bear for punishment. You should have seen what the twine did to his hands. But he stuck her all the same. I guess it was the way he acted about those blisters made Jake keep him on. He didn't let on they hurt him at all.

But he still acted funny. He'd answer you all right with that English accent of his, real slow like he was thinking over every word before he said it. Only you could easy see there was something bothering him inside. Sometimes, Jake said, he'd stop stooking and stand in the field, bareheaded with a bundle under each arm, staring out over the stooks to where the sky dropped over the horizon. Jake said he looked kind of lost sometimes, like he never saw prairie before and it scared him. I knew how he felt; prairie makes me scared sometimes. Prairie's funny.

But like I say, he didn't say so much – up till the second week he was with us.

They way I always did, I took his and Jake's lunch down to them. Jake was stooking too because all the cutting was done. They'd nearly set up the field. There's nothing prettier than a stooked field, that I know of anyway – rows marching straight across land flatter'n a platter. Wherever you looked from, there was a different pattern.

Way above without a cloud to bother him, a goshawk drifted lazy and loose – I bet our field looked funny to him, like a chequerboard and stooks for yellow chequers. While I watched he lifted higher and higher, until he went right to a pinpoint.

I sat with Jake and the stooker while they ate their lunch. After his cake, Jake reached for his tea jar, took a couple of swigs, then handed it to the stooker. Jake wiped his mouth with the back of his hand.

"She's sure a hot one this afternoon," he said. "Reminds me of the day I got throwed from my horse – durin' the Boor war. I lay there on the bald-headed prairie – 'felt' they called it – without food ner water. Couldn't move. Busted my leg when I got throwed, you see. And say! I got thirsty. My tongue swole up and cracked like summer fallow after four years' drought. Then one day I see a crick I didn't see before and I starts crawlin' toward her, and when I got no further away than that there stook, I see a dead Boor but I keeps right on goin' till I gets to the crick. I fill my hat and I'm just goin' to have my first drink in two weeks when this Boor I thought was dead lifts up his head and hollers, 'Water – water'. I crawls over to him with my hat full of water and I says, 'Here,' I says, 'git this into you. You need it worse'n me.' "

That's Jake for you. Just like Sir Philip Sidney in our fourth grade reader. But the stooker was saying something.

"In 1902 that was?"

"Yep," Jake said, "she was '02 all right."

The stooker got up, and he had the funniest look on his face, like he had some joke inside him he wouldn't let out. His left eye flickered at me – not much – you couldn't swear it was a wink. He clicked his heels together, and bowed at Jake sitting there gaping up at him from the stubble.

"I am charmed to meet you again," he said, "I was that wounded Boer." He said it like it was "boar".

For a minute Jake stared at the stooker, then he turned to me. "You better take that jug back and get it filled. Take it down to the barley. We're movin' there in an hour."

After that wherever we'd be I noticed Jake kept looking at the stooker. He seemed kind of mad about the stooker pretending to be that wounded Boor. He asked me if the stooker ever said much to me and I told him that he did talk more than he used to; about the prairie mostly, and how spacious it was. I asked Jake what spacious meant, and Jake said elbow room was what it meant.

In a couple of days Jake got over being mad at the stooker for pulling his leg. Jake can never stay mad long. Live and let live, he always says. Jake can take a joke. But there was still something bothering the stooker. Jake and I couldn't figure it out till one night by the pumphouse.

At first there was just me – me and the ground and the night sky spangly with stars. Little things seem to get lost at night on the prairie, and she gets so quiet you feel left dangling. Like you were the only person in the world, listening to the night wind lapping in the poplar's leaves. Over in the hen-house a rooster let half a crow out of him, then shut up. Way out on the prairie a coyote howled because they don't go in packs like timber wolves and he was lonely. His howl was lonely too. It grabbed up the prairie stillness around itself. I heard a clinking.

The stooker was getting a drink at the well, and it was the tin cup on a chain made the noise. He said "Good evening," and I said, "Hello." I couldn't see him so well. I watched a torn cloud slipping across the moon. In the fall the moon looks like a yellow tiddlywink – a harvest moon. Just as the cloud finished wiping off the moon's face, the stooker said:

"Such nights we do not have where I come from. To stand here – it . . . When I was a boy, my uncle had a paperweight – crystal – a fly was in the centre."

"Was it alive?" I asked him.

"No," he said, "in the crystal it was fixed. When I was a boy I too wondered that, but now of course I know it was dead." He didn't say anything for a minute. I thought it was kind of funny anybody talking about a dead fly like it hurt them. All the same I'd sure hate to have been that fly if it was alive. Just when I was thinking that, he said the craziest thing. He said:

"All my life I have that fly been." I felt kind of sorry for him.

"That's just the way night on the prairie makes you feel," I said. "It makes me feel funny too."

" 'Nough to scare a dog from a garbage can." That was Jake. "She was a still night like this–except there wasn't any moon–before Vimy. I remember a fellow come up to me and said . . ." He stopped, and I could see him look at the stooker. "Say," he said, "you wasn't at Vimy too, was you?"

The stooker didn't answer him right away. "You Canadians at Vimy Ridge did well," he said.

"We sure did," Jake said, "Canadians is fighters."

"My father's in England now," I said. "He's a sergeant in the S.S.R. They got a gold antelope on their hats."

"What is this antelope?"

"Like a deer, only it's got short horns," I said. "They got a white patch on their pants and can run like anything. They belong to the prairie."

"The prairie," he said. "I do not imagine that they–that–All this space they like, do they not?"

"Never got a chance to ask one," Jake said.

"Canada has much–much openness."

"Elbow room," Jake said.

"And horizon it has too."

"But no room fer dick-taters," Jake said. "Nobody lines up Canadians like they was stooks in a field."

"Miss Henchbaw does," I said.

"She is a dictator?" the stooker said.

"My teacher–and real bossy."

"I also think this prairie has not got room for dictators. Before tonight I would not believe it possible that such a difference elbow room could make."

From then on our stooker was the same as anybody else. And he was fun. I told him all about the Little Daisy BB gun. I wrote my father all about him. He played Night Patrol with me and Jake all the time.

And then one morning just at the end of stooking, my mother sent me over to Tinchers' to borrow Mrs. Tincher's flat-iron.

I felt pretty good going down the highway and it stretching out ahead of me, thinning to where someone squeezed it out of a toothpaste tube, without jiggling their hand. Between our place and Tinchers' I shot two gophers, a magpie, a goshawk, and twenty-five glass knobs off telephone pole crosspieces. Five times going to Tinchers', my throat plugged up, just thinking about having that gun. What it'd be like when I really had her!

Vera, Tinchers' hired girl, let me in, and when I got in the kitchen it was dinnertime, and Mr. and Mrs. Tincher and the boys were sitting around their radio, listening to the news.

We can't afford a radio at our place. That was why we hadn't heard about three Nazis escaping from Brokenshell Camp two and a half weeks ago. The announcer said they caught two of them, but the third one, who was a count or something with a long loopy name, was still loose. He could speak good English and was wearing a brown jacket and dark pants and had grey eyes and was slight and five feet eight. Then the announcer started saying to save gasoline for the war and he was through, and Mr. Tincher got up and snicked off the radio and I didn't feel so good.

Mrs. Tincher asked me to stay for dinner but I wasn't interested in any dinner, not with my whole throat aching like it was doing. I wanted out of there and I left without even asking for the flat-iron. I felt sick.

Our stooker was a Nazi!

As soon as I got in our gate I heard Jake behind the house, sawing birch chunks and the red bucksaw going whee-haw, sort of impatient with what it was sawing. Jake didn't see me come around the house.

"Jake," I said, and he looked over his shoulder, then

straightened up and stood there with one hand on the buck-saw, wiping the sweat off of his forehead. "Jake," I said, "I found out something awful."

"Did you now!"

"Our stooker's a Nazi!"

"Sure he is and I'm Churchill, but you can call me Winston fer short."

"Honest, Jake! I just heard it on Tinchers' radio. Three of them got away from Brokenshell Camp and the Mounties caught two but the third one's still loose and he's our stooker!"

"They couldn't learn him to speak the kind of English he speaks in a camp."

"The announcer said he could speak English so you couldn't tell he was a German hardly. He's our stooker, Jake."

While Jake looked at me, a hen walked past us, lifting her feet careful, like she had an elastic stretched between her ankles. "Yeah," Jake said, "I guess it's our stooker all right." Like he was bunged out of a slingshot, a grasshopper looped through the air and lit at Jake's feet. "Ever since I heard the way he said 'boar' for 'boor', I figgered he wasn't no English-man." Jake looked away from me and stared off beyond the woodpile where wind off the prairie was bending soft waves through the grass. "I felt her in my bones," Jake said, "but I didn't dare say nothing for fear she was true. Now we know, but what the hell are we gonna do?"

I could see the grasshopper good in front of Jake's feet, with his shanks all bulgy and his knees stuck up ready for another jump.

"She's gotta be did," Jake said. "I don't know when I met a nicer fellow, but she's gotta be did. We gotta turn him in."

"But he isn't like a real Nazi, Jake. He doesn't . . ."

"He's one of the enemy and he's . . ."

"But Jake! What about that night by the pumphouse – what about what he said? You heard him!"

"Sure, I heard him. But he's still a . . ."

"It's different now he isn't a dead fly any more. We can't turn him in. Why can't we keep him here and . . ."

"I don't see how we can do it. She's gotta be did and that's all there is to it. We gotta do what's right. I only wish it wasn't us had to do it, that's all."

"But . . ."

"Sometimes when two persons cannot make a decision a third can help."

Jake and me stood there by the woodpile and you could've heard a pin drop. Here we'd been shouting our heads off about the stooker and not thinking where he was. Jake's mouth snapped shut like a gopher trap.

"Mebbe you got something there," he said. "The Kid and me have got us into a jackpot."

"Yes?" the stooker said.

"Supposing you knew a fellow and supposing this fellow was, uh, well – a lot like a dog that's all the time tied up – mean, tricky. You couldn't turn yer back on him for fear he'd go after you."

"And this man of whom you speak – he also has been tied up?"

"Yep. Where he hailed from there wasn't no elbow room. It was real stuffy, but he got away from there. And he got himself a job stookin' – and out there on the prairie with all that horizon and all them stooks under all that sky, he started in to wonderin'. For the first time in his life, he got a chance to take a look at himself and he wasn't so fussy about what he seen."

Jake stopped for a minute and we just stood there with the sun kissing the back of our necks. Then Jake started talking again.

"Then one night when the chores was done and the pigs had quit hollerin' and she was real quiet the way prairie gets, this fellow did some more thinkin'. From that night on he ain't been the same fellow. He ain't been like a dog that's all the time tied up. Me and the Kid don't know when we met a nicer fellow."

For a minute a Jake looked at the stooker. He looked without winking his eyes a bit. I never noticed till then how foggy they were – not bright blue like I thought, more like old skim milk. Then Jake was talking again.

"Trouble is now, there's some other fellows that don't know about what happened to the stooker. They figger he's still the same way he was. I and the Kid, we know we oughta turn the stooker in, but we hate to do it. And that's how she is."

"That is your – jackpot?"

"Yep," Jake said.

"I do not think it is such a bad jackpot from which to get out. These men who want this stooker, they will take him away and he will be put in a camp."

"Yep."

"But the camp will not change this stooker. It will not be the same man who goes back to the camp. It will be one who has found out the meaning of elbow room – who no longer could be satisfied with being a – a stook fixed in a row. This man has freed himself from an imprisonment of which he was not even aware until he saw more horizon flung round him than he had believed existed. He is not – he never will be the same man."

"That the way you got her figgered out?"

"It is only what I think."

"Well, that's good enough for us," Jake said.

And when Jake had gone in the house to phone, and the stooker went back to the barley field, I thought it over. I still hated to see him go, but after what he said I figured it was the only thing to do.

It only took the Mounties about fifteen minutes to get to

our place after Jake phoned. They piled out of their car and they had guns. I didn't see what happened. Ma didn't let me go with them.

There wasn't any shooting. I listened at the kitchen door but I didn't hear a thing. Afterwards, Jake told me the stooker saw them coming, and dropped the bundle he was holding and bowed to them kind of and said good afternoon like they were farm inspectors and he was a farmer waiting for them to come take a look at his crop. He had handcuffs on when they brought him back to the house.

Looking at those handcuffs I didn't feel so sure we did the right thing in turning him in. I only saw him through the kitchen window but it made me feel awful funny in the stomach. For a minute I thought of running out and asking them to let him stay with us. I figured maybe if I told them about his uncle's paperweight they might let him stay. Only I didn't do it. I just watched through the kitchen window. Jake got in the front seat of the car and leaned back to the stooker between two Mounties in the back. He handed the stooker some money – stooking wages, he told me after. Then the car started up.

Jake didn't come back till just before supper – he got a ride out with Magnus Petersen. I was by the back stoop, washing up for supper, and I saw him come in the gate. He wasn't walking so spry, his knees were half-bent the way they always are when he walks. He had a parcel under his arm.

When he got up to me, he stopped. He didn't seem to know what to say. He just stood there with his shoulders kind of saggy under that old coat he wears whenever he goes to town. I could see the furrows ploughing down past his mouth and the silver stubble all over his face. I guess in Crocus where they hire on soldiers, they're right.

Jake held out the parcel he had.

"Here," he said. "Here's your Little Daisy."

He knew how I felt when I saw the handcuffs and he'd got me that BB gun so I wouldn't feel so bad. "Thanks," I said. "Thanks for getting it for me, Jake."

"I didn't," Jake said. "Our stooker did."

I felt kind of sick again.

GETTIN' BORN

WITH HIM SITTING IN THE PEW IN FRONT I COULD SEE MR. Tincher's neck good, and it was all creased crisscross like somebody pressed chicken wire up against her real hard. Jake has the same kind of a neck; she's what you might call a prairie neck. By looking across Ma I could see Jake kind of hunched down in his seat, with his chin down on his chest. Every once in a while his head would go like somebody yanked her with a piece of binder twine. It isn't so easy to keep awake when you can smell the spring slipping in through the church windows and Mr. Stoddard's going on, up and down, up and down. He has what you might call a humble voice.

But I wasn't having any trouble to keep my eyes open. I'd got to thinking about my down-east Aunt Margaret that's married to Jim Matthews, and the reason I'd got to thinking about her was the way Mr. Stoddard was going on about the flesh like he always does. Every time he gets to the flesh I think of people getting born or dying. This time it reminded me about Archie Winters that sits behind me out at Rabbit Hill. His mother died when he was born. He told me. I'd just as soon he hadn't, because I'd already heard Ma telling Mrs. Tincher over our phone about how my Aunt Margaret was going to have a baby.

So there was me sitting in church, thinking about how come Archie's ma died, and about my Aunt Margaret that might too, and I wasn't so glad about having any new cousin. I'm funny about my Aunt Margaret.

Right in the middle of thinking about my Aunt Margaret going to have a baby, Mr. Stoddard said about being born again. I never heard that one before. I never even heard Jake say anything about it, and he's getting on some. You'd think if somebody was going to get born again it'd be Jake, with those fellows in Crocus keeping telling him he's too old to fight. If there was any way for Jake to get himself younger he'd've been right over there with the South Saskatchewan and my dad. I figured I better ask Jake about it after church.

From outside the church a meadowlark sang. I started counting; he let me get to nineteen. I started over; on twenty he tar-tar-tickely-booed. Next time it was twenty-seven. I didn't get another chance to try him, because Mr. Stoddard had quit, and I had to find number 242 for Ma.

I saw Jake didn't have hold of any hymn book so I grabbed another from the back of the pew to see if I could find the place before they got singing. I beat them to it. Jake, he looked kind of startled when I handed him the open book, but he took it, and when the singing had started I saw his head sort of bobbing, and his chin going.

After Mr. Stoddard let down both his arms from spreading them out over everybody Ma leaned forward with her head in her hands for a minute. She always does that just before we leave church. It's about my dad. She never told me but I know. Her eyes are some different after she straightens up.

Outside the church Jake and me headed for Baldy and the democrat, and I was still squeezing my eyes shut till the sun wouldn't be so bright, when Jake said:

"If she's all the same to you, Kid, never mind findin' me no place in no hymn book. I don't figger to do so much singin'."

"You was singin', Jake."

"Nope. I try real hard, only my throat gits kinda taunt.

Them there notes keeps right on pilin' up so by the time church's out I got three, four hymns harled up agin my Adam's apple."

I guess singing's about the only thing Jake can't do. He can play the mandolin real sweet. He's a two-war veteran. It was him took care of Looie Riel and Chief Poundmaker when she looked so black for Canada in the early days. Miss Henchbaw, she says if there was many more like Jake loose it couldn't look any blacker for Canada right now. She says Jake's careless with his history. Jake, he says she wasn't history when he did her; that came later when some fellow wrote her up in a book – wrote her up all wrong.

✑ξ ⧽✑

It was while Jake was taking off Baldy's nosebag, I remembered.

"Jake," I said.

"Yeah?"

"How does a – how could a person get born twice?"

"Huh!"

"You know, what Mr. Stoddard was saying about?"

"Guess I musta missed that part."

"Well – have – did you ever run across anybody like that?"

"Why, I . . ." – Jake didn't seem so tickled about what we were talking about.

"Would he have the same folks?"

"Mebbe – if he was fussy about 'em."

Then was when I remembered about the runt pig I fed out of a medicine dropper so he wouldn't get hit over the head with a hammer. "Take that there runt pig, Jake. He oughta had another chance. Will he get born over again?"

Jake stood there with his arm lying over Baldy's neck and he looked down at me. He looked real serious. He said, "She's a hard one to answer, Kid."

"Doesn't seem to make so much sense."

"Not right off," Jake said. "Look – you fellas playin' agates yet?"

"Yeah."

"What kind?"

"Chase, plunks, poison."

"Ever takin' aim, an' somebody sorta jiggled your elbow?"

"Yeah."

"Don't go exac'ly the way you figgered?"

"No, it . . ."

"Could call her a runt-shot, huh?"

In his head Jake thinks a lot like I do. I'm fussy about Jake.

Only I should have told Jake about what happened to Archie's ma, and got Aunt Margaret straightened out, too. I didn't because of the way they acted whenever I started in talking about her. I could tell I wasn't supposed to know about her going to have a baby from the way they always looked at each other, and that made it worse knowing about Archie's ma. Getting born must be awful if they won't even talk about it.

Riding home in the democrat with Ma and Jake, I didn't do so much thinking. When she's spring it isn't so easy for a person to think anything but goofy thoughts – like wondering what she'd be like to bounce off clouds. Over top of us the sky was what you might call a luke-blue. All alongside the road the fields were green with new wheat. There isn't any green like young wheat green stretching out spang to the horizon, bright green like to yell at a person. Looking back I could see the Crocus elevators with their shoulders flat against the sky.

She was spring all right, with gophers sitting up to watch us go by, and millions of crocuses along the ditches and a real soft spring breeze sort of teasing a person, making the back of Ma's Sunday dress go out like a balloon.

Spring has winter skinned a mile. In spring look what there is: colts with their tails, maybe a calf with a wet nose, baby chicks, and catching gophers; little pigs are something else. Spring has a lot of things that never lived before.

Just when we got to our place, and I was holding open the gate while Jake drove the democrat through, I heard Ma say not to unharness so he could go over to get Aunt Margaret. I asked why she was coming over, and Ma said she wasn't feeling so well and Jim was going to eat at our place while Margaret stayed with us.

I pretended like I didn't know and I said, "What's the matter with her?"

"She'll be better after a while."

"Is she sick bad?"

"Not very," Ma said.

"What's she got?" Ma didn't say anything. "Do you figure she might die?"

"She – look! A gopher – over there. See him?"

In our front yard there's always a whole slew of gophers playing, winking their tails to you as they go down their holes. You'd think Ma'd seen a badger the way she pointed him out. I was wishing Archie hadn't told me about his mother.

‿§ §‿

I guessed the only thing to do was talk to Jake, and a couple of days after Aunt Margaret came over, I did. It wasn't any use. Jake, he wouldn't say anything either, and when I kept on he said to get. He doesn't say to get very often, so I knew Aunt Margaret wasn't doing so well. When Ma told Jake that Dr. Fotheringham was coming out to see her, I was sure.

There was only one thing to do, and I did it. While Dr. Fotheringham was up seeing Aunt Margaret, I hung around the kitchen. Ma was still upstairs when he came down. He said hello, and so did I. He said I was getting to be big, and I said I guessed he was around when a lot of babies were born. He said, yes, he did happen to be there. He's got a way of chewing all the time so his moustache gets to moving, and he looked down at me, and his moustache was moving from chewing. I said:

"Do you often have them not turn out so good?" I could see the rusty streaks in his moustache, and smell his bitter smell. He looks a lot like an old collie. He said:

"Just one."

"What happened?"

"As soon as he was born, he started to grow. He kept right on."

"Aw . . ."

"Of course with his father a sergeant in the S.S.R. overseas – have to have a man around the farm."

He's a Parliament member, and I was sure glad I talked with him. If he wasn't het up, then there wasn't likely any reason for me to worry about it.

But I did. I started in worrying the next Saturday when me and Mr. Churchill Two went out after gophers. Mr. Churchill Two's my red and white fox terrier Jake gave me after Mr. Churchill One got lost, and that Saturday all the time I was doing noon chores he kept jumping up on me. That meant only one thing – going after gophers.

But while we headed for the south pasture I wasn't so sure it was a good idea; she looked like rain. She was a funny sky, full of cloud stuff that went black along the horizon. Over top of us Somebody had stuck Their finger through, and yanked one long, ragged blue rip in her.

She was real still in all that empty prairie, lonely still. Every once in a while, in the high grass, the wind took a notion to whisper some but not like she really meant to. A meadowlark dropped some of his notes off a straw stack; the prairie quiet grabbed them up like a blotter does ink. She wasn't letting anything spoil her quiet.

I guess I'm not so fussy about the prairie when she's still

before a rain; she's too much like in school when Miss Henchbaw looks up, and you don't know who's in for it – before-the-
strap quiet.

I stood still for a minute to listen for a gopher squeak. Mr.
Churchill Two sat down with his neck bent so proud, and his
ears standing right up except where they flopped at the ends.

He started making little crying sounds in his throat; he up
and lit for a clump of rose-apple bushes. I waited to see where
he'd chase the gopher, only he came running back. Then he
off again with a pale butterfly blinking its wings over top of
him. I followed.

It was a gopher we'd killed a couple of days before; I'd left
him there after I took off his tail for the municipal office,
where they give you three cents. Just as I got up to him, a
black cloud of flies lifted up off of him real quick.

He had his paws held out ahead of him like when a person
prays. His eyes were open; they were more like dead black
beads. I didn't feel so good.

~§ §~

I was remembering about a train I had once – the kind that
winds up with a key – and how she wouldn't go after I busted
the spring. I couldn't make her move at all till Jake fixed her
with some solder. That was a funny thing for a person to think
about when he was looking at a dead gopher. A person sees
a lot of dead gophers. Only this one was different. He was
dead, and the prairie wind was whispering careless, and another gopher hidden off somewhere was squeaking like he
didn't care either.

This wasn't an agate game, and slingshots, and somebody
jiggling somebody's elbow. Jake couldn't solder this.

I wished my Aunt Margaret wasn't going to have any baby.

Something hit the back of my neck; another one spanked
itself against my nose. Rain. I hit for home.

In the barn I waited for Jake to come in from the field. After he showed up and I was helping him unharness, I said, "Jake, what–which is the worst, getting born or dead?"

"Huh?"

"Which one would you say was the–well, would you say one of 'em was more important?"

"I don't git you."

"If you had your choice–which one?"

"There ain't no comparison."

"What's that?"

"Jist there ain't no comparison."

"Do people send flowers when a person gets born?"

"I guess a person might."

"Well, take the way she is with spring and winter. Which, if you had your pick?"

"How the hell could you die if you wasn't born, er, how could you git born if you wasn't gonna die?"

"But just . . ."

"Look." Jake held out the end of Baldy's belly-band. "Them buckle holes–what makes 'em? The leather or the ain't leather?"

And that was all I got out of Jake. I didn't even say about Archie Winters's ma, or getting born again.

I wondered whether I should maybe talk with Aunt Margaret's husband, Jim, about it. But the way he hung around the house with his eyes looking sort of sick, and asking Ma was there anything he could do to help, I knew I better not. When I came home after school I'd get him to help with my chores, and at night after homework we played rummy on the kitchen table. A person's wife going to have a baby can sure spoil their rummy game.

All the next week she kept right on raining, just as bad as two years ago when Mr. Ricky made enough to pay for seeding his crop out of that low stretch of gumbo that runs past his front forty. Mr. Ricky, he's fussy about money; most folks in our district wouldn't charge a nickel to pull a person out of the mud.

Every night when I went to sleep I could hear the rain noisy on our roof, gurgling loud down the rain spout at the corner of the house. Rain is a sad thing, even if she is good for the crops. And one night about a week after she'd started in raining, Jake and Ma weren't looking so glad either. Jake, he didn't do the chores, and we had our supper early, and that was funny. Jim Matthews, he just sat there at the table with his great big hands lying in front of him, and his shoulders kind of slumped, and he didn't eat at all.

◆§ §◆

Three times while we were eating Ma got up and went to the phone. She was phoning Crocus for Dr. Fotheringham. She wasn't getting any answer, because he's a bachelor doctor, and central said Mrs. Sawyer that keeps house for him had gone to Broomhead so her daughter could have a baby, and the doctor must be on a call.

Jake got up from the table after supper, and he reached down his coat and cap from the wall, and he said he guessed he'd take Queenie and the democrat and go into town and bring out the doctor, and for Ma to keep on phoning.

Ma said for Jake to take Jim with him, and Jim said maybe he'd better stay. Ma said for goodness sake to go with Jake so as not to be under her feet all the time. Jim went.

"Why didn't they wait," I asked Ma, "till she clears up?"

"Dr. Fotheringham has to come tonight," Ma said. "With those roads the way they are now, he won't be able to get his car through." Ma's mouth was a tight line across her face.

All the time I did arithmetic and spelling on the kitchen table Ma was either upstairs or on the phone. No wonder I got eight wrong, especially the way I kept thinking about Archie's ma, and that gopher, and my Aunt Margaret. When I'd finished my homework I didn't feel so much like going to bed. I just sat there and watched the raindrops sliding down the window – slow at first, then crazy fast.

The phone rang, two long and a short. That was us. I grabbed her. It was Jake. He was phoning from Ricky's.

He was stuck. He was stuck and when he unharnessed, Queenie bolted. He said he phoned so we wouldn't worry while him and Mr. Ricky went out to catch a horse, and it would take a while because the horses had been out all winter and they were kind of wild.

When I told Ma, her mouth got straighter than ever. She said I better go to bed, and I said maybe I better stick by the phone and keep on calling. She looked at me a minute and then she said all right.

But I didn't get any answer out of Dr. Fotheringham. I kept her up till Jake phoned the second time. Him and Mr. Ricky couldn't catch a horse; he was going to walk her to Tinchers' and try and get one there. I figured there wasn't any use telling Ma about that.

About twelve Ma came downstairs and told me I better get to bed. I just started out of the kitchen and our ring came again. Ma listened for a minute, then hung up.

It had been Jake, and all the Tincher horses were over at Winghams' where they were seeding, because Mr. Wingham lost all his from the sleeping sickness last fall. Jake was on his way to Gatenby's.

Then was when Ma told me to go saddle Baldy.

As I went out the back door Ma was talking with Jake again, telling him she was sending me in, and for him to come back in case she needed him.

She'd let up raining, and the sky wasn't dark any more. Behind some torn black clouds I could see a big, pale, tiddly-wink moon. Like they do after a rainstorm, frogs way off in the night were singing in their sloughs. The air smelled cool and washed.

I didn't bother with no saddle and I didn't go by Government Road. Straight across the prairie I headed Baldy at a full canter bareback and him going whumph-whump-whumph under me, and me thinking how pretty my Aunt Margaret was, and how nice she smelled with the soap she uses, and about Archie's ma, and that gopher lying there on the prairie.

And other things I thought: the time Jake had to shoot Duke; the way Jake's knees don't kink so much in the spring when he walks; the way he used to get me to plant wheat seed in tin cans, then Easter morning tell me it was the Easter rabbit had nipped the sprouts off. And about hatching chicks in the oven, and the big grape-and-red-coloured window in our church, the one with Jesus carrying a baby lamb with all its legs hanging down. There wasn't any sense to what I thought except about Archie's ma and that dead gopher, and my Aunt Margaret going to die if Dr. Fotheringham didn't get to her.

⁋ ʕ▶

In Crocus I turned Baldy round the Baptist church corner and headed for Dr. Fotheringham's.

With my legs tingling like they weren't my own, I ran up the front steps, and I knocked a lot but nobody came. It was when I turned around I saw the car lights come along the street.

They were Dr. Fotheringham's and he'd been out to Forbes' so their baby could come. When I told him how the roads were our way he made me get in the car and we started for the livery barn. We woke Pete Botten up, and he said there wasn't any rig around, but there was the big paint that belonged to the Hershel boy, only there was no saddle because he was still buying the horse off Cam Secord, and he only made two dollars a week delivering for MacTaggart's, so he hadn't got around to buying a saddle.

As soon as we got started bareback I knew why the doctor

said for me to come with him on the paint, and why he told Pete to throw me up in front instead of behind. Every time the paint lifted, Dr. Fotheringham bounced, and between bounces he jerked out that he hadn't ridden since he was twelve. So I told him to kind of grip his legs, and roll his backbone kind of so he wouldn't get her so bad.

The Hershel boy sure didn't get stung on that paint.

At our gate the doctor sort of fell off, and he lit pointed for the house and running with his satchel in his hand. As I took the paint to Baldy's stall, I heard Mr. Churchill Two whimpering over by the house.

I hated to leave that barn; I hated to go find out what happened. And walking back with the old-time lantern that we most always left in the barn, to where the house windows let yellow squares of light through the dark, I'd've given anything to forget about that dead gopher.

Mr. Churchill went again – louder.

I wondered if I'd brought the doctor in time, and about the belly-band of Baldy's harness.

The henhouse, the hog pens, the old rack, the pumphouse were born into the lantern light as I went past them. They died right away out of it.

Mr. Churchill whined some more.

At night a lantern's a magic lantern, making things come and disappear where she melts into the dark, and you're all alone in your light cave.

Mr. Churchill Two went louder, real strong from inside our home; only it wasn't Mr. Churchill Two like I thought. He didn't have like hiccups when he cried. This was different. It wasn't anything I ever heard before. It was new – like spring wheat, and calves, and colts, and everything else in spring! It was thin and it quit, then went again, and it came right through the walls of our house!

I lit out running . . . .

Jake was in the kitchen.

"Jake! Is – did . . . ?"

Jake, he just took his hand and sort of brushed at his face, and he was looking straight ahead. "She's all right," he said.

"What . . . ?"

"Boy," Jake said. I could see by the coal-oil lamp flame he was sweating, and his face showed how she was all creased like baked drought land gets. "Remember that there question, Kid?"

I said yes with my head.

"Gettin' born's got the other beat a mile. I can't say her so good, but if anybody should ask you, you tell 'em she's what your old man's fightin' for in England. Spring, he's fightin' for, an' she's the opposite of winter. Gettin' born. An' that's the opposite of gettin' dead.

"An' mebbe they's gonna be a lotta winter before they's any spring, but she's worth it. There's a whole shaganappy world gonna git born agin – an' born right."

From upstairs I heard my cousin cry again.

JACKRABBIT BABY

When she commences to be fall, I get to thinking about Indians, and that's because Indians are wild. Fall is wild too, and sad like an empty shack on the bald-headed prairie is sad, but mostly wild. You have wild geese flying high, and straw stacks that look like your ma's thimble, only smoking to beat anything against the horizon. Jake, he gets real wild with his rheumatism 'round about threshing time. Fall is a wild time of the year.

So there is why I was thinking about Indians when I found Jake by the oil barrels, talking with Ralp Harper. Most folks just call him Harp. I heard Jake say, "Until I see they got somethin' the matter with 'em."

"Steal you blind, Jake." Harp had his mouth sort of foldy. He carries his teeth in his pants pocket. He only uses them to eat with. "Why I knew a fellow . . ."

"How the hell do you know they will?"

"I'm just tellin' you they . . ."

"They're humans the same as anybody else," Jake said.

"Why, sure, but they . . ."

"Canadians, ain't they?"

"Could call 'em that. Same as gophers an' kiyoots an' jack . . ."

"You ain't . . ."

" . . . rabbits is Canadians." Harp, he laughed sort of snorty. "Jackrabbit Canadians – that's what they are – Jackrabbit

Canadians." He laughed some more with his mouth open. Harp's tongue is real fat.

Jake, he was staring at Harp. There was a manure fork hanging out of his hand. Jake has the hands with the big knuckles. Jake isn't the mean kind; he's the kind to move a prairie-chicken nest out of the way of the discs; in spring he's always bringing me home a baby jackrabbit in his pocket. All the same I knew Harp better quit laughing. He looked up and he saw Jake's face.

He quit laughing. "What's eatin' you?"

Jake just looked at him.

"Look like you're gettin' so's a fellow can't have him a little joke without . . ."

"I ain't so fussy about them kinda jokes."

"Why – what'd – I was only tryin' to warn you – ain't got no call to fly offa the handle just because you went an' got you a coupla, uh, a . . ."

"Canadians."

"She was just a little frien'ly advice. Never thought for a minute you'd take her the way you done." Harp, he sounded like it was Jake stepped over the britching; he sounded real hurt. "I was only tryin' to tell you about this here fella which had only one eye an' he . . ."

"All the same I'm keepin' 'em."

"Don't say I didn't warn you."

After Harp had left I said to Jake, "Who was he calling Jackrabbit Canadians, Jake?"

"Couple of stookers I got – fellow an' his wife."

"Stookers! His wife isn't gonna stook, is she?"

"That was the understandin'. They got 'em a kid same age as ours." Jake meant my Aunt Margaret's baby.

"They're going to stook . . ."

"Just him an' his wife. The kid ain't had no experience."

"But what did Harp . . . ?"

"Blackfoot. They're from Hanley Reserve a hunnerd miles east of here."

"Indians!"

"Yep."

"Living on our place?"

"Gonna set their teepee up back of the woodpile."

"Real Indians!"

"What the hell other kind is there?"

"What's their name, Jake?"

"Rolling-in-the-Mud."

Till late at night I lay in my bed, listening to the fall wind washing in the leaves of the poplar outside my window. *Wheeeeyew*, she went gentle through the screen. Fall was walking right through my dark room, and me thinking all about Indians.

Next morning after Jake told me they'd come during the night, I could hardly wait. Ma told me three times not to bolt my mush. I was out the back door with Mr. Churchill Two, my fox terrier, right behind me. I saw the horses then. Right in our front pasture they were, paints and bays and greys and sorrels. I counted eleven. With the morning sun warm against the back of my neck, and the wind whispery in the dry grass all around me, I walked across the yard. Past the windmill and the old rack, past the blacksmith shop I went; past two fighting roosters throwing themselves up in the air one after the other, like those toys you wind and the two fellows go up and down. I walked to the fence, and I stood, and I looked, and I felt funny.

Over and over again the wind in the dry grass was saying something to me, and I didn't know what. From clear across the prairie it had come to tell me while I stood looking at the colt, the little, stilty colt with the proud neck. The colour of pull taffy with the fall sun lying on him, he stood close to his mother's side with the wind blowing through his dark mane

and his dark wool tail, with the sun lighting the hairs underneath his chin. Whatever the wind was saying through the
grass, it was saying for the little buckskin colt, too.

I heard a scuffle noise behind me and I turned.

He was dressed just like a white man, only he had on high-
heeled shoes instead of farm boots, which are flat. He was
wearing a bright green windbreaker, and when he said hello I
could hear his voice in the middle of my stomach. I said hello
and he took off his hat. His hair wasn't braided at all; it was
cut real short and bristly. His eyes were kind of tight-looking
at their corners, but he wasn't red; he just had a good tan –
what you might call a purpley tan.

He ran his hand through his hair and he said, "Where's the
fellow?"

"Jake, he's still in the house," I said. "Are – do you – these
all yours?"

He nodded. "Got more too." He said it like he was real
proud. "Feed's bad at Hanley."

"You got any – any more like that – that there buckskin
colt?"

He nodded again and he was looking at the colt. "Damn
fine colt." He started for the house. He was bowlegged.

The colt let me pat him through the fence. It was kind of
hard starting back for the house to do the morning chores.

It was by the woodpile I saw the Rolling-in-the-Mud teepee, only it wasn't a teepee. It was just an ordinary tent.
Across the front it had stamped, "Be sure your camp
fire is out, Worder Tent and Awning Company." While
I was reading it, Mrs. Rolling-in-the-Mud backed out. Her
hair hung down the front of her pink dress in two straight
braids. She said good morning – real clear – just like a kid's
voice. After she hung some diapers on the rope from the
ridge-pole, she went back into the tent. She came out with
the baby all wrapped up in a thing Jake told me later was a
yo-kay-bo.

He didn't look like any Indian baby except for his eyes. He was pale. And except for having a lot of black hair, he didn't look much different than Aunt Margaret's baby. His nose was running.

All morning, propped up near the chopping block, he watched me haul water for Ma's boilers; he never smiled any, just stared at me from his *yo-kay-bo* while I chopped wood. I got to thinking about the baby jackrabbit Jake caught for me last spring. Their eyes are different from a tame rabbit's eyes; they stare like an owl's, like those they put into a bird that's stuffed. The Rolling-in-the-Mud baby's eyes were real watching, but he wasn't any jackrabbit baby. Like Jake I wasn't so fussy about the way Harp talked about Indians.

Noontime Harp showed up again. He seemed real pleased about the horses. When Jake came in from the binder, he said, "Goin' in for horses, Jake?"

Jake didn't say anything.

"Started raisin' hot bloods, eh?"

Jake, he just looked mad and uncomfortable. You could tell Harp was tickled to death.

"Twen'y-eight heada fox feed," he said. "Five weeks they can eat up lotta pasture. You're sure payin' high wages for them stookers."

You could tell he just came over to get the laugh on Jake about those horses.

Right through dinner Jake was quiet. Just when we were finishing, a knock came at the back door. I went. It was Rolling-in-the-Mud. He said, "Have you got some kinda grease?" He kept looking down at the ground.

When I took back the cup of butter Ma gave me, he said, "Maybe you gotta little flour, too?"

After I brought the flour he still stood. "I don't s'pose you got an old bone – for some kinda soup?"

"Go into the shed and get him a sealer of that sausage." That was Ma behind me. "Come into the kitchen, please."

When I got back to the kitchen, Ma was saying, "Have you people got any oatmeal – salt – sugar?"

Rolling-in-the-Mud, he looked over at our baby in his high-chair and he said, "Damn fine baby. How old?"

"Ten months," said Aunt Margaret.

"Mine too. Thank you for the grub. Damn fine baby." He went out.

Ma turned to Jake. "I don't think they have a thing in that tent, Jake. Perhaps you'd better see."

Rolling-in-the-Mud was sitting on his heels by the wood-pile, his baby asleep in the *yo-kay-bo* right beside him. Its nose was still runny.

"What you need?" Jake said.

Rolling-in-the-Mud just looked down at the ground.

"Better go in to Crocus this afternoon while I fix that there binder. Order whatever you gotta have. I'll phone Mac-Taggart's an' we can put her against your wages." Jake started to turn away, then he stopped. "Uh, them horses – you gotta lotta horses there."

"Got more at Hanley," Rolling-in-the-Mud said, and like when he said it that morning, he sounded proud of it.

"Kinda thin, ain't they?"

"Got all thin on the reserve. They'll pick up soon."

"Yeah," Jake said, "they sure will, uh, did you have to bring . . ." He scratched the back of his head while he looked down at the baby. "Lotta horses – Ain't that there kid gotta cold?"

Rolling-in-the-Mud said yes.

"Whatta you doin' for it?"

"Skunk oil."

"Skunk oil! That ain't wortha whoop – you got no goose grease?"

"Skunk oil's good." He sounded real sure of it.

"Used goose grease all through the Boor War," Jake said.

"Goose grease for the outside, coal oil for the inside. I got some in the house. Better rub some onto him."

"Skunk oil's good." He sounded just like Jake when somebody tries to tell him different.

"Oughta use goose grease. Bad time of the year to have a cold. Liable to catch pneumonia. Skunk oil ain't worth a good goddam."

Rolling-in-the-Mud got up. "Skunk oil's good. Them horses."

"Oh," Jake said, "yeah – fellow only uses so many head of horses. They gotta eat, you know. What – how many of them is broke?"

"Six," said Rolling-in-the-Mud.

"Six! That all? What're you keepin' 'em for, then?"

"Me," Rolling-in-the-Mud said. "I like horses."

"Oh," Jake said, and that was all he said.

✺

Nearly every day after that Harp dropped in at our place to see how our Indians were coming along. When he heard Jake advanced them money for groceries he clicked his tongue so it went like water dropping slow onto cement, and he told Jake all about two Indians that collected wages ahead of time then didn't show up to do any stooking. Jake, he said the Rolling-in-the-Muds were fine stookers, and even if the horses were using up feed, it was worth it to have such good stookers. Harp said there wasn't an Indian alive had the stick-to-her and Jake'd be left holding the bag. Only Harp didn't seem so sure of what he was saying after he saw them stooking, with Rolling-in-the-Mud setting up the bundles two at a time and Mrs. Rolling-in-the-Mud leaving the baby in his *yo-kay-bo* at the end of each row till she came up to the next one and could move him over like you do a jug of water. Jake suggested maybe when our stooking was done, they could come over and give Harp a hand. Harp just snorted.

Just before he left he said, "They ain't clean."

"They are *so* clean," I said. "Mrs. Rolling-in-the-Mud washes her baby every day the way Aunt Margaret does – in the stock trough."

"I seen the way them two kids is playin' together on the same blanket. Wouldn't let no baby of mine near any nitchie kid. Liable to catch somethin'."

"T'ain't likely you're gonna have no baby," Jake said. "Your age."

⊷§ ও๛

It was just a couple of days after that our baby's nose started in running like the Indian baby's. Aunt Margaret told Jake it wasn't anything and that the bottle of dark stuff that Dr. Fotheringham gave her would fix it up. Jake, he wasn't so sure.

"Got to keep her from goin' into his chest," Jake said. "Ever try goose grease?"

"I think the nose drops . . ."

"Goose grease for outside, coal oil for . . ."

"Between you and Rolling-in-the-Mud . . ."

"Him? What'd he . . ."

"Skunk oil. Brought me a jar of it this morning."

"Just superstitious, that's all. I told him. Why, I knew a fella used skunk oil. Rubbed her on – dead in two days."

"From using skunk oil, Jake?" I said.

"Yep. Neighbours' dogs smelt it on him – chased him clear over the prairie in the middle of winter – caught him the death of pneumonia."

Aunt Margaret didn't use either the goose grease or the skunk oil, and the baby didn't get any better. He just sat in his high-chair with his eyes looking like he'd been crying a lot. His mouth was open all the time and he didn't seem to have such an easy time breathing.

"Listen to this kid's chest," Jake said.

Aunt Margaret listened. "Seems to have a little rasp," she said.

"Rasp, hell!" Jake said. "Whistlin like the seven-ten freight on a clear winter night! You gotta phone the doc."

After Dr. Fotheringham had gone over the baby with that listening thing, he said, "Some congestion there." He bent down over his bag and he brought out a bottle. "Every four hours you can steam him with this in about a pint of water."

"Ever use goose grease at all, doc?"

"Lot of folks use it," Dr. Fotheringham said.

Jake, he looked sort of pleased.

"Some swear by skunk oil, too," the doctor said.

Jake's face dropped. "But which one . . . ?"

"We'll try that bronchial inhalant, and if it doesn't work we can give your goose grease a try." Dr. Fotheringham's eyes went sort of twinkly, but I didn't see what was so funny.

Ma put kettles on the stove while Aunt Margaret laid a blanket over the baby's crib. They stuck the spout of the kettle under one corner so the steam filled the inside.

The Rolling-in-the-Mud baby didn't seem to be so much outside as he used to be. I figured that was the rainy weather that started in and held up the stooking. Mrs. Rolling-in-the-Mud was all the time sitting in the opening of their tent, just sitting there looking out. Every time I headed for the pasture to take a look at the little buckskin colt, she was watching out of their tent.

With his hide wet that colt was prettier than ever. I used to think a paint was the best, but I knew better now. I sure was fussy about that buckskin colt. Patting him made me feel just like holding our baby. The way Rolling-in-the-Mud said, I like horses.

I don't know when we started getting real worried about

our baby. He didn't get any worse or any better for three days. We didn't take him out of his crib much, and he lay there with us steaming him every four hours. He slept a lot, only it didn't look like the kind of sleep that would do him much good. He didn't fuss; he just lay there.

The fourth day after Dr. Fotheringham called, I came into the kitchen for breakfast, and I knew right away something was wrong. Aunt Margaret was there with Ma, and she looked like she hadn't slept all night. I never saw her eyes look that tired before.

You could hear the baby breathing all over the kitchen, loud and raspy. Jake was sitting there just staring at his pancakes.

It was raining out. All day Jake and I hung around the yard trying to find something to do. Every once in a while we'd go back to the house to see how the baby was. He wasn't any better.

And each time I passed Mrs. Rolling-in-the-Mud sitting there in the tent opening, just sitting there like her baby hadn't given our baby a cold from its runny nose, just sitting there like nothing was the matter with our baby, I felt something boiling up inside of me. The way I felt, I wasn't so fussy about their buckskin colt any more. I wished they'd never come near our place. I wished we'd listened to what Harp said. I wished they'd never brought their jackrabbit baby near our baby.

I finished my chores real late that night, and as I headed for the house, Mrs. Rolling-in-the-Mud was sitting there in the front of the tent. She had a long saskatoon branch and she was whittling on it, lopping the twigs off. She didn't care.

Inside the kitchen, the lamp was flickering and the moths were batting themselves up against the glass chimney and falling in it and dying there. Aunt Margaret, with her face all glisteny and her hair down around the sides of her face, was holding the baby in her arms and looking at him. One of his arms hung down. Straight down.

The lamp light was gleaming on the stubble of Jake's three-day beard, and the corners of his mouth were sort of droopy. He got up and walked across the kitchen and then he walked back to the woodbox. I thought about the grey coyote the Cobblenick boys kept in a chicken nesting-pen, and the way it sort of stitched back and forth, turning twitchy just the way Jake was doing.

Every once in a while the baby would cry, just like a hurt pup. Each time he'd cry you sort of cried inside right along with him, then you waited for him to cry again. And while I sat there I got to thinking and wishing I wasn't a human being. It isn't safe to be a human being, because you have to be so careful for fear something gets busted.

Jake swallowed loud. "I'm gonna phone for the doc. That kid's real bad."

"All right, Jake." That was Ma. "Perhaps if you could get him to swallow a little water, Margaret."

"He can't keep it down." Her voice sounded real dead.

I went outside and sat on the stoop.

It was a real skinny moon hung high in the sky; real light out, so light out I could see Mrs. Rolling-in-the-Mud sitting in front of her tent, exactly the way she was when I came in after chores. She had the saskatoon stick she'd been whittling on, held in one of her hands. All in a rush I hated her – a lot.

Just as I got up to go into the house there came a sound drifting down from high in the sky, real faint like it was only in your ears and not real. I looked up and saw a wobbly black vee with one long arm, strung out. Geese give you that lost feeling the best I know.

When Dr. Fotheringham finally came and he saw our baby, he clucked his tongue. He took some pills out of his bag, but he didn't give them to Aunt Margaret. He stayed. Ma made up the couch in the parlour for him. Jake and I sat up with the baby. That was when I told Jake about the saskatoon stick.

He was sitting with his hands sort of between his knees and his head down. I told him twice. He sat up like he was shot.

"Huh!"

"She was just sitting there whittling a saskatoon branch."

"Saskatoon branch! How long was it?"

" 'Bout three, four feet."

Jake up off of the woodbox like a scared jack. "Get Doc — *go get him!*"

"But . . ."

"She was whittlin' a yardstick."

"Yardstick!"

"The way they do – for measurin' thuh kid!"

Then it sank in. Her baby had pneumonia, too. She'd been cutting a yardstick. It's easier to build a coffin that way.

I hit for the parlour.

They brought the Indian baby in. Dr. Fotheringham looked at it and he didn't say anything, just shoved two pills down its throat. It wasn't dead.

All that night we took turns with the babies. Every once in a while we gave them those pills.

◆◆

It was a clear morning like fall has, with the air sparkling like pop. Stretching clear to the horizon you could see our forty-bushel crop all thimbled with yellow stooks. In front of us a couple of tipped-up hens were pecking in the dirt. Rolling-in-the-Mud was sitting on his heels. Jake was sort of drawing in the ground with a twig. His eyes weren't so pouchy now he'd got a couple of nights' good sleep.

"Knew that the baby was gonna be all right – ours," Jake said.

"Me too." Rolling-in-the-Mud's eyes were kind of squinty and he was looking off into the distance. "Damn fine baby." He meant his.

Jake was looking pretty pleased about something. "Still fussy about that there skunk oil?"

Rolling-in-the-Mud bobbed his head. You couldn't tell whether he meant yes or no.

"Whilst I was taking my turn with him that bad night," Jake said, "I rubbed him good with goose grease."

I'd been watching the buckskin colt getting dinner from his mother. I turned around.

"Did you, Jake?"

"Oh, them there pills mighta helped a little, but she was goose grease pulled him through."

Rolling-in-the-Mud stood up. "You like that there colt?"

For a minute I couldn't even say yes with my head; the way he was looking down at me meant only one thing.

"You keep him – pay for all that feed." He turned to Jake. "Damn fine colt. Me too – I rubbed on skunk oil. Damn fine baby. Damn fine skunk oil."

JAKE AND THE MEDICINE MAN

THIS TIME OF THE YEAR – LATE IN THE FALL, AFTER HARVEST, winter about to set in – nothing all that exciting happens around Crocus district. Aunt Lil's thinking about heading for Victoria, and the Allerdyces for Jolly California. Just curling and chores to look forward to. Kid's Ma's on that pump organ of hers in the parlour a lot more. Me, I'm in the kitchen picking at my mandolin, wondering where the hell *do* the flies go in the wintertime.

A lot more fellows are setting round the stove in Mac-Taggart's store or over at Repeat Golightly's barbershop. But whenever we get to talking, everybody remembers when Professor Noble Winesinger first showed up in Crocus. Just a twinge of rheumatism or a touch of brochitis – maybe a sneeze or two – that's enough to make a fellow remember Winesinger.

Don't see fellows like the professor much these days. Travelling through town, stopping off, setting up their wagon. They'd usually have another fellow who played a banjo or a guitar and sang to draw the folks. Then they'd get up and show you a sort of a map of a human critter's insides, all bright and cheerful and red, with the liver and gizzard and lights. Then they'd sell bottles of their medicine.

Guess the professor must be about the last of his kind. Kind of hate to see them go. Real entertaining – educational. And that there medicine seemed to work, too. We'll miss them, though I suppose nowadays you can get the same stuff in Pill

Brown's drugstore, ads in papers, magazines, on the radio. Same stuff these old medicine men used to hand out, I figure.

⋅⋗ ⋖⋅

Last fall was the first time I ever run across Professor Noble Winesinger. I'd just took the Kid's ma into Crocus to deliver the eggs and cream, dropped her off at MacTaggart's Trading Company store to pick up the stuff for her new slipcovers. I headed for Repeat Golightly's barbershop. Haircut.

"One ahead of you, Jake. I say, there's one ahead of you."

I could already see that: fellow in a white bib in the chair. He had a Vandyke beard.

"Meet Professor Winesinger."

"Professor," I said.

"Jake Trumper," Repeat said.

"How do you do, Mr. Trumper," the professor said.

"I 'spose it's ten years since I trimmed a beard. Hooterites never come in, and I guess they got the only beards in Crocus district. Yes, ten years since I trimmed a beard."

Repeat was almost right. Albert Ricky has a beard. George Solway has one. Just like the professor's, George's is a Vandyke too, only on him it puts you in mind of a goat. Malleable Brown's goat.

" . . . was a senator – head of a land and mortgage company, I think," Repeat was going on. Way he usually does. "He stopped off fifteen years ago and he – stopped off –" Repeat straightened up. "Now – what was I – how did he come into the – oh! *He* had a Vandyke beard. Grey . . ."

"What about it?" I said.

"I trimmed it."

"That's nice."

"I trimmed it over fifteen years ago, and now here's the first one I've trimmed since then."

Repeat probably had that right. No way Albert Ricky's ever gonna pay for somebody to trim *his* goatee. He is the tightest fellow in Crocus District, of which he owns and farms nearly half.

"If you'll pardon the personal nature of the observation, professor – you have the finest Vandyke beard that I have ever trimmed."

"Thank you. I do not mind in the least."

"Pleasure. Pleasure. I always like to see a beard on a man. Yep. Pity they've gone out of fashion. Beards. Dignity. Give dignity to a man, you might say. True dignity. Essence. Essence of the male. Vee-rul." He cleared his throat. "How's things with you, Jake?"

"All right, Repeat."

"Professor here is a man of medicine."

That didn't surprise me any. "That right?" I said.

"An itinerant healer, sir. The beard Mr. Golightly has admired is the badge of my profession."

"That's nice," I said. "Critter? Human?"

"Both, sir. Mine is not the healing of the knife but rather an entirely natural remedy that uses nature's own restorative and therapeutic methods and powers."

" 'Lightning Penetration Oil and Tune-Up Tonic'," Repeat said.

"Yeah! Yeah!" I said. "I should've known! And you're Professor Wine . . . !"

"My remedy's gentle and beneficient healing and revivifying powers are equally bountiful for either man or beast."

"Sure are!" I said. "I had an eight-year-old mare once and she came down with . . ."

"In man and horse alike the greater part of the systolic period is occupied by systole of the ventricle . . ."

"She started in wheezin' an' there was nothin' . . ."

"Only about one third by *auricular* systole. The specific gravity does not vary greatly. In man, ten-fifty-five. In the horse, ten-sixty. The haemoglobin is almost identical in every way."

Repeat had took off the sheet, shook it, and stood back from the chair.

"She died," I said.

"I have not the slightest hesitation to recommend my remedy for man or beast. I beg your pardon?"

"This here mare – I was sayin' – she died."

"Was she afforded the inestimable benefit of Lightning Penetration Oil and Tune-Up Tonic?"

"Nope. That was what I meant to say – my neighbour. It was years ago – Manyberries way – fellow name of Flooger, Herb Flooger, his horse come down with the same thing. One bottle of your medicine saved *her*."

"All done, professor," Repeat said. "Step up, Jake."

"One of thousands, sir, still walking the face of this earth . . ."

"Here's your collar and tie . . ."

"Thanks to the timely use of Professor Noble Winesinger's Lightning Penetration Oil and Tune- . . ."

"Seventy-five cents," Repeat said. "Regular shave rate."

Working at his tie, the Professor said, "No doubt through relaxation of the vagus nerve which frequently inhibits and controls the respiratory movements."

"Nothing extra for the Vandyke trimming . . ."

"Expansion of the lung is associated with some stimulation of the pulmonary termination of the vagus . . ."

"Seventy-five cents is what I usually charge . . ."

" . . . which checks inspiration. Expiration then follows passively as the lung contracts, the stimulus is withdrawn from the vagus endings, inhibition spontaneously ceases and the act of inspiration starts anew . . ."

Professor, he was headed for the door, Repeat right behind him.

" . . . in forced breathing the sterno-mastoid and posterior portion of the trapezius muscles . . ."

Door slammed shut behind him. Repeat was standing there

with his hand still held out. He turned to me. "Next, Jake. I say, you're next."

"You, uh, didn't collect from him, Repeat."

"I guess I didn't. I guess the Professor can beat a bill just about as painless as any fellow I ever run across. Just about as painless."

Anybody gets out of Repeat's shop without paying for a haircut – shave – he's a champion. Repeat, he kept going on how the Professor hadn't paid him. I told Repeat I'd look him up and remind him he hadn't paid.

I found the Professor a while later, in Drew's pool hall. He wasn't playing.

"Professor."

"How do you do, sir? Have we met be . . ."

"In Repeat's shop. Half-hour ago. Trumper. Jake Trumper."

"Oh yes. Yes. I believe you treated a grey mare with my . . ."

"Friend of mine did. Herb Flooger. Uh, I, Repeat asked me to tell you that, uh, you forgot about your trim."

"No, no," he said, "I've just had it."

"*Payin'* for it."

"Oh, did I, didn't I – ? Ah well, I shall pass that way again, soon. Ah, uh, little game, sir? Billiards? Snooker? Fluke?"

"That'd be nice, Professor. Uh, snooker, I guess."

"Perhaps a small wager . . ."

"Well, uh, I, I don't know how you . . ."

"Just to make the game more interesting. Or shall we play a short one – enough to see – to gauge our respective talents on the baize?"

"Okay, Professor. Just for fun."

He wasn't all that good. Grabbed his cue too far back, didn't bend over enough to get his balls lined up true. After the first game I took him by thirty-three points, I said, "Sorry you had that – you seemed to run into a streak bad luck there . . ."

"The eyes, sir. Getting on. A man must have the eyes."

"We better keep her just for fun then. Hate to take your money . . ."

"My suggestion," he said. "I shall stick with it. On the next – a small wager, say, a dollar?"

Dollar a game ain't small. Not in Crocus.

"Well – if you you really want to."

"Or two?"

"Well, we usually play for . . ."

"Three then. You won. Your break, Mr. Trumper."

He didn't run into any streak bad luck this game. Or the next. Or the next.

"Twelve, thirteen, fourteen and five makes nineteen."

"Thank you, sir."

"Your eyes sure picked up a hell of a lot – after we jumped up the bet."

"Light had shifted. My vision seemed to clear."

"Yeah! Sure did!"

"As the winner, sir, may I – will you step into the Maple Leaf with me? Or, no, perhaps a cup of tea at the Canary Inn. I, uh, little matter I haven't straightened out at the Maple Leaf."

"Usually go into the Sanitary Café."

"Slight, uh, strain there too with Mr. Wong. But, yes, we can go there."

Wong as usual was sitting behind the cash register in the Sanitary Café, his fly-swatter in his hand.

"Hi, Jake, you in town again and – and – ah . . ." He saw the Professor behind me.

"It's all right, Mr. Wong," Winesinger said, "I happen to have a few dollars . . ."

WHAAP! Wong don't often miss a fly lands on his counter.

"Thirteen dollar fi'ty cen' – yes, you say hesta'day – day be-foh, you say-ee same day. Every day you say you be pay-ee thirteen dollah fi'ty cen'."

"Precisely the reason I've come in with Mr. Trumper. Pay a little on my account . . ."

"You pay-ee – thirteen dollah . . ."

"Five dollars – the rest tomorrow. Here, take our order, Mr. Trumper and I will have a pot of tea . . ."

"Oh no, must have thirteen dollah – no thirteen dollah, no tea – no thirteen dollah, no steak – pie-ee, oh no."

"I have just given you five on my account . . ."

"Never mind, Wong," I said. "This one is on me."

"Oh no, *I* invited *you* in. I couldn't let you."

"A couple of steaks, Wong – for me and the Professor. On me."

"But I can't let you . . ."

"That's all right. How'll you have it?"

"I – I wouldn't think for one moment of, ah, very rare, please."

After Wong took down our order and headed for the kitchen the Professor said, "Very kind of you. Thank you, Mr. – ah . . ."

"Trumper – Jake Trumper."

"Thank you indeed."

"S'all right. You, uh, you sellin' your medicine in Crocus, Professor?"

"At the moment, no. No, incredibly unfortunate turn of events finds me – not selling."

"Things a little sticky?"

"Sir?"

"On your uppers?"

"Mr. Trumper, for fifty-one years I have travelled the length and breadth of this Dominion, coast to coast. I have seen bad times and good, taken the bitter with the sweet. But never, not at any time, have I come upon times quite so unmitigated in their misfortune."

"Come again, Professor?"

"As a man of science I do not believe anything is to be

gained by railing against fate – cursing luck – but, sir, you see me now when the sound of the grinding is low. Very low."

"What I figgered. What's happened?"

"Pelvis. The little town of Pelvis, nestling upon the richest black loam in these western plains. Rheumatism and neuralgia endemic – great deal of goitre – exophthalmic – a little hamlet that in past years has welcomed me and my Lightning Penetration Oil and Tune-Up Tonic with open arms. A town of fat wheat cheques and easy taps, uh, wealthy agriculturists."

"What happened to you in Pelvis?"

"I was run out of Pelvis. Matter of a hundred-and-seventy-five-dollar licence fee."

"Oh."

"Blackhead, Saskatchewan . . ."

"Heavy license again?"

"Not even permitted to *buy* a licence. Three years before, I made a killing – ten dozen bottles."

"Ought to've been glad to see you back again, Professor."

"Bad batch," he said.

"Them folks in Blackhead sure are . . ."

"My remedy, I sold three years ago. Ah, seems to have leached away the enamel of their teeth. I was run out of Blackhead inside of twenty minutes."

"That's too bad," I said.

"When we got to Conception – oh, I might say I had with me, till we reached Conception, a young man who was serving his apprenticeship with me. In the town of Conception, where he was to set up the pitch, uh, where it – instead of playing upon his guitar and bringing people round for my lecture, he left me."

"Why?"

"Little girl, waitress in the Palm Café. Claimed he had found his true love. It was not love."

"What was it?" I said.

"In his own words: his belly was taut as the skin on an

Indian dancing-drum. He stayed to marry the waitress and to *eat* – regularly."

"So you lost your guitar fellow?"

"Just out of the town of Brokenshell, my car went out of control, left the road. Lost my entire stock of medicine. The Fourway Garage towed me into Crocus. There were extensive repairs to be made on the car. They hold it now for a bill of eighty-nine dollars and sixty-five cents. I am a week behind on a room at the Royal Hotel. As you know I have imposed upon the kindness and trust of Mr. Wong far beyond the limits of his generosity, patience, and endurance."

"Yeah – yeah."

"No assistant – no car – no Lightning Penetration Oil and Tune-Up Tonic."

"That's tough, Professor. Uh, just what is that stuff made out of?"

"I can divulge no more, sir, than to say that it is com-pounded from herbs and flora indigenous to this very soil of ours, which has nourished the noble red man and the pioneer – grown from the very loam which nurtured the mighty herds of buffalo and over which now blow these limitless fields of golden grain."

"That don't tell me much what's in . . ."

"It is an ancient remedy given me by an old Peigan medicine man as he lay upon his death-bed under canvas-filtered sun. His old hooded eyes flickered as he drew the last breath of his life to say to me, 'Professor Winesinger, take this recipe, take it and go far and wide alleviating the suffering and ail-ments of the Assiniboine Territories.' This I did. It has been my dedicated mission ever since."

"But, just what is she made out of?"

"Would you have me betray the trust of a dying medicine man, sir?"

"Oh no," I said. "Hell no!"

"Suffice it to say that my greatest obstacle to obtaining a stock of my remedy would be, ah, bottles."

"Bottles! That all?"

"And the labels."

"Well now, Professor, I sure hate to see you in a jackpot like this, all them poor folks that ought to be gettin' your medicine – them critters. We ought be able to work out a little matter of bottles and labels. Have another piece of pie, Professor, whilst I think her over."

Felt kind of sorry for the old fellow. Stranded. Like Repeat would have said, dignity – he sure was dignified. And he sure was hungry the way he tied into that steak and Wong's pie. Date cream. Three pieces! Time he was through, I had an idea. We headed for Pill Brown's drugstore.

"So we was wonderin', Pill, if the Professor here could pick up some bottles, uh, on credit."

"Bottles?" Pill snuffed. Pill's always sure to have a head cold. "What kind of bottles?"

"Twelve ounce, clear, graduated," the Professor said. "And corks."

"Why, I have quite a supply of those – but what did you want them . . ."

"Professor here – he's in sort of the same business as you are, Pill," I explained. "He's short of bottles . . ."

"Well, how many bottles?"

"Gross," the Professor said, "or two."

"Two gross! Good heavens, man, I can't let you have two . . ."

"In that case then, one gross will do. And labels."

" 'Fraid I can't help you there." Pill blew his nose.

"We'll drop over to Chet's at the *Crocus Breeze*," I said. "He'll be able to fix Professor with labels."

"Was there anythin' else?" Pill said.

"Yes – yes, I'll need a few things – oil of peppermint . . ."

"Yes, yes . . ."

"Capsicum, acacia, anise, ethyl . . ."

„&#65533; &#65533;›

Not so much stuff goes into that there medicine of Winesinger's. I helped him haul all those bottles to the Brokenshell River, behind the power plant. Near as I could see she was mostly water that old dying Peigan medicine man told him in that receipt of his. He filled up the bottles, pasted on the labels from the *Crocus Breeze* printing company. Looked good when he was done with them. Kind of dark and murky. I tasted a little of her. Tasted like medicine all right. Medicine or . . .

"Yee-uck! She's sure strong, Professor."

"Yes, bracing. Guaranteed to restore . . ."

"Tastes awful lot like coal oil to me!"

" . . . normal tone of all organs in any condition of debility – invigorates, builds up, imparts unbelievable vigour."

"What's next, Professor?"

"Tonight, sir. I lecture – before the gathered multitudes of, uh, before the – oh!"

"What's the matter?"

"In the excitement of preparing my remedy, I – we've – overlooked one important thing. People."

"People?"

"Customarily I have had my man to sing and play, to gather them round."

"You mean the fellah you left behind . . ."

"That's right," he said. "In more ways than one he was essential. His selection of music was important . . ."

"You mean light cheery stuff?"

"Mournful. Sad," he said.

"Like 'The Homesteader's Lament'?"

"He frequently opened with that very ditty."

" 'The Terrible Death of Roundhouse Pete'?" I suggested.

"Ah yes. As their throats choked up I used to swing into the respiratory ailments."

" 'My Wild Rose of the Prairies Is Faded Away', 'The Shade of Annie Mae'?"

"Internal complaints," he said.

" 'Let the Coyote Howl, Let Him Howl'?"

"Nothing like them. True ballads – sad ballads. Uh, just a minute. You know them?"

"Sung 'em all my life. Accompany myself . . ."

"Guitar!"

"No, my instrument is . . ."

"Banjo?"

"Mandolin."

"Wonderful, wonderful!" he said. "Tonight then – just opposite the post office."

"Well now, hold on, Professor . . ."

"Saturday night. You will be in town?"

"Yeah, yeah I can be in town – but . . ."

"I'll count on you, sir."

ᴥৡ ঌᴥ

Professor, he sure had a way with him. Didn't argue, just sort of – well, I felt kind of sorry for him and he knew how to use it. Had supper with him at Wong's Saturday. On me again. Then along about eight o'clock while the post office was still open, just before folks was on their way to the Hi-Art Theatre, Professor, he set up a box he got from MacTaggart's general store. Apple box. Lot of folks in town. I stood there feeling kind of foolish with my mandolin under my arm. Winesinger climbed up onto the box.

"Ladies and gentlemen, may I have your attention for a few moments that may change the course of your lives!" He leaned down to me. "Tuned up? Ready?"

"Yeah," I said. The mandolin was. I wasn't. First time I ever performed in public. Wished to hell I'd ordered a half dozen more in the Maple Leaf.

"First, a little entertainment. Not the complicated art of the concert stage – a few simple songs by one of your own fellow citizens. Those simple melodies which have had their birth in the hearts and emotions, the very grass roots, of these spreading plains of ours. First from Jake Trumper, 'The Home-steader's Lament'! Hit it, Jake!"

I done that.

> He lay upon the prairie
> When the light of day was low;
> He lay upon the prairie
> And knew that he must go.
>
> He lay upon the . . .

"Hold it, Jake." He turned out to the folks had gathered in front of us. Maybe a dozen of them. "We all know the hard-ships suffered by those first homesteading pioneers who pushed their way west. We all know the bitter winters and the relentless summers of drought and plague. Inadequate diets – lacking in the necessary vitamins – in a country where the frosts of winter, the heat of summer, the back-breaking toil of the soil, brought upon man all those respiratory com-plaints of bronchitis, pneumonia, pleurisy, galloping consump-tion, influenza, sinusitis, asthma – Okay, Jake, next one."

> The sweetgrass, the sweetgrass
> Was borne on the gentle breeze;
> The sweetgrass, the sweetgrass
> Never his pain could ease.

He let me finish 'The Sweet Grass'. All nine verses of her, while he set up his folding weasel and unrolled a map of the human body. More than one, actually, because she had layers to her like an onion has. Now he had an audience of almost *three* dozen.

He lifted up his pointer. "Let us start here with the trachea, then go down the esophagus, where we find a gradual transition from striated to non-striated muscles commencing at the limit of the upper and middle third or quarter. Internal to these muscular strata . . ."

> The call of the kiyoot is a sad one;
> The call of the kiyoot is wild;
> The call of the kiyoot is lonesome,
> As the heart of a motherless child.

"Foot-and-mouth disease is transmitted from cattle not only to sheep, horses, pigs, cats, goats, and dogs, but also to man. Further, it is not only in man but in many other mammals that the so-called ante-stomach is absent, whether as in the horse and pig it takes the form of portio-oesophagea or . . ." He lowered his pointer, leaned down off of the apple box to me, whispered, "Now! All stops out, hit them with 'To a Wild Rose I Was Married'!"

I was glad to oblige. That one's my favourite of them all, and I had a hunch them fifty people out there would feel the same as me about it.

> To a Wild Rose I was married
> Upon the prairie wide.
> We lived an' laughed together
> Until she up an' died.
>
> Where the tiger lily blows,
> There I buried her last night.
> Where the purple crocus blows,
> My own dear heart's delight.
>
> The wind cries from the west land,
> The wind cries o'er the sod,

The wind cries all around me,
For now my flower's with God.

She lays there; oh, she lays there
With the prairie for her bed.
She lays there; oh, she lays there
With a foxtail at her head.

" . . . entrusted to me by an old and dying Peigan medicine man as he lay upon his bed of pain. Look to that tree – brittle and dead with age, with the fall of the year, bare of leaves – but just as sure as this: when the sweet, mild, kiss of spring touches those roots – just as sure as this, the sap will stir and rise through that dead trunk. So too the healing power of Professor Winesinger's Lightning Penetration Oil and Tune-Up Tonic will stir that sluggish blood within your veins, and you will feel the years drop from you as the leaves from that tree – you will feel the sap of life to your very fingertips!"

No bingo players in the credit union hall. Hi-Art Theatre empty. Hardly a soul in the Maple Leaf Beer Parlour. Most of Crocus District were out there in front of the post office and the Professor up on his apple box.

I'd opened up the cartons of bottles the way the Professor told me to do.

"Well may you draw your breath and gasp in sheer surprise. Well you may, but I repeat, tonight I am giving away free the large-sized bottle – three months' supply – of Professor Winesinger's Lightning Penetration Oil and Tune-Up Tonic, which ordinarily sells for two dollars and forty-nine cents. I am *giving* it away with every purchase tonight of a regular-sized bottle. Only *two* dollars for both to one and all! Male and female! While they last!"

My part wasn't over. I wouldn't be singing or picking that mandolin any more. I'd handed it to Old Man Gatenby to hold for me. I was loading up with bottles.

" . . . bottles of youth and vigour for old, old veins that have not pulsed with the true joy of living for lo these many years! Bottles of zest! No, sir. Mr. Trumper will take care of you. Please! Do not crowd up to the front!"

I had my arms full and I was handing them out, but it was the Professor taking their two-dollar bills. He folded them and he stuck them between his fingers. *All* his fingers, both hands with bills fanned out of them.

Even before they got them bottles home, drank a drop, their faces was all lighted up. The years was dropping away from them like the Professor promised, like leaves dropping from a tree in fall.

Kind of sorry the Kid and his ma hadn't been there to see me perform, to hear the Professor's educational lecture. She don't approve of Professor Winesinger *or* his medicine.

"I'm surprised at you, Jake," she said next morning. "Standing up there in front of everybody and playing for that — for . . ."

"Professor Winesinger."

"Medicine man!" She said it like it was them words she don't like me to use in front of the Kid. Or anywhere else.

"He was in a bad spot," I said. "I *had* to help him out."

"You know that his medicine is just a patent medicine! I'm sorry you . . ."

"Now look here. I watched them folks whilst he talked at 'em. I saw their faces. Professor, he done 'em a lot of good. He give 'em their money's worth."

"Maybe," she said. "Certainly his *medicine* won't do them any good."

"Oh, I don't know. I don't know. He gives 'em a lot more than was in the bottle. Pretty good stuff. And that there lecture of his — educational. Done a lot of folks a lot of good. Know more about their insides now. You might call the old Professor a faith healer. Sort of."

"Have you ever used it? For your bronchitis? For your lumbago?"

"Aaaah, no – no, not yet. Herb Flooger, out Manyberries way, he had a eight-year-old mare an' . . ."

"Just what do you mean 'not yet'?"

"Uh . . ."

"Did you buy a bottle last night?"

"No," I said. "Not a bottle."

"What was in the carton you carried in last night? Took up to your room?"

I didn't know she seen me. "Why – it was – they was . . ."

"How many, Jake?"

"Uh – it's good for critters too, you know, Queenie's been bloatin' again."

"How many!?"

"He gave me a real bargain."

"How many bottles of that . . . ?"

"Couple of dozen."

"Two dozen!"

"I didn't pay *cash* for 'em. Just a couple meals in the Sanitary Café – some money he won off me in Drew's pool hall. His idea. He just squared with me for helpin' him out when he was broke an' starvin'."

She just looked at me and shook her head slow. "Jake, I don't think I'll ever understand you."

"That's nice," I said. "Oh, by the way – Albert Ricky."

"What about him?" Kid's ma isn't very fussy about Albert. She's on Crocus School Board, and Albert's chairman of that. He is the meanest, stingiest, tightest fellow in all of Crocus district.

"Ricky bought eight bottles," I told her. "Would've bought more but the Professor had run out."

KING OF ALL THE COUNTRY

JUST ABOUT OVER NOW, BUT EVERY YEAR YOU GET IT IN Crocus district. Like the stuff hits the jackrabbits every so many years – plague, epidemic. Bad brand of it in Crocus. Starts round about the fifteenth September – busy time of the year, harvest – runs through October and then she quits dead, fifteenth November. One nice thing about it – leaves most the women alone. Not many men.

Double-barrelled sickness that comes out of the sloughs. It gets a fellow the worst just at sunrise, and again at sunset. Gives him a high fever, aching shoulder, stiff joints, shooting pains, and black specks in front of his eyes. Attacks young and old and for a couple months every year, makes widows – goose widows – butterball widows and blue-wing teal and pintail widows.

From fourteen to eighty I guess there's hardly a fellow in Crocus district doesn't come down with duck fever or the prairie-chicken complaint or the partridge plague. If they miss him, he gets laid low with the worst of them all: the grey honker horrors. Whether it's upland game or ducks and geese, when the hunting season opens you'll see fellows with their shotguns over their arms, their dogs at their side, heading for McConkey's slough or Yellow Grass Lake or the general direction of the Brokenshell River. There's your real epidemic in this country: duck hunting and goose hunting. Here this fall the Kid and me nearly got cured of it, whether we wanted or not.

One morning early in October, just before daybreak, I heard the Kid yell. His bedroom's right next to mine.

"Hey, Jake – hear 'em? Geese – thousands of 'em!"

Way it is with geese: a couple of dozen of them can *sound* like a couple of hundred.

At breakfast the Kid was still real excited. " . . . just like bein' waked up by a thousand dogs barkin'! Sound asleep an' the next thing I knew – in bed, holdin' my breath, all cold inside of my elbows – settin' straight up in . . ."

"*Sitting*, son."

"Must have been five hundred of 'em!"

"Maybe fifty, Kid."

"Jake – would they be northren geese?"

"Northern geese, son."

"Sure," I said, "They're northren geese, all right."

"Wavies!?"

"Kid – Kid – you been raised better'n that. Honkers. Grey Canada geese. Honkers."

"The sound of northern geese coming down is a sad sound," Kid's ma said. "Frost has blackened the flowers – there's a sadness. End of another year . . ."

"Not all that bad," I said. "Harvest's over an' she's time to get out the old twelve-gauge!"

"Yeah! Oh, yeah! I swear I could hear their . . ."

"Eat your pancakes, son."

" . . . wings. When they passed over I bet they scraped their wishbones on the ridge o' the house!"

"Let's just wait till after we've finished breakfast."

"What's wrong with talkin' about a flight o' geese went over . . . ?"

"Nothing! *In* its place."

"Where's its place?" I said.

"Not at meals."

"I'm not so hungry," Kid said.

"That has nothing to do with it. Eat your breakfast."

Kid's ma used to be a schoolteacher. Don't get me wrong
– hell of a fine woman.

After the Kid left for Rabbit Hill School, she said, "Perhaps
I *was* a little sharp, Jake. I've said I'm sorry."

"Like anybody else the Kid was just interested in them geese
flew over this morning."

"All right. I've admitted I was a little short. You know just
as well as I – how he is. The middle of his breakfast wasn't the
time for it. I have enough trouble getting him to eat his breakfast without – a growing boy has to have a decent breakfast. I
know I'm just a little on edge."

"A little?"

"Today."

"What's special about today?"

"This afternoon is my turn for having the Athenian Book
and Discussion Group."

"Oh," I said. "That case I'll stay clear the house the next
fourteen hours."

"Now, Jake, there's no need for you to . . ."

"Yes there is! You got a bunch them girls comin' in for tea
an' lady fingers an' – an' that stuff. You'll be shinin' up your
kitchen linoleum – polishin' floors – buffin' silverware – rubbin'
up table tops – I know."

"You know what!"

"I know when to get away – when you're snuffy . . ."

"I am not!"

"You wasn't so sweet at breakfast . . ."

"It had nothing to do with . . ."

"Maybe not – but I'll just steer clear till the tea cosy's put
away an' the cake crumbs is all swep' up an' the gossip is
all . . ."

"We do not gossip!"

" . . . over an' you kind of lay back against the chesterfield an' sigh an' say how glad you are it's all over an' you hope you don't have to do it again for a thousand years."

"Jake Trumper!" Then she laughed. "All right, all right. You win."

"I got lots pilin' up in the barn – saved for a rainy day or when you get the Atheniums in. Me an' the girls."

"Girls?"

"Nora an' Naomi an' Ruth an' Irene an' Eglantine got a meetin' we been puttin' off for a long time now. I got to get ready – same as you – I'll have a holt the business end of a manure fork instead of a teaspoon, but I'll be pitchin' the same sorta stuff as Mrs. MacTaggart an' Mrs. Doc Fotherin'ham an' Mrs. Abercrombie an' . . ."

"Jake!" Then she started laughing again. Kid's ma, she ain't all bad.

I don't know why I keep putting her off so long every time, grabbing a pitchfork regular and cleaning her up. But I guess I ain't alone in the manure matter. Look at that olden time Greek fellow. Kid read all about him – Herb – Herm – Herk-somethin'. He run up against real stable trouble. Kept right on coming back in as soon as he threw her out. I know just how he must've felt.

Up at that house the Atheniums were still going at it strong when the Kid came home from Rabbit Hill school. I guess that's why he stayed with me in the barn.

"Gee, Jake!" he said as soon as he led in his buckskin pony, Auction Fever, "I seen – saw 'em landin'!"

"A-ha! Feedin' early! Grab a fork, Kid."

"*Two* flocks of 'em! Onto Mr. Ricky's!"

"Where else?"

"Yeah. Isn't that funny the way they hit for Ricky's right from the start?"

"Nope. Geese is smart. They know Albert Ricky don't let nobody shoot over his land. They talk it over amongst their selfs. That manure fork's hangin' up right next Baldy's stall."

"Talk it over?"

"Mexico – South America – word gets around down there. 'Head for Albert Ricky's stubble, up there in southern Saskatchewan,' they honk. 'Head for there when you're flyin' south an' you're home free.' "

"I bet Mr. Ricky waits till they're all in there then he takes a crack at 'em himself."

"Nope. You're thinkin' of Pete Botten. Nobody touches a grey honker on Albert's land, includin' Albert hisself."

"Anyways," the Kid said, "they really started piling in there. Maybe won't be long before they start landing on that barley stubble of ours."

"Yeah. Honkers prefer barley – hey! Kid! Watch where you heave it!"

"Sorry, Jake."

"S'all right. Mostly straw."

"Jake?"

"Yeah?"

"Willis Tincher's almost a year younger than I am."

"Mm-huh."

"He knocked down a goose last fall, back last fall. His dad took him out."

"Yeah?"

"Stevie Kiziw goes helps his dad pit in – shoots. I was wonderin' – Gee, Jake, she'd be real nice if a person could have a shotgun – if he was old enough to . . ."

"Uh-huh."

"I was wonderin' if maybe this might be the fall I could . . ."

"It might be, Kid. Just might be."

"Shotguns, they cost a lot of money, don't they?"

"Oh, I don't know. Fellow picks up one secondhand, single-shot twenty-gauge – I don't know."

"Oh – Jake!"

"Next time I'm in Crocus. See maybe if Mac has any secondhand guns, ah, single-shot."

"Gee, Jake – that'd be – I'm one lucky kid!"

"Are you?"

"Way I got born."

"Huh?"

"Saskatchewan. Why, I might've been born all kinds of places – I might've got born in B.C. or – or in Ontario!"

"I guess you might."

"Or in a city!"

"Uh-huh."

"All the places a person could get born, and I go an' get born plunk in the middle the central flyway for all the geese of North America!"

Kid and me hung in with the manure forking well after the Atheniums had finished theirs and took off. Almost suppertime. We came in, Kid's ma was on the parlour couch, laid back and her feet stretched out ahead of herself, just like I said she would be. "Certainly glad that's over for another year. It went off well."

"That's nice," I said. I picked up the new *Crocus Breeze* off the coffee table. "We can take her easy till she's your turn with 'em again."

"Say whatever you like, Jake. All over without a hitch."

"Uh-huh." I opened up the paper.

"They all said it was a rewarding session. We finished up Free Trade and Tariffs with Elsie's paper."

"That's nice," I said. "Are we gonna be able to read all about it in the *Crocus Breeze* next issue when she comes out?"

"Oh, Jake!"

"Like – in 'Newsy Notes From Round About' in here. 'A sumt-you-us lunch wound up the afternoon with a double ring cake by Mrs. Totecole . . . assisted in openin' the gifts by her sister, hauled in on a beautifully decorated wagon – ' Hey! Hold on . . ."

"The Totecole shower," she said.

"What they doin' haulin' her in on a decorated wagon?"

"The gifts – they do that . . ."

"Oh! – ah, 'Our side-delivery rakes can't be beat' – 'Auction three miles west. Colonel Hepner – ' Say!"

"What's that?"

"Doc Fotheringham and the Reverend Cameron – Mayor MacTaggart . . ."

"What about them?"

"Their limit!"

"What?"

"Yellow Grass Lake – barley field – they hit the jackpot beginnin' the week – got their limit grey honkers!"

"Oh."

"Barley field – now I wonder whose . . ."

"Oh, Jake, don't you think we could forget goose hunting for a while?"

"That'd be two mile south an' a quarter west of Arley's place maybe – past South Conception schoolhouse."

"You know, Jake, there's a lot to be said for Albert Ricky after all . . ."

"An' I bet there was just the three of 'em in on it – three's the right number for a goose hunt . . ."

"For all he may be mean and – and untrustworthy, you can say one thing for him." Kid's ma should have known better. She's on Crocus School Board. Ricky's chairman.

"Two ain't enough to get 'em in a cross-fire. Four or five – there's sure to be some damn fool won't wait for the signal."

"Goes to show you – there's something good in everyone."

"Huh? Who?"

"Albert Ricky."

"What about him?"

"He's no goose killer."

"Oh – I though for a minute you knew somethin' *good* about him."

"I consider it to his credit that he has made his place a sanctuary for wildlife. Albert Ricky is a close, hard man, but it shows that he has a soft side to him that perhaps finer men we know – haven't."

"Albert! Him!"

"You don't hear of Albert heading out to slaughter . . ."

"O' course you won't. Shells cost money! He ain't about to go blowin' nickels into thin air!"

"*And* he won't let others do it on his land either! I think it's pretty nice that weary birds can rest in peace and comfort on their long trip south in the fall, and know they're safe from humans' guns."

"Ah-hah. Albert Ricky may be runnin' a sort of a wild goose sanctuary – but it ain't because he loves 'em. It ain't the softness of his heart. He is as tight as the bark on a saskatoon . . ."

"I didn't say he wasn't – but you might give him credit when he deserves . . ."

"Fertilizer."

"Whaat!"

"Albert Ricky figures goose manure is the greatest fertilizer there is."

"Now, wait a minute."

"That's right. He's kickin' his heels together thinkin' of all of them geese workin' for him for nothin'. Every single second they're on his land they're enrichin' it an' him. It figgers."

"Jake – that's ridiculous!"

"Sure it is, but Albert doesn't think so . . . ."

"Come on, Jake."

"Free fertilizer. Simple as that. Other fellows get a bang out the sound of their wings when they come up off the horizon – ploughin' the mornin' sky, callin' wild an' free an' thrillin'. Other fellows is out there in a frosty goose pit with their hearts in their throat. Albert he rolls over in bed an' says, 'There they are again – another load of free goose turds onto my land'. How low can a man sink!"

She got up off of the couch, and heading towards the kitchen she turned back at the door.

"Speaking of fertilizer, it does not smell like sweetgrass in here. I suggest you have a good hot bath tonight. Both of you!"

The Kid and me did have a bath in the kitchen after she'd gone up to bed.

❧ ❧

Couple of days later, Thursday early when I was out on the manure spreader, the geese started coming in on our place. Lucky I hadn't started on the barley stubble. I watched them land and decided to put off spreading manure for a few days. Give her a chance to rot a little more. Kid got home from Rabbit Hill. I told him.

"How many, Jake?!"

"Thirty to fifty of 'em."

"Gonna blast 'em in the mornin', Jake!"

"Nope. That's just the first of the party, Kid. Tomorrow they'll be double. Fifty, hunnerd."

"And the next flight, two hundred, then four, six – why, we wait a week we'll have . . ."

"We ain't waitin' that long, Kid."

"But, Jake, what about that twenty-gauge . . ."

"We'll take care that, Kid – we'll keep our eye on them geese. Tomorrow's Friday."

"Yeah – yeah!"

"I got to take the cream can an' eggs in. Let 'em rest an' increase till, oh, maybe Monday morning . . ."

"Jake, I can hardly wait . . ."

"You do your best, Kid. Tomorrow I'll be pickin' up material for your ma's new drapes at MacTaggart's store. Aim to take a look at what he's got in there, way of shotguns."

"Oh, Jake!"

"Ah, wouldn't say nothin' about that to your ma. Not quite yet."

Her drapery material wasn't in yet, but a Couey single-shot

twenty-gauge was. I was cleanin' my own twelve-gauge in the bedroom when she showed up in the doorway.

"Mr. MacTaggart promised the material would be here *last* week."

"He said she didn't come . . ."

"What's that you've got there!"

" . . . an' he phoned 'em an' they promised . . ."

"Jake, what . . ."

" . . . they'd get 'em down for sure beginnin' next week. Drapes is difficult, Mac says."

"Jake, what is that?!"

"Anybody can see it's a gun."

"Gun!"

"Shotgun."

"*Another* shotgun. You already *have* one."

"That's right."

"Well, what's the other one?" She'd caught me by surprise. The Couey was laying across the foot of the bed.

"One I got off of MacTaggart. Twelve dollars."

"You didn't say anything about getting another shotgun."

"Nope. Just seen it there in Mac's fall gun display – second-hand ones he's took in on new guns. Twenty-gauge. Single-shot."

"Is it!"

"Hardly any kick at all to a twenty-gauge."

"Isn't there."

"Nope. You take Reverend Cameron, he uses a twenty-gauge on everything. Not just on prairie chicken – partridge, ducks, too, an' geese. He claims a good shot don't need no twelve-gauge cannon . . ."

"Jake, did you get that gun for . . ."

"Way he figures it, an' he may be right – he figures what you lose in pattern you gain in accuracy. He claims you get this sort of unconscious flinch with a heavier gun."

"I hate guns!"

"Sure, sure. So your kid's first shotgun just naturally oughta be a twenty-gauge single-shot. Don't cost much. He learns proper right from the beginnin'—no flinch. He's gotta be accurate—make his first shot tell . . ."

"That gun is *not* for my son!"

"Who else?"

"You take it right back to Mr. MacTaggart!"

"Huh!"

"I wish you'd said something to me first, Jake."

"But I ain't—I can't. Look, he's old enough—I half promised him this season . . ."

"Unpromise him! You had no right to go ahead . . ."

"I don't see what's wrong with it. Willis Tincher, Stevie Kiziw, they been goin' out with their dads couple seasons now."

"My son has no father, Jake," she said. "That's—you—we depend on you."

"He's a good kid. I'll teach him to handle it careful. I'll learn him right."

"That isn't it, Jake. I don't intend him to have a gun—at all—ever. He—hasn't seen it yet?"

"No. But I did tell him . . ."

"All right. It won't be so bad then."

"It'll be bad."

"I'm sorry, Jake. If you'd let me know first—we could have saved him disappointment."

"All right."

"Just don't let him see it. Take it back."

"Yeah. Yeah. I'll hide it outa sight. I'll *sneak* it back to MacTaggart's. I'll just kind of *lie* an' tell him Mac didn't have a Couey single-shot this fall."

"It won't be as bad as that. I'll explain to him. He'll understand how I feel about it—how I'd like him to feel about it."

"I was only trying to do the right thing."

"I know you were, Jake."

"Hadn't no business . . ."

"It's all right, Jake."

"Kid raised on the prairies – part of his education – duck huntin', goose shootin' . . ."

"Not my son."

"Well, he's your kid. But the way I see it – well, it ain't natural."

"It's going to be natural for my boy."

"So long as you feel right about it. Me, I don't like forcin' stuff on other people."

"I'm not *forcing* anything on him!"

"I don't see what you got against huntin' anyways," I said.

"Just a conviction and a distaste for needless killing, Jake."

"Needless! You seen the ducks swarmin' over the swathes! They cleaned out thousands of acres a hunnerd percent! Needless! If they wasn't shot up we'd be up to our hips in mallards and pintails an' canvasback an' teal!"

"That's no answer to what I mean. I mean killing for sport, Jake. I think it's cruel and – and inhuman!"

"I'd say she was one the human-est things I know."

"I don't like to think what it must do to a man's character," she said.

"Just what do you figure it – does – to a man's character?"

"Coarsens it," she said.

"Oh."

"Unleashes the primitive instincts."

"Oh."

"The world can do with as little of that as possible."

"Can it," I said.

"Any way you look at it – it's not right."

"Look, it ain't all that easy. Them geese, they got a fair fight. Ain't they? Don't you . . ."

"No."

"How do you know? You never been in a goose pit. You never took a shotgun an' tried to knock down a . . ."

"They're not shooting back at you."

"Whaaaat!"

"*Then* it would be a fair fight," she said. "Or if you were starving – and you had to shoot them for food or die. *Then* it would be a fair fight, Jake. But not for *fun*. Killing for fun – that's weasel killing!"

"Look, it ain't all as bad an' wicked as you – it – all right, all right! Coarsens a fellow's character – makes him, uh, gives him – starts up his, uh, instincts – all right. Look at Doc Fotherin'ham. Just look how coarse and primitive he is!"

"I didn't say he was."

"Oh yes you did. You said it coarsened a man's character, an' Doc, he spends just as much time with the goose as he does with the stork!"

"Jake. It isn't a matter of . . ."

"An' Reverend Cameron. He's a fine man, ain't he? All the same – he's just as interested in flocks o' mallards as he is in that human flock o' his down in them pews every Sunday mornin'. He's just as deadly with his twenty-gauge on a high grey honker as he is on a blue-wing sin!"

"Look, Jake . . ."

"For that matter," I bust in on her, "seems to me the Bible says somethin' about duck an' goose huntin' . . ."

"It does not!"

"Somethin' about the Lord puttin' critters of the earth an' fowl of the air here for man's use."

"If you mean *need* – yes – but I'm sure there was no Divine intention that man should kill – destroy His life for pleasure."

"I ain't sure what He had in mind at the time. One thing I do know – Doc Fotherin'ham an' Reverend Cameron ain't coarse fellows!"

"Of course they aren't. They're both fine men. But couldn't

they have been *finer* men? Suppose when they were tempted, they had resisted. Suppose they hadn't allowed themselves to be carried away by the excitement of – of – the kill."

"Why you keep harpin' on that! It ain't – a fellow ain't thinkin' how he's killin'! That ain't what makes it . . ."

"There are lots of men who aren't half the men Doc Fotheringham and Reverend Cameron are, who do not shoot. But, oh, Jake, believe me, I know what I'm talking about! You can't . . ."

"Look – what did you have last night for supper?"

"What?"

"Pot roast," I said. "That come off a critter. That critter was slaughtered so's we could eat him."

"That's no answer at all. I would disapprove just as much of a man who worked in a slaughterhouse for the fun of it. We eat to live. I'm talking of killing for *fun*. Why do you shoot geese, Jake?"

"Huh?"

"Have you ever asked yourself that? Have you?"

"Why, I, the reason a fellow – you don't ask yourself – I like it!"

"Why?"

"Because – I don't know – look – it's none of your goddam business!"

"But you must have wondered . . ."

"You wanta know why? Because they're up there, and I'm gonna knock 'em down!"

"That's no answer, Jake."

"Because – they're up there! That's why!"

"All right, Jake."

"I guess it ain't – any answer. But – but – woman – there's lots of stuff a human does he ain't got a solid square six-by-six reason for. Maybe that's what a fellow does a lot of things for because they *don't* make no sense – they don't make him a nickel – he just does 'em to *do* the thing. Maybe it's the way a human critter is."

"All right, Jake. Perhaps you know how I feel about it, though."

"Yeah. I guess so."

"Please put that gun away."

"Don't worry. I don't aim to torture him. I'll get it outa sight – till I can take it back."

⊰ ❧

Live and let live, I always say. Maybe I argue more than my share. Maybe I don't change round to the other side the fence so easy. It's her business how she wants to bring her kid up. All the same – I – I didn't take that gun back into town Saturday night. I stuck it in the bottom drawer under my underwear.

She was a full moon Saturday night. Kid shook me awake.

"Jake, Jake! Hear 'em! Real close! I think they're landing on our barley field!"

That was when I had to tell what I promised his ma about the twenty-gauge. He took it good.

"You going to . . ."

"Yep. Soon as they take off tomorrow mornin'! I'll be lookin' for droppin's – pittin' in."

"Can I come with you?"

"Uh-huh."

"I don't care if I haven't got a gun."

⊰ ❧

They was in our barley field, all right. Kid and me found their droppings. We pitted in. We didn't set up the decoys. Do that Monday morning when we'd know which way the wind would be coming from. Great decoys. Made 'em myself, bodies cut out of stove pipe, neck, and head out of apple-box wood, listeners and watchers and feeders. Work a hell of a lot better than those twelve-dollar ones of Doc Fotheringham.

Just before daybreak Monday morning I shook the Kid awake.

"Ah, uh, Jake . . ."

"Shhhh! Almost daylight in the swamp. Roll out."

"What time is it?"

" 'Bout a hour before daybreak an' the morning flight."

The bedsprings creaked and twanged. His feet hit the floor thudding like a pile-driver.

"Easy! Easy, Kid! Want to wake everybody from here to the correction line!"

"They can't hear us clear up . . ."

"Ain't the *geese* I'm worried about! Get dressed."

"I am! I am! Wore my pants and socks and shirt to bed." Then he saw the single-shot twenty-gauge. "You got *two* . . . !"

"Yeah. Yeah, an' I'm liable to get shot with one or the other of them if you don't whisper, Kid! Take your shoes off and *carry* them!"

Till we got right up on the pit, the Kid couldn't even remember or see it. We'd dug her deep and roomy, covered her with the chicken wire lid wove with straw. We set our decoys upwind from the hide. Eighteen of them.

"Gee, Jake! They look real!"

"Yep. Now, Kid – no shell in that gun till I say."

"Uh-huh."

"Safety off till I tell you to snick . . ."

"Uh-huh."

"Just me doin' the lookin'. You keep your head down till I yell."

"Uh-huh."

"Get down in there."

We got in, pulled the lid over us. Lots of room. I always dig a pit for three. Within fifteen minutes we heard 'em way off. They must've been taking off from the Brokenshell River. Then we saw them heading our way. Oh, they was coming straight and sweet! Drifting free on the horizon – low and straggling like thin and thready smoke against the morning sky! Only you don't get smoke in a wide, shallow honking vee.

Then I saw this figure running across the barley stubble towards us, the wind whipping her skirts. It was the Kid's ma! She pulled up just the other side of our decoys.

"Jake! Son! Where are you!"

"Shee-yit! She's gonna ruin it for us!"

I yelled at her, "Here! Over here!" I didn't want to stand up with the geese coming in on us. "Come a-runnin' belly to the ground! You're gonna ruin it for us just when we got 'em by the tailfeathers on a downhill puuuulllllll!"

I yanked her down with us. She landed on top of the Kid.

"Jake! You promised!"

"Shuhduuuuuuup!"

They come! They come, sifting sidewise and the sound of their wings was like a rush of wind – like she was our own blood whanging in our own ears! Then we saw them lower and lower – gaggling – barking shrill and untidy! Crazy – crazy wild! Peeling off and wheeling down, tilting this way and tilting that! So low you could see their feet getting ready. Then:

"SUH-LAWWWWWTER THE DARLINGS!"

I dropped two out of my three shots. Then there come the lighter twenty-gauge shot and another one planed down, then tumbled to thud on the stubble to our left.

"Good goin', Kid! Knocked down your first . . ."

"It – I never . . ."

We was all out of the pit and Kid's ma was holding the Couey single-shot, smoke breathing out of the barrel. She was looking down at it, sort of dazed. Then she looked up at me and I seen the wind had took out her hair and laid it across her cheek to the corner of her mouth. I seen the tears, too.

She handed the Kid the gun and she turned away and she didn't say nothing. She didn't say nothing.

I watched her walking away across the barley stubble, and I was wishing – oh God, how I was wishing I kept my promise to her!

WELL, WELL, WELL

Trouble with old man gatenby — he's got no tact. Most *un*-tactful man in Crocus district. Lives down Government Road from us. Yellow grasshopper-coloured house just beyond the correction line. Always coming out flat-footed about how he knows everything. *Un*-tactful. Old Gate and me, we don't see eye-to-eye on nothing and it don't stop there. He's all the time trying to ram what he thinks down my throat. Take when Gate and Ben and me was passing the time of day late last June, wondering when she was ever going to rain. Old Gate was setting on the edge of our stock trough, his knees up like a grasshopper all ready to bung up into the air, looking kind of squinty the way he does. It was a lazy sort of day.

Ben Tincher said, "Gettin' awful low on water our place. We been going careful two weeks now, but I'm afraid she'll be dry in a couple days. Looks like we're gonna have to dig a new one. I don't know why ours always has to go dry before anybody else's in the district."

"Yours is a shallah one," I said. "You're just gettin' surface water out of her, Tinch. Gotta go real deep you want a *real* well. Like ours here."

"Like *mine*." See what I mean about Gate. "Best there is — witched her myself."

"Now you take ours," I explained. "Five years old now and . . ."

"Mine's fifteen."

I tried once more. "Now – you take our well . . ."

"Witched her with a willah wand. Water outa my well is just as clear as . . ."

"No clearer than the water outa our well," I said.

"Maybe. But I ain't fussy about water that tastes a touch brackish."

"Ain't brackish at all!"

"Must be the Glauber's salts in her then," Gate said.

I got to admit there's a touch of Glauber's in our well. Isn't a well in Crocus district hasn't got *some* Glauber's in it. "Glauber's is good for a fellow's system. Keeps you . . ."

"When you witched that well, Jake, did you . . ."

". . . reg'lar."

". . . use a willah wand?"

"Hazel."

"Hazel! Who ever heard of hazel for witchin' water?"

"Most witchin' wands I ever heard of was made out of willah, Jake." That was Tinch. He don't say much most of the time. 'Specially around Gate.

"Hazel ain't worth a whoop for divining!" Gate said.

"The hell it ain't!" I said.

"Look around – where do you find willah growin'?" Gate said. "All where there's water. And where do you find hazel? Anywheres."

"All right, Gate. All right." I said.

"Willow does grow near water, Jake," Tinch said.

"Willah knows where to *find* water," Gate said. "Willah *loves* water."

"Willah's been near water so long – it's had a belly fulla water! Ain't interested in water no more," I said. "Willah's water-*logged*!"

"Is not!"

"Is so! But hazel – because it ain't been soaked up with water – it *wants* water. *Got* to have water. *Thirsty* for water . . ."

"In a pig's ass!"

"All right, Gate, you go ahead and use a pig's ass for water witching – go right ahead!"

"I didn't say I . . ."

"You said a pig's ass was good for water witching!"

"All I said was – what I meant – aaaah . . ."

I had the edge on Gate now. "I found out how good hazel was years ago when I was living in Medium Rock – up the line from Little Rock, just down the line from Big Rock – and I . . ."

"Willah . . ."

". . . and a friend of mine, fellow name of Fladiger, Sudbury Fladiger, Suds Fladiger we called him for short. He went lame in the left knee. Bad. He was a section man . . ."

"Willah's the only thing for witchin' . . ."

"Doc, he couldn't do a thing for Suds. Tried everything – had him beat."

"What's all this got to do with witchin' a goddam well?"

"I looked at Suds' knee and then I remembered this here lovely hazel witchin' wand – been give to me by a Cree medicine man . . ."

"Sure, sure," Gate said. "Chief Weasel Tail, you're always goin' on about. How you saved him an' the whole South Blackfoot from starvin' to . . ."

"Nope, Elijah One-Thin-Man – he had his own personal hazel water witching wand . . ."

"Dumb medicine man if he thought she was good for witchin' water . . ."

"Wise old medicine man."

"What's that got to do with this fellow with the bum knee, Jake?" Tinch said.

"Oh yeah, that. Why, well, I took this here hazel wand. I held her over top his bum knee. Say! She flipped right over and turned down – hung straight as a plumb bob. She was so sensitive, she ree-acted to Suds Fladiger's knee – water on the

knee! Doc knew just what to do then – cured Suds by drainin'
off the water."

"Of all the *ex*-aggerated, *un*-likely stories I ever heard!"
Gate sputtered.

"Now just you hold on, Gate, that there was the most sensitive wand I ever had. Still got her. She's got more an' more
sensitive more wells I witched with her. Right now she's
worked down so fine she can shiver to a drop of frog spit."

"Practical," Gate said. "Awful handy to know where there's
frog spit."

"Just shows you what hazel can do."

"Well," Tinch said, "looks like you're the boys for me – got
to get somebody to divine me a well . . ."

"Glad to, Tinch," I said.

"Glad to, Tinch," Gate said.

"Only which one will do the witchin'?"

"Hazel will do her," I said.

"Willah will do her," Gate said.

"Looks like I'll have to use the both of you," Tinch said.
"Have sort of a well-witching contest."

Now, I told Gate and Ben I still had that hazel wand, the
one I used to witch Ma's dandy well with five years ago. I was
wrong. I looked and I looked for it: in the machine shed, the
harness room, the back stoop, my bedroom. I was pulling out
drawers in the kitchen counter when the Kid's ma came in.

"What are you doing? My kitchen draw . . ."

"Figured she might be in one of 'em."

"What might be . . ."

"Sure she was in the harness room but she wasn't. Gotta
be somewheres in the house!"

"What must be . . ."

"Wand."

"Wand! What do you mean a wand?"

"Wand – wand – hazel . . ."

"Hazel who!"

"Hazel nobody. Hazel wand – I'm looking for her. Gonna divine a well for Tinch."

"Well, there's no wand around the house."

"Yeah, yeah – that's just what I'm findin' out!" I slammed shut her goddam kitchen cupboard drawer.

"Jake, why ever would you think your wand would be in my . . ."

"Only because five plugs of chewin' tobacco was," I said, "An' a package razor blades an' my toenail clippers!" I didn't tell her I found the clippers in her sewing basket.

Then it was the Kid's turn. Had to wait until he came home from Rabbit Hill school.

"Kid, I been lookin' for something all day. High an' low. She was up on the top shelf in the harness room – ain't there now. Ain't nowhere. Dammit!"

"What, Jake?"

"Witchin' wand. Hazel witchin' wand. You seen it any-wheres?"

"That sort of a forked stick, Jake?"

"That's right."

"Sure, I saw it."

"Great! Where? When?"

"Harness room. Last summer. I didn't know it was a witching wand, though. Last summer me and Stevie Kiziw were in the harness room."

"Yeah?"

"Stevie, he – Stevie's a real good shot with a slingshot."

"What the hell has that got to do with my hazel witchin' wand?"

"Last year Miss Henchbaw, she took Stevie's slingshot off him – made him hand it right over – after he got Mr. Bollington right in the . . ."

"Where is my hazel wand?"

" . . . when he was bending over to put the lid on the sweeping compound after four. So Stevie, well, he needed a new
slingshot . . ."

"Go on, Kid."

"Well, uh, he's got him a *new* slingshot."

"Sheeee-yit!"

Generally I'm careful about using language around the Kid.
Even when his ma isn't there. I gave him royal hell for fifteen
minutes, took it up with his ma, and I don't do that very
often.

"How can I witch Tinch's new well without any hazel
wand!"

"When is this divine event to take place?"

"Day after tomorrow."

"Perhaps – why don't you just go down to the Brokenshell,
find yourself a wolf-willow crotch and make a new . . ."

"Because willah's no good for witchin', that's why."

"Isn't that what diviners always use?"

"Gate's usin' willow. I need hazel. That's the best. Hazel I
used for our well . . ."

"Simple. Get yourself some hazel then."

"You looked out your kitchen window lately?"

"Of course."

"You are now livin' plunk in the centre of the bald-headed
prairie. Just where the – where would I find me a hazel tree
between here an' the North Dakota border!"

"No need to get so snappy about it, Jake. I was just trying
to help, that's all."

"Sorry."

"But it *is* awkward. I mean, I don't see what you can – is
there anything else you can use? Don't – couldn't you make
one of something else – bamboo?"

I didn't say 'shee-yit!' to her.

"She's got to be sensitive," I explained, "got to feel them

there invisible water waves – got to be sort of a cond – cond – conductor."

"Wire?"

"Nope. Ain't the same as electricity. Say!"

"What, Jake?"

"What conducts water?"

"Pipe."

"That's it. That's the thing! Some sort of pipe! I'll bet you copper pipe – tubin' – I'll bet that'd make a real witchin' wand! I'll just take a trip into Crocus! Visit Pipe-fittin' Brown."

Pipe-fitting's place is right next to Barney's Vulcanizing. It's the Pipe has the well-drilling rig and he'd be the one doing Tinch's well. I decided no point telling him what I wanted the copper pipe for. He was in there with his assistant, Flush Spring. "Flush" ain't his real proper name. Can't recall offhand *what* it is.

"Jake," Pipe said, "Right with you." He turned to Flush. "On your way! She's yellin' about her waste an' overflow. Then Killikers' sump-pump an' after that, uh, Mrs. Barnell, her – let's see. Wrote it down. She's havin' trouble with her – no, that's Mrs. MacTaggart. An' drop by Aunt Lil, too."

Flush took off.

"What's wrong with Aunt Lil's plumbin'?"

"Nothin,' not a thing – hummin' along jist fine – but she's in the hospital with her gald bladder. Doc Fotheringham operated on her three days ago, after she turned yellow at the Burning Fundamental Church of Nazareth Ladies' Auxiliary chicken supper, yellow as butter. Doc had her up on to the operating table – lifted out three gald stones size of hen's eggs out of her gald bladder. Ordered a basket of fruit made up for her at MacTaggart's. What can I do for *you*, Jake?"

"I was wonderin' if you had any spare pipe layin' 'round."

"Black, galvanized – what kind, size – half-inch, three-quarters?"

"Copper – not pipe exac'ly – tubin'. Got any copper tubin'?"

"Sure have. How much?"

"Oh, about, uh, a six inches – no, foot – times two. Four foot oughta do me."

"That all!"

"Yep."

"What you want her for? Radiant heatin' in a gopher cage?"

"Nope. How much is she a foot?"

"Twenty cents."

"I'll take five foot."

"Then there's my twenty-percent commission."

"For what?"

"I don't know," Pipe said. "But I always get it on all plumbing supplies."

"This ain't plumbin'."

"What is it then?"

"Nothin'. How much'll she be?"

"Uh, dollar twenty. Only I got to install it – you drop into the town hall – get a permit . . ."

"I don't need no permit. Ain't plumbin' I'm doin'."

"What *are* you doin'?"

"Why, well, I'm making somethin'."

"What?"

"Bean shooter, Pipe."

"Well, why didn't you tell me in the first place? Makes some sense – that's, hey, what's a fellow your age doin' with a bean . . ."

Next stop: MacTaggart's Trading Company Store.

" 'Day, Mac."

"Jake. Right with you. Got to get this basket of fruit made up for Aunt Lil."

"Yeah, I heard over at Pipe-fittin' Brown's."

"Ladies' Auxiliary three days ago – turned yellah as a lemon. Doc took out half a dozen stones – size of turkey hen's eggs."

"Gald stones sure got a way of growing," I said.

"Uh-huh – now what was it you wanted, Jake?"

"Handle-bar grips," I said.

"Handle-bar grips!"

"Bicycle handle-bar grips," I said. "Them black rubber things, you got 'em?"

"Over in the hardware section. What you want them for?"

"How much are they?"

"Fifty cents. What you need them for, Jake?"

"Oh nothin'. Apiece?"

"Yeah, just got one pair left. They'll look real nice on your bicycle, Jake."

"I ain't got no bicycle."

"Oh, then what, uh, you using them for?"

"Thumb stalls."

"Thumb stalls!"

"Yeah, in case I happen to mash both my thumbs on the same day sometime."

⤙ ⤚

Next stop: Malleable Brown's blacksmith shop. He was whanging away at something on his anvil.

"Got a little job here for you, Malleable."

"Why sure, Jake."

CLANG! CLANG! CLANG!

"Soon as I'm through with this. Heard about Aunt Lil?"

CLANG! CLANG! CLANG!

"Turned yellah as a canary Ladies' Aid supper three days ago. Doc Fotheringham . . ."

CLANG! CLANG! CLANG!

" . . . dozen gald stones out of her . . ."

CLONK! SPLOSH! SSSSSSSS . . .

" . . . size of your fist. Now then, Jake – what was it you were wantin'?"

"This copper pipe, Malleable. Cut in three then welded back together in the shape of a 'Y'."

"What for, Jake?"

"I drew out the plans here – length the stem an' the arms. They got to be exactly the same length, the arms."

"Why, sure. What's she for?"

"Slingshot."

"Oh."

"For Aunt Lil."

"For Aunt Lil!"

"So's she can take an' bung them dozen gald stones of hers outa the hospital window."

⊷ ⊶

Malleable done a real fine job on her for me. Those bicycle handle-bar grips were great. I figured they'd insulate and make her more sensitive. When I got back home, me and the Kid took her out into the yard.

I explained to him the way you got to hold her: "Straight up. Thumbs right along the inside the arms. Not tight, mind you. Loose so's you tell when she shivers. Now watch how I walk – real slooooooooow . . ."

"Isn't doing anything, Jake."

"Give her time. Giver her time. Aaaaah – there!"

"What, Jake!"

"Twitch! Didn't you see her give that little twitch? No? Well, maybe you couldn't see her with the eye. I guess I just *felt* her give a sort of a shiver. Now, we'll keep mooovin' ahead – slower now – see if she gets stronger."

"Gettin' stronger, Jake?"

"Nope. Nope. Now – back up again till – right back the way we come baaack up, ah, there!"

" 'Nother shiver, Jake?"

"Yep. Now. Try her to the right – slow – sloooow."

"Gettin' stronger, Jake?"

"Nope."

"Now, Jake?"

"Nope. Got to go back to where she shivered. Ah, there she is—now—the only other way we got to go—we ain't tried—a few slooow steps an' wow!"

"Shiver again, Jake?"

"Shiver! Going like a kootchie dancer! See her—see her, Kid?!"

"I sure do! Look at how it's . . ."

"Can't stop her, Kid! Pullin' and twistin'—an' bowing . . ."

"There she goes, Jake—right over and down!"

"Yep."

"That mean there's water, Jake?"

"Water! Water! Why, I never had a wand flip over like that on me before! There must be a artoosian well down there! Now—let's see—just where are we . . ."

"Jake . . ."

"We're just between the blacksmith shop and the stock trough . . ."

"Jake, you know where we are?"

"Sure. Just between the stock trough and the blacksmith. Hey—that don't seem right . . ."

"It sure don't!"

Where we was—we was standing right over top of where our tractor fuel drum is buried. Five hundred gallons. I told the Kid wasn't any point mentioning this to anybody. We gave her another couple tries, got a few twitches, that was all.

Kid's ma, she wasn't all that interested in going over to Tinchers' with us, said she had plenty more promising things to do in the way of finishing the new drapes. I guess there's a lot of folks like her, that don't even believe in water witching.

When the Kid and me got over to Tinchers', Pipe and Flush was already there with their well-drilling rig. So was most of Crocus district folks. *They* believed in water witching.

Everybody came up to look at my copper-tube wand.

"Funny lookin' hazel," Gate sneered. "Most ree-dick-you . . ."

"Is not!" I said.

" 'Way I got her planned out," Tinch said, "you two a couple hundred paces apart and moving the same direction from a point of startin' you can both agree on. Now, where *both* your wands go down . . ."

"His hardware ain't gonna go down nowhere!"

"She sure will!" I said. "Just wait an' see!"

"I'll be too busy findin' water for Tinch."

"That set-up suit you fellas?" Tinch said. "Jake?"

"Sure."

"Gate?"

"Uh-huh. He can witch all the way to Moose Jaw an' back and he ain't gonna find no wat . . ."

"That so! That so! Well, now let me tell you somethin' – this here is a ay-tomic wand!"

"What!" Gate said.

"Yep. Right in her crotch she's got a little lump – radiant ure-ureenium."

"That is a lump of pure bull . . ."

"All right!" Tinch yelled, "let's go!"

Kid, he walked alongside of me, except every few minutes he would trot over to Gate and then report back to me.

"How's Gate doin'?"

"Nothin' yet. You gettin' any action?"

"Nothin' yet, Kid."

We'd been at it a good hour when we heard Gate yell.

"Huppa-yay-eye-oooooooow!"

Everybody headed for Gate. I could hear them over there. Damn it.

"Just look at that!"

"There she goes!"

"Take willah every time!" Gate crowed. "Here's where your well goes, Tinch! Right here! Depend on willah every time!"

Tinch came over to me. "How's yours, Jake?"

"Nothin' yet."

"Come over to where Gate is and see what your – wand shows."

I had no goddam choice. She showed nothing.

"There you go," Gate said. "Shows you . . ."

"What it shows," I said, "is that wand of yours – shows water where there ain't – water!"

"Hell it does!"

"Can't be any. Ain't showed up with my wand!"

I went back to where I left off. I didn't take a dozen steps before that copper wand started dancing!

"Yip-eeee-eye-aw-hooooo! Told you! Told you! Just like a kootchie dancer! Block-an'-tackle couldn't pull her back up!"

Tinch came running back to me. So'd most the other folks. "Now ain't this a nice set-up. Gate's got a showin' . . ."

"Not like this one!"

"You got one. One of you says dig here – other one says . . ."

"Right here, Tinch! Tell you what, you just take and put your hands longside of mine on the arms this ay-tomic wand – you feel the pull an' the pressure. Then you go over to Gate's, feel his – see which one has the strongest water pull to her."

"Well, now, seems fair enough. Uh, where do I – how do I . . ."

"Right over my hands. See – let your thumbs run along over mine – there – there . . ."

He did.

"Holy diddle!"

"Didn't I tell you! Now you go over feel the feeble little puny sickly pull you'll get out of Gate's old-fashioned willow wand."

Wasn't no comparison.

"We dig here," Tinch announced, "where Jake's aytomic wand says to. Strongest pull wins. This is her!"

Just before they started up where I showed them to, I said, "You'll get a showin' about fifteen feet, Mall'able. Maybe twenty. Pull this strong's goin' to be real close to the surface – real close."

We didn't.

"Can't figure it out, Tinch."

"Thirty foot now," Tinch said.

"Right through the gravel," Malleable said. "Dry as the Ladies' Aid."

"You'll get something. Keep goin' – 'nother five foot. Guarantee you."

So much for *that* guarantee.

"Jake – what's the matter with that wand of yours?" Tinch said. "Any good there'd be water now. Hundred foot!"

"She's there, she's there, Tinch. That wand don't lie . . ."

"I'm beginnin' to think maybe she does!"

"I told you to try her where mine showed!" Gate said. "I told you!"

"Try her another little bit, Tinch. She's got to be there."

Wrong again. At a hundred and thirty Malleable shut her down.

"She's a dry hole, Tinch."

"Just a few more foot, Malleable," I said.

"This rig's reached her limit, Jake."

Malleable and Flush moved the rig over to where Gate's willow said there was water. They started her up, just went down nineteen feet and hit water. Flowing about fifty barrels to the minute. A real gen-you-wine artoosian well. Me, I felt pretty small with Gate preening and primping hisself all over the place like a Banty rooster. Strutting – aaah!

Thing that bothered me the most was it all happened with the Kid there. I'd give anything if he hadn't been. All those folks patting Gate on the back, snickering at me behind my back.

Kid said, "Don't pay any attention to them, Jake. I know that wand of yours is a good one."

"Thanks, Kid."

"You'll show 'em. Next time . . ."

" 'Fraid there ain't gonna be any next . . ."

"Hey! You fellas smell somethin'?" That was Malleable over by the puddles of water all around Gate's hole.

"Yeah – yeah!" Gate said. "Jake's well witchin'!"

"No. Serious," Malleable said. He had his head up and back and he was sniffing. "From over there." He pointed over to where Pipe had dug for me.

Pipe said, "Yeah. Somethin' must've died. Wow – some critter – real ripe!"

She was stronger than that, more like when Baldy breaks wind. Or Gate does.

"Stronger now," Tinch said. "Powerful!"

Everybody headed for my hole. No mistake – that was where that smell was comin' from. Awful!

Next I knew, Tinch opened the door of his pick-up, came out with some newspaper. "Anybody got a match?"

Malleable did. Tinch lit the paper and leaned over the hole to look down. "I'll just drop her – let her float down . . ."

Well, sir, Tinch's eyebrows an' moustaches have just about growed back in again. Johnny Totecole's out of the hospital now. Old Gate, he only had first-degree burns. It was Holgar Petersen got the worst of her, the way he was bending right over the hole when she went off. Right shoulder outa joint, sprained back – she kind of lifted him straight up and lobbed him towards the burnin' harrah.

Like I said to the Kid after, "Yep. That there gas is dangerous stuff. When she explodes. I witched all kinds of wells.

Deep wells, shallow wells, alkali wells, hard, soft, artoosian wells – first time I ever witched one the like a that. Gas well."

Ma says, "Mrs. Tincher is tickled right up the back. Says she doesn't know how to thank you, Jake."

"Oh, well . . ."

"Says gas is going to be wonderful for cooking – getting a gas refrigerator in – gas radiant in their fireplace."

I guess you could say she was the most successful well I ever witched. Gas well – natural gas well. Like I told Gate in the first place, she's all in the wand. Sure, willow's all right for ordinary everyday witching for water – but for a real well, takes that modern aytomic wand. Mine.

Maybe I ought to patent her. One thing for sure, Kid's Ma – don't think she's so sure that wand witching's just silly. Not any more.

LO! THE NOBLE REDSKIN!

Poetry's something i don't know all that much about. Take grain farming, horses, beef–hogs. I know just about everything there is to know about *them*. I ought to. Been mixed up in them most of my life. My business. I'm a hired man. So why *would* I know anything about poetry, any more than ninety-nine out of a hundred folks in Crocus district?

I do know one thing: when I read or hear a chunk of poetry and it gives my ass the raging heartburn, then I know she's bad poetry. 'Specially the kind of stuff a poet name of Belva Taskey cranks out. I figure she's upped the sale of baking soda one hundred percent in southern Saskatchewan. That's just for starters. Her poetry's as bad as sow thistle or pigweed when it comes to spreading. Everywhere! Regina *Leader-Post*, *Winnipeg Tribune* and *Free Press*. She's a regular in the *Crocus Breeze*.

Sometimes she's over the "Complaints of Cattle Horses and Poultry", or the "Too Late to Classify" – but she's there, every rosy-fingered Thursday morning. All about the meadowlark spring or the shivering crocus! Aaaah! Can't get away from her. Turn on the CBC for noon wheat prices and there she is:

> While I've never failed at anything I've tried and
> have now done everything I ever dreamed of doing,
> I have not ever forgotten the simple things in life!

If I have anything that gives me more pleasure than a genuine interest in people, well, I just don't know what it is.

I *love* history. Somehow it's hard to put into words what history does to me. To get into touch with the past, the dead dead past, it thrills me! When I read of the Riel Rebellion, or of those noble savages who roamed our great Western plains – I get a squeezy feeling. You know what I mean. Oh, it is enough to . . .

. . . give a badger's ass the heartburn. That's only one of her programs: "Belva Tells a Story." Then just when you're ready to listen to the evening news you get her again on "The Poet's Corner" – CHAF, Moose Jaw. Mulroney's Funeral Chapel.

What is it about Indians that thrills us all? Why is it that I find them so exciting? Is it so with you, too? With you, my friends, my half million listeners? You women who listen to my radio shows, you women who are my host of good friends? Indians just ask for poetry – that is, they are so *good* for poetry. If I had only one thing I could write my poetry about, it would be Indians and the olden days of our glorious history. My pen has been busy with Indians these past months and today for you I have my favourite poem, "Song of the Blackfoot Warrior":

On the prairie wide and tawny,
O'er the grasses bended low,
Rides he now the savage hunter
With his mustang hot pursuing
The hump-ed Bison, cloven hoof-ed.

'Neath the teepee tall and pointed,
Sits his loved one, Kug-ah-dee-shah.
Comely maiden, dark-eyed, waiting,
Loved and savage one, Kug-ah-dee-shah,
Mate of warrior, Eto-bee-coke-ee.

See what I mean? Kid's ma and me, we don't see eye to eye
on Taskey. Take a couple weeks ago. We was setting in the
kitchen, chores all done. Ma had her tuned in on the radio:
" . . . and so I think back to my simple childhood – as a
barefoot prairie girl on a prairie farm and I . . ."
Snicked her off!
"But, Jake I was . . ."
"Can't stand her! Raises the shackles on the back of my
neck . . . !"
"I think she has a great deal to say. Her poetry is lovely."
"Aaah!"
"We can't all like the same thing," she said, "have the same
tastes."
"That's right. That's right. Can't pick up a paper or turn
on the radio without her gettin' in your crop. I think her
poetry is the . . ."
"Jake!"
"That stuff she calls poetry is the shee . . ."
"Jake! That's enough!" She turned the radio back on.
I headed outside to throw down some bundles for Queenie
and Baldy. Before I went back in, I went out to the box.
Thursday. The *Crocus Breeze* was all there was. Radio was
turned off when I got back. Kid had got home from Kiziws',
where his ma had let him stay over for supper. I just got the
Breeze open when she brought up Taskey again. I kept my
nose buried in the paper and let her run on and on about how
great Taskey was: the voice of women and the voice of the
prairies.

"I don't care what you say, Jake, her poetry is . . ."

"Shaganappy! I can show you better po'try up a gush – haw – cuss . . ."

"What did you say, Jake?"

"He said '. . . show you more poetry up a goshhawk's . . .'"

"All right! All right, Kid." I went back to the *Breeze*.

Wouldn't you know it! She ain't on the radio. Kid's ma quit going on about her. But not the *Crocus Breeze*.

"Listen to this one," I said.

> His hands are rough
> but his heart is kind
> As an ash is tough,
> That has fought the wind.

"Hell, that don't even rhyme."

"'*Wynd*', Jake," she said. "'That has fought the *wynd*.'"

"Like you do a clock," the Kid said.

"Aaah. Uh-huh. There's more:

> The seasons ebb and the seasons flow
> Through the old old veins
> Of a farmhand, I know . . .

aaaaahhh!"

"What a wonderful tribute to a farmhand," she said. "So true – the image – comparison to a tree that – why, Jake, she could be talking about you!"

"Me! *Me!*"

"Yes."

"Yeah," the Kid said.

"In a pig's, uh, left ear, she could! '*Old* old veins'!"

"Well, perhaps not that part but – the rest of it."

"What does she mean?" Kid said. "'The seasons ebb and the seasons flow' . . . ?"

"How should I know! She don't! She just figures it *sounds* good! Ain't half what she says makes any sense!"

"But it does, Jake. Her poems are bright and they're cheerful. She's brought a lot of – of – they're inspiring and they're pretty nice to run across. Life is sad enough without . . ."

" . . . her makin' it worse!"

"I'm sorry you feel that way about her, Jake."

"I sure do! Her yappin' on about Indians. What's she know about Indians?"

"Evidently she's made a study of them, Jake."

"Her and Henchbaw – figure they know everythin' about everythin'. Now it's Indians."

"Gee, Ma, Jake knows all about Indians. Take the time Chief Weasel Tail an' all the South Blackfoots was starv . . ."

"All right, Kid. All right . . ."

" . . . starvin' and Jake invented the Buffalo Jumpin' . . ."

"Is that so," Kid's ma said.

"Mm-nnh . . ."

"There's a great deal of *truth* in Belva's poems. As well as beauty. Her Indian poems have just come out in an anthology . . . ."

"Whatever the aitch that is."

"Collection, Jake. A book. *Rhymes for a Yo-kay-bo.*"

"What the aitch – uh, what's a yokeee . . . ?"

"What they carry their babies around in, Kid. On their back. She's packed with moss to make it soft for 'em. Many's the time I seen Indian women gatherin' . . ."

"I understand the book is selling like hotcakes – high on the best-seller list. Martha Tincher says there's a pile of them at Brown's drugstore . . ."

"No accountin' for taste," I said.

" . . . next to the magazine racks. She tells me it looks wonderful. The cover is made to look like birchbark."

"Really! Are they made out of birchbark?" Kid said.

"No, son. Just made to *look* like birchbark."

"Just like her," I said.

"Of course not!" his ma said.

"You ain't far wrong, Kid. What I meant was, just like her – like her po'try, like her writin' poems about Indians – just *look* like Indians – ain't the real thing."

"Well, I like them – *especially* the Indian poems. And that isn't all while we're on the subject of Belva Taskey..."

"I'll say it isn't! She was bad enough when she stuck to her rosy-fingered dawn an' her pomes about her old-fashioned garden an' about her – about what she seen from her..."

"Saw," Ma said.

"... out of her privy door, but when she gets onto Indians – why, she's come over onto my reserve – territory."

"Then you'll be the first one to go to hear her."

"Huh!"

"She's coming to Crocus next week."

"Whaaaat!"

"I said she's coming to Crocus. She's giving a recital."

"Recital!"

"In the Hi-Art Theatre. She's being sponsored by the Athenians. We're..."

"Holy diddle!"

"There's going to be an autographing party at Brown's drugstore the afternoon before, and those who buy her *Rhymes of a Yo-kay-bo* will be able to get a signed copy."

"Surprised she isn't brandin' 'em."

"Branding them!"

"Sort of make it gen-you-wine. Brand 'em with her own brand, the lazy B.S."

"That would be ridiculous!"

"Mmmmmh," I said.

"While she's here, she's staying with Miss Henchbaw."

"Henchbaw!"

"Miss Henchbaw. It was through her that the Athenians Book Club got her to come and give her Indian Recital."

"Indian Recital!"

"Oh yes. It's to be her Indian poems that she's going to use most for her readings, Miss Henchbaw was telling me . . ."

"Awful – awful!"

"In costume."

"Draw more folks if she wasn't wearin' nothin'."

"That's crude, Jake! She's wearing ceremonial Indian costumes. She's . . ."

"Wearin' buffalo horns?"

" . . . bringing an Indian dancing-drum and she's going to demonstrate Indian dances . . ."

"Gee!" Kid said. "Gee!"

"She's gonna do Indian dances? Why, she never *seen* Indian dances! What dances – which ones?"

"I don't know. All I know is what Miss Hench . . ."

"Prairie-Chicken Dance? Dance of the Chiefs? Owl Dance? Rabbit Dance?"

"Montana foxtrot?" Kid said.

"It seems to me Miss Henchbaw said something about a snake dance . . . ."

"*Snake* dance! I know all of the Indian dances – I never heard of any snake dance . . ."

"Perhaps you don't know everything there is to know about Indian dances, Jake."

"Jake knows all about Indians." Kid said. "There was the time Chief Lazarus Three-Persons offered Jake the hand of his daughter in marriage . . . ."

"There just isn't any such Indian dance as a Indian snake dance," I said. "She made it up."

" . . . of his daughter in marriage. Her name was . . ."

" . . . an' you can't show folks a Indian dance when there ain't any such Indian dance! Dishonest. Fake! Like her!"

" . . . this here Indian maid Jake was s'posed to marry – her name was Sadie Runnin'-Cow," Kid said.

"That's pretty strong, Jake."

"Not strong enough!"

"Then you won't be wanting a ticket to her recital . . . ."

"You're goddam rights I won't!"

I got up out of my chair and headed for the back door.

"Where are you going, Jake?" Kid said.

"Me? Out to do the Indian Snake Dance. Over the hills and through the dells with the wynd in my hair. To pick the shivering crocus, the buttercup, the tiger lily, an' when I'm through doing that, I aim to start in on the cow barn. It's piled up nearly to the rafters!"

I know them all – Indian dances. I been *in* them. Bad enough hearing her spouting that awful stuff every time you turn on the radio. And her being a friend of Henchbaw, Kid's teacher at Rabbit Hill school. Me an' Henchbaw don't get on too well, anyway. Bossy. Like I say, bad enough, without her handing out a lotta stuff about Indians. Snake dance! Snake dance! Indian costume! Any real Indians I ever run across, when they danced all they wore was a britch clout. Not her!

Next morning just before he took off for Rabbit Hill school, Kid said to me, "I'm not so fussy about her poetry either, Jake."

"I got nothing against po'try, Kid. Just hers! In its place poetry's all right. For women mostly. Like – like picking out wallpaper patterns or crocheting – painting tea cups."

"That's the way I figure. The girls at Rabbit Hill, they *all* like poetry. But the fellows . . ."

"Yeah, yeah – well now, Kid, don't go by me. I, uh, there is some things that ain't ugly – poetical things. What I mean, Kid – I ain't expert on everythin'. You pay attention in school – what they dish out to you – even poetry."

"Yeah. Yeah. Sort of think she'd stick to – kind of – Jake, it would be kind of nice to see her bangin' a Indian drum and doin' that snake dance."

"Ain't any such dance!"

"Must be if she's doin' it, Jake."

"Just made it up. Just as phoney as her Indian poetry!"

"Well, her poetry gives me the heartburn, too. Miss Hench-baw reads it to us in school. There's one of 'em in the Grade Six Reader."

"No!"

"Yep."

"Holy diddle! Even defenceless little kids! You ain't got the chance of a gopher through a thirty-six-inch thrashin' machine!"

I figured the only thing to do was pay no attention to it. Forget about her coming and giving a recital – Indian Poetry Recital. Not so easy with Taskey. Turn on the radio and there she is again:

> Brothers of the Plains, I have been on a long journey. I have communed with the Great Spirit. He has spoken to me. He spoke to me with the words of the Thunder and the words of the Sun. In wampum shall the story be kept and never shall it cease from your memories.
>
> And now for my little listeners – a true tale of the Blood Indians: 'How the Chipmunk Got His Stripes'.
>
> Once upon a time when little Sammy Crazy-Horse was a little boy his grandfather, Herbert Crazy-Horse, told him the tale of how the little chipmunk got his stripes. For, you see, the chipmunk did not always have his stripes . . . .

This time I guess I must've dozed off, but not for long, because when I came to, she was still at it.

> . . . and ever after he bore the shadow of the foxtail which had hidden him that hot day – right down the middle of his back!
>
> I shall not be with you tomorrow, for I shall be

on the banks of the Brokenshell River, in Crocus, Saskatchewan. There I will see again my old friend, Mabel Henchbaw, for the first time in – but that would be telling, wouldn't it? My poem for today is not an Indian poem. It is dedicated especially to Miss Mabel Henchbaw and to those other women to whom I will give my recital in Crocus.

I guess it was because she was dedicating it to Henchbaw, I listened.

> Oh how fiercely I would like
> To be a bee in drunken flight,
> O'er the stubble spreading wide
> Flowing free in yellow tide.
>
> O'er the prairie I would roam
> With none to call me, take me home;
> None to say me yea or nay,
> None to bar my vagabond way.
>
> Loit'ring at the prairie's blooms,
> Sloughs and meadows for my rooms,
> Prairie blossoms for my fare,
> Slipping here and supping there.
>
> Flowers of flax that brightly gleam
> Next the saffron buffalo bean,
> Crocus blue and cowslip too,
> Myriad blooms of every hue.
>
> Oh how fiercely I would like
> To be a bee in drunken flight,
> A prairie bee on cellophane wings
> A-tilt on the breeze while the long grass sings.

Fierce! Tortured a fellow to think of that woman coming and telling folks all about Indian – reading them Indian poems.

Dancing a phoney snake dance. Awful! Next day I had to drive Kid's ma into Crocus. Kind of blowy as we rode in behind Baldy an' Queenie.

"All right, Baldy – Queenie. Hump your rumps, lift them hoofs an' lightly tiptoe go! O'er the . . ."

"That is *not* funny, Jake!"

"Didn't say it was. Team of poetical horses. So I figured I'd speak to them poetical! Guess she's the kind of a day Taskey likes. Real nice poetical day."

"Nice day! It's blowing . . ."

"Yeah. An' Taskey's sure gonna get the wynd through her roach."

"All right, Jake. Nobody says you have to go to her recital. You don't have to go near Brown's drugstore . . ."

"I ain't."

"I'd sure like to see that snake dance," Kid said.

"Ain't any such dance. Where'd she get – what kind of snakes could she find out here?"

"Just garter snakes," the Kid said, "or if she was lucky, a bull snake."

"Ridiculous – ridiculous," I said.

"Not so ridiculous," Ma said. "Miss Henchbaw says that the ceremonial snake plays a very important part in . . ."

"Not out west it don't. Snakes is hard to come by on the prairies an' in the foothills – in the Rockies."

"Maybe she brought 'em with her – out of a zoo?" Kid said.

"Probably just stuffed ones," I said.

"Quit it – both of you!" She had to hang onto her hat with both hands against that wynd, but Kid's ma had the coal oil on her fire. "Whether she uses a stuffed snake or not, you do not intend to see it or to listen to her read!"

"Got to have snakes for a snake dance or it ain't a . . ."

"Shut up, Jake!"

I done that. Rest of the way in to Crocus. Funny thing: I yet got to see a woman fussy about snakes. Even garter snakes.

I dropped Kid's ma and him off at Brown's drugstore, hitched the team and democrat up at Pete Botten's Livery, took a dangle down to Repeat Golightly's barbershop. Didn't notice any more folks than usual in town.

Like he often does, Repeat was sitting in his barber chair. Book on his lap. Repeat probably reads more than anybody else in Crocus district, every one of them historical books about Egyptian princesses that take on a new fellow every other week, or Roman Empires that tie a dancing girl to the belly of a donkey and – History can get pretty disgusting!

"Jake."

"Repeat. Thought you'd be over at Pill Brown's for Taskey's autografting."

"Got mine. First in line." He held up the book. "Birchbark. Looks just like birchbark."

"Mmmmh."

"*Rhymes for a Yo-kay-bo*."

Then I saw he had *two* books in his lap. "Uh-huh."

He held up the one wasn't birchbark. "She signed this one for me, too. Sister volume, you might say, to her new one. Called *Prairie Gleanings*. Hard to come by now. Out of print."

"That's nice," I said. "Makes her real valuable."

He opened the book up.

"Hold on, Repeat!"

"I think it's still my favourite book of hers. Certainly has my favourite . . ."

"Repeat, I just remember . . ."

" . . . poem of all her poems."

"If she's all the same to you, Repeat, I ain't . . ."

" . . . called 'To a Prairie Fieldmouse'."

"I come in here to get away from . . ."

"Simple little thing. Just about a mouse. Fieldmouse. Hits a deep wellspring of real human feelings . . ."

No stopping him!

Bright button eyes
And toy ears.
Rodent tooth
But instinct wise.

You love grain
A human plants,
Harvests,
for his gain.

You are a mouse;
The brown earth,
Fertile, kind,
Is your house.

Thus he pays you, the
Two-legged creature
Who plants:
He slays you!

"Slays me, too," I said. With Repeat you can get away with
saying stuff like that. He talks a lot, but he don't listen good.

"That's the *old* Belva Taskey. No rhyme. Sprung quatrains.
Simple. Now, what's really exciting with this . . ." He held up
the birchbark one. "She has entered a new field: trochaic
pentameter. Matter of fact it suggests the beat of the Indian
dancing-drum . . ."

"How the aitch would you know what the beat of a . . ."

"Her recital tonight will be mostly this new – but not new
for her – *return* to more traditional poetry. *And* it's *Indian* poetry. Wild."

"Ah-hah."

"That recital tonight is going to be one of the high points
of my life! I am really looking forward to her interpretation of
the Snake Indian dance . . ."

"Look, Repeat, I heard of the Owl Dance, the Rabbit
Dance, the Prairie-Chicken Dance. I known Indians to dance

what they call the Montana foxtrot, but I never heard of any
snake dance."

"Well, you ought to go tonight, take it in, Jake. See something new – see something . . ."

"Ain't interested. Tell me something, you wouldn't know
what this snake dance is like, would you?"

"Matter of fact I do. From talking with her and . . ." He got
up off of his barber chair, reached under his instrument shelf
and came out with a folder. "She gave one of these to everybody that came in the drugstore. I guess they'll have them at
the Hi-Art tonight. That's her on the cover in her Indian
costume. Ceremonial Indian costume."

"Yeah."

"At the climax of her program – see what she's holding up?"

"Basket."

"That's right. Wove out of sweetgrass. She told me that.
Self-same sweetgrass basket used for years for this ceremonial
snake dance."

"*She* told you."

"She did," he said. "She also explained – at the very end of
the dance she takes out – see that snake she has in her hand?"

"It's a snake, all right," I said. "Hanging straight down. Ain't
very lively-looking one to me."

"Oh, Jake – it wouldn't be a *live* snake."

"Didn't think so. I never seen one that big our part the
world."

"It is quite large. Quite large," Repeat said.

"South American maybe. Repeat – just where does a fellow
pick up a ticket for this recital o' Taskey's?"

Pill Brown's drugstore or MacTaggart Trading Company
store or Chez Sadie's Beauty Box. Dollar. After I picked one
up, Baldy and Queenie and me took a little trip along the
Brokenshell River. When I got back to Crocus I went over
and had a talk with Charlie Golley, who runs the Hi-Art. He
took me up on stage, showed me the dancing-drum, peace

pipe, the big basket. Had a lid on it. She was wove out of sweetgrass, all right. Nothing smells nicer than sweetgrass does.

I was in luck. Charlie said he had to go down in the basement, open up some windows, said he promised Pill Brown. Pill's always sneezing, and Charlie wanted to air out the theatre well ahead of time, so Pill wouldn't interrupt the recital.

Just a handful folks showed up. Hi-Art seats about a hundred. I counted maybe thirty. Most of them women. Didn't notice anybody from Hanley Reserve, in or out of ceremonial costume, in attendance.

Curtains parted. She come on stage. White doeskin, fringed and beaded. Headband with a feather up out of the back of it. Crow or raven, my guess. No war paint.

> See the stubble
> In the sunlight,
> Yellow.
> In the moonlight,
> Mellow.
> See the stubble,
> Upright,
> Crisp.

Didn't seem all that Indian to me, *or* poetical. She was just *saying* it like she was talking to somebody, but that was just for starters. She changed her headgear for a eagle feather war bonnet. Then she began to whang that rawhide drum and she begun to dance, stooped over so her ass stuck out and her head kept bobbing up and down while she shimmied round and round the stage. She quit dancing but kept on with the drum.

> Dance we now, oh brother warriors!
> Dance the dance of ancient times
> 'Round the fitful campfire light,
> Through the shadows of the night!

> Nearer, nearer dance we now!
> Touch it – leave it – dance away –
> Nearer, nearer to the serpent;
> Flirt we now with brother Death!

She dropped the drum and she picked up the sweetgrass basket.

> High we lift it, proudly high,
> 'Ere we take him from his nest . . .

She lowered the basket and took off the lid.

> High we lift him now again
> Toward the happy hunting grounds
> Then we lower and we grasp . . .

She stuck her hand inside the basket.

> To reveal him in the campfire's – EEEEEEEE-YAAAH-YUCK-AAAHRRRH-EYEEEEE-YIKE!!!!!!

Sure brought the house down. Or up and out. Way she flang that sweetgrass ceremonial basket and twenty-four snakes out into the audience. You could call it a gen-you-wine Indian snake dance all right.

Indian *garter*-snake dance.

THE MAN WHO CAME
TO RUMMY

TAKE A CAT AND A DOG OR A BADGER AND A KIYOOT OR those two roosters of ours – Rhode Island Red and the Winedot – they can't get along. Just the same with Jake and Old Man Gatenby. Old Man Gatenby lives down Government Road from us. Jake and him, they're always going at it. Never let up. The worst was a while back time the blizzard hit Crocus district. I guess that was the worst.

You ever run across Old Man Gatenby, you're looking at an old fellow with a face like an apple. *Old* apple. Wrinkly. Like a *bad* apple. Jake, he's the long skinny kind. Just Jake and me and Ma on our farm. We raise wheat and oats and barley and cream and eggs.

The worst argument Jake and Gate ever went at it was last winter. Middle of January. Happened when Gate came over to our place to play rummy. I guess they argue the worst over cards:

"I'm up on you, Gate. Good fifty points."

"You won't be. You won't be if you ever get them goddam cards out."

"Why, Gate, you was just tellin' me I didn't shuffle 'em enough last hand."

"Leave the spots on 'em – leave the spots on 'em."

Jake looked over my way. "Okay. Kid, time you was in bed, ain't it?"

"I got three more arithmetic questions to do."

"All right. Tie into 'em. Might take a look at the thermometer."

"I just did. Twenty-six below."

"Hmm. Goin' down fast. Probably hit thirty before mornin'," Gate said.

"Real wind comin' up, Jake," I said.

"Yeah, figgered there would be. I can tell. Tell every time."

"Tell what?" Gate said.

"Weather."

"You ever gonna get them cards out?"

"Sure, sure." Jake flipped out a card to Gate. "Pressure. Tell her by pressure."

"Tell what?" Gate said.

"Weather. Fair or foul. Any change, pressure registers. I got a back like one them barom – uh, oh, sorry – flipped that one face up, Gate."

It was the ten of hearts.

"Bury it, bury it," Gate said.

"What's seven times eight?" I said.

"My back," Jake said, "right where she curves in just below the middle and just above my . . ."

"What's seven times eight?" I said again.

"Fifty-eight," Gate said.

"Sixty-three," Jake said. "Ah, my lumbago hits me there an' I can tell . . ."

"Give me Dr. Carter's Little Liver Pills Calendar Almanac for weather prediction every time," Gate said.

"Fifty-eight doesn't work out," I said.

"Any kind of weather. My back can tell rain to the fraction of an inch. Sleet, hail, snow," Jake said.

"Dr. Carter's Little Liver Pill Almanac was right nine times out of ten the last year," Gate said.

"And it doesn't work for sixty-three, either."

"Oh – he ain't so dependable," Jake said.

"Called every single shower last year, didn't he?"

"One way I get this fellow sellin' nine an' five-sixteenths cows – Gate's way I get an' seven-eighths cows . . ."

"Gate, you was yellin' a minute ago you wanted to play cards – you ever gonna pick 'em up?"

"Yeah – yeah," Gate said. "Try forty-nine, Kid."

"Take snow," Jake said, "my back's real good for snow . . ."

"Four of spades. Superstition – superstition."

"Five an' six-tenths cows. Can't sell six-tenths of a cow . . ."

"I'll never forget the first blizzard crick of my back predicted . . ."

"Ain't scientific like Dr. Carter's Little Liver Pill Almanac," Gate said. "Three of diamonds."

'I remember – way back in . . ."

"Three of diamonds."

"Back in Ought-Six an' -Seven," Jake said. "Never forget. I remember I was . . ."

"Three of diamonds."

" . . . in the Maple Crick district, an' I was the only one knew that terrible winter of Ought-Six an' Ought-Seven was on her way."

"Look! We playin' cards or aren't we playin' . . . ?"

"Workin' for a fellow name of Smith, Horseshoe Smith. Say! he had him a real herd of cattle, almost nine hundred of 'em. An' this mornin' late in the fall – real fall nip to the air – an' I was choppin' wood when my lumbago took me real hard without warnin'. Now, I says to myself, she never come at me without warning before. I ain't wrenched my back. Well, sir, that night there come a flurry of snow – just a little spit . . ."

Gate looked up startled. "Little what!"

"Spit," Jake said. "That thermometer dropped twenty degrees. Had a two-day cold snap, then my lumbago let up right away. You know how I knew that cold snap was gonna let up?"

"Took a look at Dr. Carter's Little Liver Pill Almanac . . ."

"Nope. I was choppin' wood again. 'Nother twinge. That night the thermometer went *up* thirty degrees in one jump. An' I knew – I knew I had me a built-in weather predictor."

"In a pig's ass!" Gate exploded.

"No, in my back. I watched her. I tested her. She worked. She predicted the blue snow. I went to Horseshoe – 'Horseshoe', I said, 'this is gonna be the winter of the blue snow! The awfulest winter the West has ever seen'. That was the winter that . . ."

"Dr. Carter's Little Liver Pill Calendar Almanac made his reputation."

"He never predicted the bad winter of Ought-Six an' Ought-Seven," Jake said.

"He sure did. He . . ."

"That's just about enough of that!" Ma had come in. Generally when Gate comes over to play rummy with Jake, she stays out in the parlour. "Just once I'd like to see you two over cards without all this arguing!"

"I was just explainin' how I predicted . . ."

"I was just tellin' Jake he can't tell weather in his goddam bones – ain't scientific."

"Watch your language around my son, Mr Gatenby."

Hell, I've heard lots worse than what Gate or Jake ever use. Every day on Rabbit Hill school grounds, or in and out of Brokenshell River when we go swimming. Maybe out there in the parlour Ma mistook Jake when he said "a little spit", the way Gate did.

"Ma, what's seven times eight?"

'Fifty-six, son."

"What I told him." Gate said.

"No, Mr. Gatenby, you said . . ."

"Has to be a explanation for it," Jake said. "I *can* tell weather by the twinges in my back . . ."

"I'll keep on tellin' her by Dr. Carter's Little Liver Pill Almanac."

Ma said, "I've noticed – when the pipe in the well is beaded with moisture it's sure to rain."

"Eight," I said.

"Look, Jake, we gonna play this game or aren't we!"

"Comes out even with fifty-six. Fellow sold eight cows – no fraction of cows left over."

"C'mon, play cards! That two of diamonds . . ."

"Huh? Oh, two – of diamonds – that mine?" Jake said.

" 'Course it is! C'mon, play cards!"

"Yeah, yeah – need that one!" Jake picked up the two of diamonds. "Rummy."

Just like the Wine-dot and the Rhode Island Red. When I finished up my arithmetic, I stepped outside, just before I went up to bed. Sure cold. Kind of grabbed inside your nose and at the back of your throat when you took in a breath. You could hear the wind lifting – first just a long soft sound you couldn't tell where she was coming from, then yelling longer and louder, licking up the snow off of the yard and firing it in your face. I went back inside.

Jake looked up from his cards. "Ain't you in bed yet?"

"I'm goin'."

"What's the thermometer say now?"

"Twenty-eight."

"Lot colder with that wind," Gate said.

"She'll never be as bad as the winter my lumbago predicted in Ought-Six an' -Seven. What we got! Winter! This ain't real winter! Just a long skinny sort of fall, that's all she is! Any snow? Hardly any till last week. Blizzard? Not a twinge, uh, not a blow. No siree, Bob. There ain't gonna be one . . ."

" 'Cordin' to Dr. Cart . . ."

"In Ought-Six she was so cold you could see the jackrabbits across the prairie – froze in the middle of the air! Height about two foot off of the ground! Where they leapt an' got froze . . ."

"We'll have her again this year, too. Dr. Cart . . ."

"One day I seen a jack sort of spraddled over a rose-apple

bush, an' about three foot behind him a kiyoot with his hind feet sort of drawed up right under himself ready to spring on that jack. Come spring – spring of Ought-Seven that is – come spring the jack unfroze first – him bein' a lot smaller'n the kiyoot – an' he got a head start on that kiyoot an' . . ."

"Both the jack an' the kiyoot had lumbago which predicted the weather ever after that!" Gate said.

"Huh!"

"If I didn't know it before, I know it now. Time for me to head home. When you get to talkin' tall like . . ."

"That's right – holler quits when you get beat. Set down – still time for one more game . . ."

"Nope, nope. She's blowin' up for a bad night. Gonna go real low tonight, stay low for ten days. 'Cordin' to Dr. Carter's Little Liver . . ."

"She'll never be like she was in Ought-Six an' -Seven. Why, that was the winter Old Man Froomby . . ."

"Late, Jake. I got to go. Tell me some other night . . ."

"All right, all right. Kid, to bed."

"Okay, Jake. Okay."

Jake went out with Old Gate to start up his car, but they found her froze up tight. Motor just groaned three times and died, Jake said. Ma suggested maybe hot water might help, but for a change Gate and Jake agreed it wouldn't. Gate was going to have to spend the night with us.

"You can bunk in with me, Gate," Jake said. "We can get in a few more hands rummy before we turn in."

"Real nice of you folks."

"Of course not," Ma said. "We're glad to have you."

"Son, up to bed. Way past your . . ."

"I'm goin'. I'm goin'."

In bed that night I could hear the wind whining away at the weather stripping – could feel the whole house shudder with her. Scarey, in the dark. Then was when I remembered our barn cat, Milk. I'm fussy about her. She was due to have her kittens any day. I hoped she was all right out there. When I came down next morning, Ma was at the stove, Jake and Gate finishing up their breakfast.

"What's the thermometer doing?" I said.

"Thirty-one," Jake said. "Driftin' bad too. Hardly see ten foot ahead of yourself. By the way, Kid, Milk had her kittens . . ."

"Really! How many!"

"Five, near as I could tell. They're up in the loft."

"This awful – this cold! How'll Milk and her . . ."

"They'll be all right. All snugged up with hay. Don't worry about them, Kid. How's your stock gonna make out without you, Gate?"

"Ernie'll take care of 'em all right. I phoned him whilst you was outside."

"Had an aitch of a time makin' it to the barn," Jake said. "Ain't the temperature so much as it is the goddam wind . . ."

"Watch it, Jake!" That was Ma at the sink now.

"Hits a fellow right between the eyeballs. Same back in Ought-Six an' -Seven when I . . ."

"Just like Dr. Carter's Little Liver Pill Calendar Almanac predicted this year."

Whenever Jake and Gate start up an argument, they don't let go of it in a hurry. Whole night later and next morning they pick her up again without missing a stitch.

"Your lumbago tell you this was comin' on?" Gate said.

"Well, no – but it ain't anythin' out of the ordinary yet. Not yet. Just your average winter."

"Terrible cold blowy winter for an average winter, ain't it?" Gate said.

"Kid, you're gonna be late for school."

'Isn't any," I said. "Mr. Tincher phoned Ma and said the roads are all drifted in."

"That's right," Ma said. She took up Jake's plate and knife and fork and spoon.

"And he said he wouldn't be surprised if it didn't drop down to sixty below. Jake, Milk and her kittens!"

"Don't worry, Kid. It ain't gonna drop to sixty below. Even if it did they'd . . ."

"I wanta go out an' see . . ."

"Oh, son, I don't think . . ."

"Sure," Jake said. "He can come with me. She ain't sixty below yet."

"Finished your coffee, Mr. Gatenby?" Ma said.

"Yep."

"How's your back this morning, Jake?" she said.

"Fine. Just fine."

"Then I guess this is one time that built-in weather predictor of yours wasn't working," she said. "If we're in for a winter like nineteen . . ."

"It ain't gonna be like nineteen ought-six an' -seven!"

"I sure think she might," Gate said. "Way I remember that winter . . ."

"Don't you folks worry about no blizzards. Ain't gonna be blizzards again like we had that winter. Old Man Froomby nearly went west that year. Stormin' so bad he strung a rope from his back shed to the barn to feed the stock."

"Gonna have to do that this time before we're through," Gate said.

"Nope."

"What happened to Old Man Froomby?" I said.

"He followed the rope. Got hisself lost when he let go the rope an' stepped inside of the barn."

"How come?" I said.

"No barn. Wind had took her right off of the door an' blowed her clear into the next township. Old Man Froomby froze so bad before they found him, Doc had to saw off his right leg."

"Gee!"

"Remember Old Man Froomby well," Gate said. "He figgered he could tell the weather lot like you – with his rheumatism. In his leg."

"The one that the doctor had to cut off?" I said.

"Yep," Gate said. "And there's a funny thing. He told the weather just about as bad *after* he lost his leg as *before* he lost her."

"He did not," Jake said.

"He did so!"

"Well, he could still tell the weather better with that there amp – amp-you-tated leg he lost than you can with Dr. Carter's Little . . ."

"Like the Kid's ma, I didn't notice your back warnin' us about this blizzard!"

"All right," Ma said. "Let's not get upset about a little weather. Looks as though we're all going to be together here for a while. Don't want to have cabin fever spoil it."

I never heard of cabin fever before.

"Jake, when we going out so I can see those kittens?"

"In a minute, Kid."

We've had Milk over a year now. I don't know where she came from; she just adopted us. Showed up on her own, moved into the cow barn. She's mostly white, which is why I named her Milk. Also she is fussy about milk. She is so fussy it didn't take me any time at all when I'd be stripping, to get her to sit up and open her mouth while I tilted a tit and squirted into it. One smart cat!

When Jake finished his coffee and his arguing with Gate whether or not we were in for another winter like nineteen-six and -seven, and Ma made me put on seven layers of clothes and told me four times to keep my scarf up tight and high, we headed for the barn.

I heard them mewing first, and Jake wasn't kidding, they were all snugged up in hay and Milk. There were *six* of them. Didn't have their eyes open yet. The ones I could see weren't mostly white like Milk was. Jake said that was because we'd never know who the aitch their father was, and he could have been any colour.

"One thing for sure, Kid, them tails on 'em."

"What, Jake?"

"Ain't stubbed and they ain't got tossels on their ears."

"Yeah?"

"Sure as aitch their Daddy wasn't no bobcat."

I wouldn't have minded that at all!

Before we went back to the house, I said, "Jake, when Ma said that about cabin fever. What did she mean – cabin fever?"

"Oh, that's – why – it's what some folks can come down with."

"How?"

"Well – like us folks snowed in here. You, me, your ma, Gate."

"Is it a real disease?"

"With Gate it is! It can hit bad. Fellow's nerves get all unstrung."

"Run a temperature?"

"With Gate you could. High one."

"Is it that bad, Jake?"

"Known to been fatal."

"Killed people?"

"Yep. Knew a fellow out the Gladys Ridge district – back in 1910 – died. Out of an axe in his skull."

"Huh!"

"Cooped up together, fellows get so bad with cabin fever, they go kind of crazy."

"You figure Gate'll go crazy, Jake?"

"Nope. He's too ornery for that. It's me I'm worried about. If this weather don't let up soon."

"Oh," I said.

Thermometer dropped to thirty-three. Wind didn't slack off at all. Nights you could hear it howling along the eaves, rat-

tling the doors. Jake and Gate just went out in it twice a day
to look after the stock. Jake strung a rope from the back stoop
shed to the barn, but only after Gate kept going on about how
it was going to be nineteen-six and -seven all over again.

That cabin fever – I began to see what Jake meant about it.
Our meals got real prickly. Take when we had soup:

"Gate, uh, kind of hard for a fellah to hear himself think."

"Think? Think what?"

"What he's thinkin'."

"Dinnertime, ain't it? What kind of thinkin' does anybody
do when they're eatin'?"

"That there slurp solo. Soup. With your soup. Awful loud!"

"Oh," Gate said. "Is it now?"

"Just thought I'd mention it."

"Mmph!"

"Don't want to hurt your feelin's, but if you sort of put –
way you've been hurtin' ours – put the *whole* spoon in your
yap before you suck her up out of it, then . . ."

"Way I been eatin' soup alla my life. Way I'll go right on
doin' it the resta . . ."

"Just a suggestion," Jake said.

"SLLRRRRR-URP!" Gate said.

Then it was Jake's turn. His tea.

"SLURP!"

"Jake! Hey, Jake, maybe if you'd wait for her to cool off
some . . ."

"SLURRP!"

" . . . you wouldn't make nearly so much noise with it. Gets
on a fellow's nerves . . ."

"Is that so! Well, let me tell you somethin'. I am doin' it
dee-liberate! Just to show you – SLURP – how awful it –
SLURP – sounds when you do it with . . ."

"Thirsty horse at a waterin' trough don't make one half the
noise you do siphonin' that tea up out the saucer!"

"SLURRRRRRRRRP!"

Gate was wrong. Neither Baldy nor Queenie ever made a tenth the noise Jake did when he saucered his tea or his coffee.

Nighttime was the very worst. Jake and Gate's bedroom was right next to mine, and the partition between doesn't go all the way up to the ceiling, so I could hear everything clear as anything. Ma offered them a hot-water bottle. Gate didn't want it. Jake did. He got it.

"Gate, that there is *my* side the bed," I heard Jake say, "an' I been sleepin' on that side. I slep' on that side on other beds for forty years before I ever came to work for the Kid's ma. Left side of the bed *fits* me!"

"Fits me too."

I couldn't tell which one of them got the side the bed he figured fit him.

"The hot-water bottle's for both of us, Jake."

"Don't need it."

"That's nice."

They both shut up for a while, then Jake said, "Would you mind blowin' out the lamp."

"Mmmm-arrah . . ."

"Gate – the . . ."

"Aah-haaaaah . . ."

" . . . lamp, dammit!"

"SNORE!"

I heard the bedsprings creak, then Jake's feet hit the floor. The light went out, then a moment later there came a cranging sound.

"Goddam chair!"

I guess in the dark Jake stubbed his bare foot on it. Didn't wake Gate up, though. Kept right on snoring.

Then he really shifted into high gear.

"AAAAW! Ease off!" Jake yelled. "I got to get some sl . . . !"

"SNORE!"

"Gate! Choke it off. Hey – Gate! You – Gate – for – if you was to roll over off of your back then you wouldn't . . ."

"Ah – hah – umph – plumph . . ."

He must have rolled off of his back because the snoring stopped.

"That's better. Just keep off of your back an' she'll cut out automatic. Maybe now somebody else can get some sleep."

Didn't take a count of ten for Gate to start up again.

"Gate! Gate, you're on your back again!"

"SNORE!"

"Gate! Get the hell back over onto your side!"

"SNORE!"

"Gate! Wake up! Cut her off! Gate – hey Gate – I've had enough! One more snore outa you an' – Gate – you ain't stayin' in this bed with me! Once more . . ."

"SNORE!" Gate snored.

"All right, you son ova – uh!"

The bedsprings twanged like telephone wires in a high wind and there came a whump and a clump from the other side of the partition.

"Hey! What the hell! What am I – How come I'm down . . ."

"I warned you! I give you fair warnin'! I ain't puttin' up with your goddam snorin' one more goddam minute . . ."

"I wasn't snorin'!"

"Sure was!"

"Never snored in my life!"

"You just been snorin' your ass off!"

"I never snored in my whole . . ."

"How can you tell!? Can't hear yourself when you're asleep, an' most folks don't snore *until* they're asleep. You can't tell worth a whoop whether you're snorin' or you're not snorin'!"

"I can so!"

"You can not!"

Then I got it from the *other* side of my bedroom. Ma pounding on the partition.

"You two in there! That's enough of that! Let someone else get some sleep!"

"I oughta know if I snore or if I don't."

"You heard her," Jake said. "Shut up!"

"Aaah."

" . . . for once in your life!"

Ma pounded on the partition again and they both of them did shut up. For about three minutes. I was just dropping off when I heard Jake say, "Gate – hey Gate!" Not loud – sort of a strong whisper.

"You heard her," Gate said. "Shut up!"

"Ssssh! Somethin's happened down there – under the covers."

"What – what!"

"Before you turned in did you forget to go take a – uh-OH!!!"

"What in hell are you – what's . . . !"

"Dammit! I told you we didn't need a hot-water bottle! This here is an *empty* hot-water bottle now, an' all on account of you this here whole bed's soppin' wet!"

I saw the light go on in Ma's room, heard her moving around in there.

"Me?" Gate yelled. "You!"

"You asked for it! You just had to have that goddam hot-water bottle!"

"You burst it!"

"I did not!"

"Sure did! When you kicked me outa bed! Lucky it's just the bottle – might've broke my back!"

"Self defence! Way you was snoring . . ."

"Now!" It was Ma. The light had left her room and was in theirs now. So was Ma. "Unless you two want to spend the rest of the night out in the chicken house, you had better settle down!"

She gave them aitch and a dry set of sheets and the kitchen-table oilcloth to go over the mattress. I went back to sleep.

Next morning Gate was a long time coming down. I think Jake must have got up and went out to the stock even before Ma got down to make breakfast. When I came down, Jake was just taking off his buffalo coat and fur hat with the flaps and his mitts. "She's awful out there!" he said.

"The stock?" Ma said.

"How's Milk? Her kittens?" I said.

"Tough milkin' Irene an' Eglantine."

"Those kittens, are they . . . ?"

"So cold it kep' pluggin' up their tits. Ice cream."

"Jake! How are Milk and her kittens?"

"Fine, Kid. Just fine. All of 'em. An' I'll check again for you when I go out to throw down feed after breakfast."

"Really bad out there, Jake?"

"Yep."

"But not too bad for me – for a kid to go . . . ?"

"Oh, son!" Ma said.

"Your ma's right," Jake said. "Quit worryin' about 'em. Day or so more an' this weather'll clear up."

"Maybe we ought to bring 'em in here . . ."

"Nope. She's a barn cat," Jake said.

"I agree," Ma said. "Heartily."

" . . . make a nest in a box behind the stove . . ."

"I tell you they're fine where they are, Kid."

"Jake knows best, son."

"How'd you like to be out in a barn with a litter of kittens in sixty below?"

"First place," Jake said. "It ain't anywheres near sixty below. Second place, it ain't gonna get to be sixty below. Third place . . ."

"She hit sixty below yet?" That was Gate showed up at the bottom of the stairs.

"No, it ain't!" Jake said. "Glad to see you finally rolled outa bed."

"Me too," Gate said. He went to the stove and started dishing his mush. "Took me longer'n I figgered to dry out!"

"Ma, why couldn't we bring in Milk and her . . ."

"Because! After last night and those two up there, I have had just about as much as I can take without a bunch of cats in my kitchen!"

"SLUUURP!" Gate was almost as bad with oatmeal mush as he was with soup, or Jake was with tea or coffee.

Ma's face tightened right up. "Now! There's a full can of cream out in the back shed and I have to get to that separator before . . ."

"SLURRRRRRRRRP!"

" . . . it does turn in ice cream! I want you to do the dishes, son, and after that you can sweep . . ."

"That's girl's work . . ."

"That's right, and the sooner you get it done you can do boy's work: hauling out the ashes and bringing in the coal." She slammed the back door behind her. Gate kept slurping and Jake kept picking his teeth while I cleared the dishes. Gate finished up and sat back and bit off a chew. Jake had one, too. Then Gate went up to his room. Jake was still there when I finished drying.

"Jake?"

"Yeah?"

"Uh, just wondered . . ."

"Yeah?"

"When you go out to throw down feed an' slop the pigs . . ."

"Uh-huh?"

"You'll be goin' out the back door an' through the stoop, where Ma is. Why couldn't I go out the *front* door . . ."

Jake's chair he'd been tilting in, hit the floor with a bang.

"I'll tell you why! I'm sick an' tired of hearin' you whinin' about them cats out there!" He got up. "Whinin' on an' on an' on . . . !"

"I ain't whinin'!" I whined.

Jake slammed the door behind him just as Gate came down the stairs. "You want to give me a hand sweepin' up . . ."

"Hell, no!" Gate said. "That's girl's work!"

I decided I better shut up about Milk and her kittens. Wasn't all that hard to do. If Jake said they'd be all right, I knew they would be. I can trust Jake. Didn't mean I didn't keep thinking about them out there, though. Hoping.

Jake and Gate kept right on snoring every night, but Ma had the answer to that. Couple nights on, just as we were turning in:

"You going outside, Ma?"

"No."

"Then what you doing with those earmuffs?"

"As you can plainly see, I am headed up to bed early. With luck and these I may get some unbroken sleep."

"Pretty bad," I said.

"I agree with you. The unfinished snore concerto has never been one of my favourites!" Ma plays the pump organ, ours and the one in Crocus Knox Presbyterian Church. While we were snowed in that ten days she was at ours a lot. I got so I hated the goddam thing, sobbing and groaning away.

Fifth day our telephone went dead. When Ma was going upstairs with her earmuffs, I said, "Can I have the thermometer?"

"It's where it always is – outside wall of the back stoop. Left of the door, and going out to look at it a hundred times a day will not lift the temperature one fraction of a degree."

"No, I mean the *human* thermometer. I want to see if I'm running a temperature."

"What!"

I explained to her what Jake had told me about cabin fever.

"Don't bother," she said. "Jake's just exaggerating again. Cabin fever does not raise the blood temperature. Just the blood pressure!"

Sixth day, Ma discovered the potatoes and the carrots and the beets and the turnips in the roothouse had all turned black. Next morning, she had trouble finding any eggs in the hen house that weren't made of concrete.

Seventh day so were all our hens, as well as the Rhode Island Red and the Wine-dot. They wouldn't fight any more like Jake and Gate.

The worst of all was the next day:

"There's no salt in this porridge!" Jake yelled.

"We're out," Ma said.

"Out! Out!"

"All gone by yesterday morning. Isn't a grain left."

"Gotta have salt! Porridge ain't porridge without salt in it!"

"I know it tastes flat without . . ."

"Stops being porridge at all without salt in it!"

"Nothing I can do about that," Ma said, "until the weather clears and they can get the roads ploughed out."

"Aaaaaaah!"

That cabin fever's bad stuff. I thought Jake was kiddin' about the fellow got the axe in the head over cabin fever. He wasn't fooling.

Irene and Eglantine were still giving milk, so we did have cream for the porridge. Until *it* ran out. Jake fixed that. He put wheat and oats through the pig feed chopper. Damn it all! I've never been fussy about porridge, with or without salt. Sugar ran out, then the coffee.

Eighth night at supper, nobody said anything. Jake and Gate just hunched over their plates and grunted at each other. She was dark in our kitchen with the coal-oil lamp flickering like a yellow moth. It kind of did things to Ma's mouth. She was holding her chin kind of high. My ma used to be a schoolteacher. When Ma set down the dessert in front of us she said:

"There you are. Something special for dessert tonight. One sealer of saskatoons hasn't gone bad. Saskatoon pie."

Jake grunted.

Gate grunted.

I grunted.

"Son! That will do!"

"Huh?"

"A polite answer doesn't hurt anybody! That goes for you two – Jake, Mr. Gatenby – also!"

Jake and Gate both grunted.

"As long as we have to be together, cooped up like this, I should think it wouldn't hurt for a few people to make an effort."

"I'm makin' an effort," Jake said.

"I have not noticed that," Ma said.

"Ain't easy," Gate said.

"I know it isn't easy. Now, how about a little pleasantness for a change? I'd like to see you two do something else besides sitting glaring at each other. Pleasant conversation aids the digestion."

"Uh," Jake said.

"Uh," Gate said.

"I take it," Ma said, "you meant 'yes' – both of you."

Jake and Gate were still getting out the cards for rummy each night after supper. Because I didn't have to do any home-work, they let me play with them. Ma, she headed for the pump organ in the parlour.

Right away when we started playing I know Jake and Gate hadn't meant "yes" at suppertime when they said "uh" to Ma. I guess they didn't agree with her that pleasant conversation aided the digestion – or rummy playing.

"Have to crack your knuckles like that all the time?"

"My knuckles," Jake said.

For the next two hands that was the only thing he said.

As he gathered up the cards to shuffle them, Gate said, "Wonder how long she'll last! This here blizzard! Wonder how long we're gonna be caught in here like – kiyoots in a trapline!"

"Umph," Jake said.

"Thermometer's still saying forty-three below," I said.

"Ummph."

"Can't your hired man here speak English!"

"Sure, but he don't when he doesn't feel . . ."

"What is he – Indian? Ugh an' umph. Bad enough – stuck here like this . . ."

"Mmmph," Jake agreed.

"What's eatin' you? Can't you talk to a fellah?"

"UMMMPH!"

All through that hand the both of them shut up. Not a word. But the beginning of the next one, Jake stared at his cards, then he threw them down and gathered up the deck.

"What the hell you doin'!"

Easy to tell what he was doing. He was slapping them down and he was counting them.

" . . . nine – ten – 'leven – twelve . . ."

"What the hell you . . ."

"Somethin' wrong with this deck – sixteen – seventeen – eighteen – nineteen an' twenty an' . . ."

"Nothin' wrong with that deck!"

" . . . twenty-four – twenty-five – twenty-six – twenty-seven – twenty-eight . . ."

"Nothin' wrong with that goddam deck!"

Jake, he kept right on counting. When he finished he went through them again. "I knew it!" he said.

"Knew what?" Gate said.

"No four of spades! I had've got the four of spades I'd've been out after my third draw!"

"Hell you would've!"

"Hell I wouldn't! An' that ain't all! That there deck is short three cards! Only fifty cards in it! Should be fifty-three!"

"Only fifty-one in a deck," Gate said.

"Fifty-*three*, stupid!"

"Don't you call me . . . !"

"I'd've won if I'd had the four of . . ."

"The hell you would've! You'd of lost her whether you had the four of spades or you didn't have the four of spades!"

"I would so!" Jake yelled.

Out in our parlour Ma was pumping away at the organ. Hard to tell which was louder: Ma on that organ or Jake and Gate at each other.

"I would not!" Rhode Island Red rooster.

"You would so!" Wine-dot rooster.

The organ stopped. "Jake! Mr. Gatenby!" Ma yelled from the parlour.

"I had as much as I can take out of you!" Jake screeched.

"Equal for me!"

Now the both of them were on their feet and leaning at each other over the table.

"You are enough to give a gopher's ass the heartburn, Gatenby!"

"Just how long can a human bein' stand! Cooped up with the likes of you!?"

"JUST ABOUT HALF AS LONG AS I BEEN STANDIN' WITH THE LIKES OF YOU!" Jake yelled back.

"And I've been standing OUT OF BOTH OF YOU!" Ma was in the doorway and she was really, really mad.

Jake shook his finger under Gate's beak. "He can't win fair, so he goes an' he fixes the deck!"

"Sam! Both of you! SHUT UP WHEN I AM TALKING!" They did that.

"You think you've had enough from each other. You don't like the way the other eats, the way he sleeps, the way he cracks his knuckles, clacks his dentures! Well, I don't like the way both of you eat – sleep – grunt – talk – argue – snap. You haven't heard me grumbling! You give each other the heartburn! The raging heartburn! Me too! You, Jake – you don't like the way Gate slurps or the way he snores. Neither do I! Nor do I like the way you slurp, Jake, *and* dunk your toast! You're both hard to live with, and you'd better start making some allowance for each other! Just as I've been making allowance for you! And if you don't – blizzard or no blizzard – you'll both go out of this house and into the worst storm since the blue snow of 'six and 'seven – out flying – to snap and snarl with the jackrabbits and the weasels and the kiyoots and the badgers for whom you are fit company!"

I guess you can get blizzards inside of you same as you can get them outside of you. After Ma cut loose the one inside cleared up quick. Not the one outside. You wouldn't believe it was Jake and Gate at the table with you:

"Would you kindly pass the butter, please, Gate."

"Certainly, Jake. Would you care for a helpin' of the pickled beets?"

"No thanks, Gate. Kid, would you care for a little . . ."

"No thanks," I said. "They give me the ragin' . . ."

"Watch it there, Kid!" Jake said.

It lasted almost a whole day. Temperature hit fifty-two below and I started in worrying about Milk and her six kittens again, out there in that loft all full of cracks and holes. Wasn't easy, but I kept from asking Ma if we could bring them inside behind the kitchen stove.

When Jake came down the morning after Ma blew up, he said, "Where the aitch is my shavin' stuff?"

"Where it always is, I suppose," Ma said. "Up in your room. Your dresser. The shelf below the mirror."

"It ain't."

"Then it must be somewhere else. Look for it."

"I did. No razor, no mug, soap. All I can find is the strop hangin' up there."

I said, "Maybe Mr. Gatenby didn't put them back in the same place when he . . ."

"Whaaaat!"

"Maybe Mr. Gatenby didn't put 'em back after he borrowed . . ."

"He wasn't usin' my King Cutter razor!"

"While ago he was gettin' hot water out of the reservoir," I said. "He took it out back while you were . . ."

"Shavin' stuff's personal! People don't use other folk's shavin' stuff!"

"What else is he going to use, Jake?" Ma said. "After all, he hasn't got his own with him! He didn't know there was going to be a blizzard. He couldn't know he was going to get caught over here."

"He don't have to shave, then! He can let his beard grow, can't he! Ain't gonna bother me if he don't shave!"

"Well, evidently it bothers *him*. He was saying that he – that it gets his neck – pricks his skin and feels uncomfort . . ."

"Let it! Let it! What's he got to shave for? Ain't goin' in to town. Ain't goin' in to church. Ain't goin' visitin'."

"Perhaps it's my fault as much as his, Jake. I believe I did say something the other day, that if there was anything he needed."

"That's real nice. He's already wearin' my underwear. I hate to think what'd happen if he was to bust his dentures."

"His what, Jake?" I said.

"Teeth! Teeth! Then he'd borrow mine! That reminds me. Black Judas. I knew I was runnin' low – but I figgered there was a plug left. There ain't."

"The last I saw was on your dresser. Coal-scuttle, son."

"I finished that one on my dresser," Jake said. "There was another one."

"That was the only one I saw," she said.

"Gate by rights shouldn't have any left," Jake said. "He only had the part of a plug when he came over with a week ago. Way he chews he'd've used it up long ago."

"He's still chewin'," I said.

"Sure he is. Took my last plug! That's it! Take a fellow's last plug of chewin' tobacco without saying a word! There is the last straw, Kid!"

Just like Gate and that Liver Pill Calendar Almanac predicted, she did drop to sixty below. Broke the winter of 'six and 'seven record. Ma sent me up to bed early. I couldn't get to sleep thinking about Milk and her little kittens out in that loft. Then I *had* to do it. I got up. Ma was in on the organ in the parlour. Jake and Gate were in the kitchen still doing at it.

"I guess I did happen to pick up a plug I thought was mine," Gate said.

"I want it back!"

"Well," Gate said. "Now ain't that an Indian giver for you!"

"I want it . . . !"

"I chewed her all up."

"Whaaaat! My last plug!"

They didn't even notice me slip out the door and into the back shed, where I began to pull on my galoshes and windbreaker and toque and scarf. I could still hear them in there.

"Us snowed in here!" Jake was yelling. "No way into town! Now – my last plug of chewin' tobacco. That's it! That's *finally* it!"

"Goddam rights it is!" Gate yelled back at him. "I've had all I can take out of you! You ain't gonna have to put up with me snorin' no more – nor usin' your razor – nor borrowin' a few chews of tobacco! I'm leavin' before I . . . !"

"I wish you could, but your pick-ups still froze – hey! Don't matter! I'll just hitch up Baldy an' Queenie to the dem . . ."

"No thank you! I'm doin' her on foot."

"Three miles through sixty below – that wind! You wouldn't last ten minutes . . ."

"When the snow melts off next spring an' you come across what's left of Samuel Titchener Gatenby, just you remember one thing, Jake Trumper! You shoved me out into the worst blizzard since nineteen ought-six and nineteen ought-seven!"

I pulled open the shed door to head out for the barn and Milk and her kittens. Wind ripped her right out of my hand. When you've never been out in sixty below, it's hard to believe how awful it can be. Sure glad that just like Old Man Froomby, Jake had strung the line between the stoop and the barn. Took me a couple minutes with my back to the wind to find it. When I turned round a real blast took me by the face, nearly knocked me off my feet. I lost the rope but I found it again. I hadn't dropped the lantern.

It had to be one step at a time with the snow right up to my knee caps, except when I got to the stock trough. Then it was up to my ass. Before I made it to the barn I felt my left ear go, then the tip of my nose, then my right cheek because I'd turned my head away to protect that left ear from getting worse.

I made it. Our barn hadn't been blown away. I climbed up into the loft. They all seemed to be fine, but it wasn't all that easy to be sure just holding up the lantern to get a look at them.

I must have been halfway back when the lantern blew out, then a little ways further on when I stumbled, and lost the rope. That wind had icicle teeth grabbing my face, my throat. I didn't have any idea where I was. I was lost in the middle of the blizzard and I had to take a rest. My legs were sure glad I did. The snow was real soft when I lay down in it, and all of a sudden I didn't feel cold anymore . . . .

"Kid – hey, Kid!"

"Son!"

"My face! My hands!"

"*You're all right*, son. Just take it . . ."

"All burny! Hurts – like blue blazes!"

"Gener'lly does when she starts to thaw out." That was Gate.

"Milk an' her kittens, they're . . ."

"Behind the kitchen stove, son."

"I just had to see how they . . ."

"All right, son. We'll talk about that later. Mr. Gatenby found you."

"An' if he hadn't," Jake said, "You'd've been froze stiffer'n a quarter of beef."

"I found you about as far as I could spit from the back-shed door."

She blew herself out that night, headed south to give the Americans aitch. Thermometer flew up twenty-five degrees before noon. They told me. Ma kept me in bed for all the next day.

I found out that Gate had struck out on foot like he threatened Jake he would, and that's how he came across me lying in the snow, and carried me back into the house. He stayed with us a couple days more.

Second evening Ma let me come downstairs. You could hear Milk purring and her kittens mewing behind the kitchen range. Dr. Fotheringham made it out and he checked me all over. Jake said when he talked to him after the examination, Doc said he wasn't going to have to amputate my head at the neck after all.

"And if you ever do anything stupid like that again, Kid, and Doc *don't* saw off your head, I will!"

Ma gave me aitch too. I guess I deserved it.

Last night before Gate left, he and Jake and me played rummy. I'd found the two of hearts, four of spades, and the jack of clubs.

In Ma's sewing-basket.

MIND OVER MADAM

MA SAYS IT SERVES EVERYBODY RIGHT: MR. MACTAGGART, Repeat Golightly. She says Jackie Bews' folks shouldn't have let a thirteen-year-old kid puff away on a cigar in front of the whole Crocus district, even if it was an imaginary one. I didn't tell her I seen Jackie with a real one in his mouth behind their barn more than once. She says no one has the right to go fiddling around with people's privacy and humiliating them in public. I thought it was kind of funny: Aunt Lil fishing out of a galvanized pail, and Mrs. Elsie Abercrombie singing "The Field Pitcher's Sweetheart" and doing a dance she called "Dawn Comes Up Over the Swathes" and then talking Ubangi. Repeat Golightly's songs were real dirty ones.

"I'll never understand why a person like the Great Dr. Suhzee that's internationally famous would come and put on a show like he did in the curling rink in Crocus. According to the posters they had up for him and his full-page advertisement in the *Crocus Breeze* he's hypnotized all the crowned heads of Europe. Quite a letdown, you might say, him coming to work on Crocus, folks."

First we knew about it was the article and the full-page ad in the *Crocus Breeze*.

" 'The Great Doctor Suhzee – World Famous Mes – ah – Mesmerust' – huh?"

"Same as a hyp – uh – notist, Kid."

"Oh! 'Hilarious And Educational – Crowds Crowds – Get Your Tickets Early.' Gee, Jake – comin' to Crocus!"

"You gathered up those eggs yet, son?" That was Ma yelling down at me from upstairs.

" 'October 17th Dr. Suhzee Will Cast His Spell Over Volunteers From Crocus Community. Curling Rink Building. 7 p.m. He Will Give a Thrilling Demonstration of Mass Hyp-uh-notism!' "

"Interestin'," Jake said.

"Son, have you gath . . . !"

"Yes, Ma!"

"And wiped them?"

"I'm doing them!" I went to the sink and got the basin and a cloth and I started doing them. "Jake, would he be one of those kind with a turbine and dark burny eyes?"

"Nope. I heard about him before. Understand he comes out of Australia or maybe New Zealand."

Ma showed up at the bottom of the stairs. "Haven't you finished those eggs yet! Martha's due here any minute!"

"Sorry, Ma. Jake and me . . ."

" . . . and I."

"We were talking about this hypuhnotist, Dr. Suhzee, coming to Crocus . . ."

"I could use him – put *you* under and get you to do your chores and your homework – get you up to bed at a decent hour every night. Which reminds me. When I come back from town I want to see that bedroom of yours tidied up!"

After she left with Mrs. Tincher, I said to Jake, "You ever seen a person hypuhnotized?"

"No humans."

"Oh."

"Just critters."

"Huh?"

"Like with doctors – human ones and critter ones – I guess you get the same with hypuhnotists."

"Really?"

"Aw, Kid. You seen me do it. Halter breakin' – goin' up to a yearlin' – talkin' low to him – rubbin' his nose an' between his eyes an' behind his ears an' along his neck – chewin' a wad tobacco an' leaning my face right up into his an' givin' him a whiff of it while I slipped that halter up an' over his head an' he didn't even know it was on him."

"Yeah! Yeah, Jake! An' then when you turned your back to him, he'd follow you, buntin' his nose against your ass . . ."

"That's right. Then the halter shank round the set post an' a jerk on her so's he comes to, and then all hell lets out for recess."

"I never thought of it that way, Jake. *Animal* hyp . . ."

"Just a amachoor at it. Like a lotta farmers – ranchers. Not Dip Highdigger in Hairy Hills district, though. Used to call him Dip. Not to his face, mind you. Sheepherder – always stank of sheep dip so we called him Dip Highdigger."

"Yeah?"

"Had a cow – always raisin' aitch when he tried to milk her. Well, sir, one day he stared at her a long time, tryin' to figger out whether he oughta keep on tryin' to milk her – or slaughter her or torture her to death. Must've stared into her brown eyes whilst he said these here same words over an' over again under his breath."

"What words?"

"Well, now, Kid – they – She'd run his patience short – well, he was cussin' – poor cusser, always repeated hisself – said the same ones over an' over again. You know what he did without knowin' it?"

"What?"

"Put that Jersey cow right under. She milked as nice an' quiet as you please, never kicked over another bucket. Almost like she was in a comma from his starin' into her eyes an' sayin' them same words over an' over an' over again. Magic cussin' words. Old Dip. Sheepherder. Sheepherders is real loners, Kid."

"Uh-huh."

"That's how come – after that Jersey cow, he went to work on a pig . . ."

"Did he hyp . . . ?"

"Yep. Easier'n a cow. Pigs is smart. He housebroke that pig . . ."

"Whaaat! Why would he . . . ?"

"So's she could move in with him. For company. I think Dip liked pigs aitch of a lot more than he did sheep, so it was nice for him to come home to that sow o' his. For about six months."

"She died?"

"Nope. She moved out. Couldn't stand the stink of Dip any longer."

"Aw, Jake!"

It isn't easy to tell when Jake's kidding and when he isn't. Few other fellows in Crocus district like that, too.

"Dip taught a crow an' then a magpie to talk."

I always wanted to do that.

"He got real good at it – got so's he could freeze a rooster right in his tracks. Fixed a gander with one foot in the air. Dropped four crows an' a horny owl out of a tree."

Yeah. Jake does get carried away sometimes. So what. I learn a lot out of Jake. He's smart.

Kind of hard to go around acting natural once a person knew the Great Dr. Suhzee all the way from Australia was coming to Crocus. Why would he even bother to stop off for a cup of coffee in *Crocus*? Just thinking about him and that awful power he had made you feel kind of scared inside.

Jake, he really knew what he was talking about when it came to hypnotizing animals, but I sure learned a lot about humans out of Repeat Golightly. He's got to be about the best well-read fellow in Crocus district. I don't think even Miss Henchbaw has read as many books as he has. Not just historical books or books on gardening, either.

Jake climbed into the chair for the shave and haircut he gets about once a month when we got time in town, and a lot of other times when Jake wants to catch up on what got caught in the Crocus trapline.

"S'pose you'll be takin' in this show the Great Dr. Suhzee, Repeat?"

"That's right, Jake. Be there. I'll be there. Wouldn't miss it. Opportunity lifetime. Wouldn't miss it for the world."

"Uh-huh. Little outa my line. Just how would a fellow like that go to work on folks?"

"As it happens, Jake – something I happen to know something about. Psychology."

"I mean this hypuhnotism."

"Ties in with psychology the sub-conscious, Jake. Frood."

"Frood?"

"Dr. Frood."

"I mean this Dr. Suhzee."

"Sigmund Frood. Great psychologist, psycholanalyst. Took the lantern hypnosis and dreams – threw revealing light into the human sub-conscious."

"Did he? Well, when a person gets hypuhnotized . . ."

"Mind darkens, Jake. Shadows unconsciousness fall. Memory stirs in the dusk. Forgotten things rear their ugly heads."

"Do they!"

"No telling what a person might find in there."

"Isn't there."

"No. Sort of like an attic you might say – in the house of the soul. Or a basement. All sorts of things a person forgot about – wanted to forget about. Hidden, shameful things."

"Uh-huh," Jake said.

"Just one short step from the beast."

"Who is? Pete Botten?"

"Me. You Man – woman – all humans. One step from the beast. Animal den, wild things in there."

"Uh-huh."

"Explains why a person dreams those dreams, you know."

"Does it," Jake said.

"That's when they creep out."

"What does?"

"Things people pushed down deep in the sub-conscious. Things they're ashamed of. Float up in their dreams. And in the hypnotic state."

I just been minding my own business, pretending I was reading one of the magazines Repeat keeps in his shop for folks waiting their turn. *Country Homes and Gardens.* Jake calls it *Country Homes and Garbage.* Mr. Golightly had quit clipping at Jake's hair and was looking over at me.

He cleared his throat. "Was there, ah, something you needed to do, Kid? Aaah – elsewhere?"

"No," I said. "I'm just waiting for Jake to get his hair cut."

"Maybe you'd like to go over to MacTaggart's – Sanitary Café – have a bottle of pop," Repeat said.

"No thanks. I already did have . . ."

Jake said, "What's – what you drivin' at, Re . . ."

"Nice-looking crops being harvested."

"Sure – month ago. But to get back to Dr. Suhzee and this here sub-conscientious of yours . . ."

"Little pitchers have big ears, Jake."

"So what. You're always sayin' clean instrument an' a clean mouth in a clean shop."

"Of course, Jake. But . . ."

"This Doc Frood – foul-mouth fellow, was he?"

"Ah, uh, it's – Well, then – his findings about the human psyche – pretty adult material, Jake."

"Is it. Well, I think the Kid's heard pretty adult stuff before. Most kids has. Nowadays."

Repeat took a minute to make up his mind about that. I just buried my nose deeper in the magazine. Repeat went back to work on Jake's head.

Got real interesting, 'specially the stuff about people's dreams.

". . . finding yourself in church taking up the collection and no clothes on. Mother naked maybe on the grandstand during Twenty-fourth of May celebrations."

I had dreams like that more than a few times.

". . . embarrassing. Embarrassing things. That's why they been pushed back into the darkness of the sub-conscious. So they won't embarrass a persons – upset him. Frustrations – complexes – conflicts . . ."

"Do they?"

"Shakes a person. Shakes a person, Jake."

"I guess she does."

"Death wish," Repeat said.

"Death wish!"

"Explains why you stumble. Explains why your hand slips with the King Cutter razor when you're shaving. Makes you tread on that gas pedal harder. Makes a person want to throw himself off of bridges, cliffs, high places. Ever noticed that, Jake? How you get up somewhere and you have this compulsion, awful compulsion, to throw yourself off – dash yourself to pieces?"

"No, Repeat, can't say I have."

"Universal. Death wish. Sub-conscious."

"Well, I might've missed it. Livin' most of the time on the prairies. Nothin' really high enough to give a fellow much opportunity – throw hisself off of it. Unless he picked one of the grain elevators – or the town water tower."

"Carry the enemy in our bosom, Jake. Hidden deep down there. Shadows the sub-conscious."

"Why, that's awful, Repeat!"

"That's right. Certainly is."

"Can't tell what might happen," Jake said. "I never heard anythin' like this before."

"Jake, where have you been all this time?"

"Mile an' a half south on Gover'ment Road."

'You've got to keep abreast. I say you've got to keep abreast of the times, Jake."

"Yeah!"

"Know the times you live in. Modern times. Day of fast living. Walking the tightrope. The tightrope of our own nerves keyed tight and tense to the twanging point. Nothing like it before on this earth. Folks live closer together now, Jake – all of us tight together and hurtling through space, careless space, to our common doom."

"That's nice."

"Hear the voices of distant humans as they never been heard before. Coming at you from north, east, south, and west. Printed word. Moving pictures, radio – Human skins are thinner these days, Jake."

"Are they?"

"Tissue paper thin with the nerves right up under the surface. This is the age of the sub-conscious. She's come into her own. I, ah, I'll be there at the curling rink. Dr. Suhzee's demonstration – hypnotic – educational."

"Gonna be real hilarious, Repeat."

"Above all – above all – serious. Fill out my reading – study human nature. What books you been reading?"

"Oh, I don't get so much time, Repeat. *Nor'west Prairie Farm Review – Leader-Post – Maclean's* . . ."

"No, no, I mean *serious* reading." Repeat, he'd quit working on Jake's hair, gone over to his instrument shelf, come back with a thick book.

"Mature. *Sanity Is for You Too*," he said.

"Huh!"

"Brilliant book. By Hungerdunger, Hungerdunger, and MacCormack, *Think*."

"Eh?"

"*Think.*"

"I do. I do," Jake said.

"*Think,* book by Dr. P. J. Flockerly. Then there's *In Spite of Yourselves.*"

"Another these here books on . . ."

"That, Jake, is the finest educational documentary program on the air. CBC. *In Spite of Yourselves.*"

"Oh."

"Explains everything. Broken homes, broken hearts, business failures. Why, if a person doesn't follow *In Spite of Yourselves,* Jake, he doesn't – he isn't conscious he's conscious."

"Oh."

"That program and this book here – always keep it on my instrument shelf – that program and *Home Psychoanalysis Made Easy* cover everything. Everything. Show how everything traces back to the sub-conscious. Way you hated your mother. Wanted to kill her."

Right about then I was beginning to understand why Repeat had wanted me out of the shop while he talked to Jake.

"Or your father. Or you wanted to strangle your sister. In your sub-conscious, that is."

"You didn't hate your mother, did . . . ?"

"No, I – Of course I didn't."

"Your father?" Jake said. "Why, I figgered you an' your father . . ."

"*I* didn't. I'm just explaining why *other* people do."

"Seems to me there was just you in your family. I never heard of you havin' any sister you wanted to strangle in your sub . . ."

"I didn't. Never said I did!"

"Then why did you . . ."

"I just said the sub-conscious explains all that. It's not simple, Jake. There in the sub-conscious you can find the explanation for everything. Conflicts, neuroses, psychoses, blocks, complexes, fixations, fetishes, schizophrenia, hebephrenia, paranoia, dementia praecox, delusions grandeur, introversion, extroversion, manic depression, regression, ascendancy-submission. Explanation of all these things lies in the subconscious."

"Well, she's nice to know they got alla that kinda stuff located – in the right township."

"Makes a person tremble to think how the children – our children – modern children are being raised."

"How's that?" Jake said.

"Blind. By blind parents don't know the dangers – the pitfalls – the terrors that threaten."

"Now look here, Repeat, seems to me the av'rage kid aroun' Crocus is doin' all right."

"Can't raise a child blind, Jake."

"Like your ma an' pa done?"

"How's that?"

"What'd they know all about this stuff?"

"Oh, there are bound to be a few lucky ones. Our home – was one the lucky ones. Mostly because of father. One of nature's noblemen, my father."

"I've heard you say, Repeat."

"Noble example to one and all. Family – exemplary – fine wise old man. He gave us constant guidance and daily advice. Wise council. Unflagging. Father never flagged."

"Didn't he."

"The Golden Rule lived in our home, Jake. Lived right along with us in our daily living. Blessing before every meal. Prayers morning and evening. We kept the Sabbath. Mother cooked everything for Sunday the night before. No cow was milked. No feed thrown down. Horses weren't watered on the Sabbath, nor was water for humans hauled in our home on the Lord's Day. No broom swept nor no dish was washed. Not a speck – a single speck of dust – was dusted on the Sabbath."

"Ah-hah. Seems to me I heard all this before, Repeat. Coming back to that sub-conscientious yours. I can't see how readin' alla them books ain't gonna make things a hell of a lot worse for a person."

"Oh, I'm not saying they can give you peace of mind by themselves. Not by themselves. Our age – paradox – gives us material comforts beyond what our fathers and mothers had. Far beyond. Can't seem to give us peace and contentment."

"I'm with you there, Repeat. 'Specially if folks got a whole bunch of wild critters lurchin' 'round down there in their sub-conscientious . . ."

"Sub-*conscious.* False security does no good, Jake. Got to face it. Can't bury our heads in the sand. Know the truth about ourselves."

"But, Repeat, *is* she the truth?"

"How's that?"

"What you been tellin' me – stranglin' your sister if you had one . . ."

"You don't quite understand what I was . . ."

"Drawin' a bead on your old dad with a .30-30."

"I was speaking only of the . . ."

"Pottin' your dear old ma with a twelve-gauge, then turnin' it on yourself for a double . . ."

"It isn't that simple, Jake."

"Now you was talkin' about them awful dreams. You never had them sorta dreams about your dad, Repeat? Repeat?" He waited. "See how ridiculous that sorta stuff is?"

"Not – so – ridiculous, Jake. Not – all – ridiculous."

Way we generally do when we're in Crocus, we dropped in at MacTaggart's Trading Company Store to leave Ma's order. There was a big poster in the store window, all about Dr. Suhzee. Another one inside.

"We're going to be there," Mr. MacTaggart said. "Guess we got the first tickets to it. Complimentary."

"Free?" Jake said. "How come?"

"Well, I guess he called on *me* first – being mayor of Crocus.

Find out what there was available in the way of a hall. Credit Union's redecorating – I told him the curling rink ought to do – holds a lot of people."

"Uh-huh."

"Then he explained what he needed. I just stuck the Softly Drowze mattress in the window there – between the cream separator and that shotgun shell and decoy display."

"What's a mattress got to do with . . ."

"Don't you read your *Crocus Breeze*, Jake?"

"Sure I do."

"His ad in there?" Mr. MacTaggart said.

"Yeah. I read the article an' . . ."

"This morning's issue?"

"Oh no. *Last* week's. We don't get it till a day . . ."

"His request for volunteers."

"Volunteers? For what?"

"Hypnotism. Somebody willing to be hypnotized. He, ah, he's coming in on the 2:10."

"Maybe he is, but what the aitch has that got to do with a mattress in your front window?"

"That's why I got the free tickets. The poster and permission to put his subject to sleep in my window there."

"Huh!" Jake said.

"Huh!" I said.

"Kind of wish I hadn't made the arrangement. Not so sure I like the idea now. Somebody in a coma in my front window, all tomorrow afternoon till the evening show."

Me, I was reading the inside poster up above canned goods, same as in the front window:

THE GREAT DR. SUHZEE
HILARIOUS AND LAUGH PROVOKING.
COME AND SEE THE WORLD'S GREATEST
PRACTITIONER OF THE ART OF MESMER.

Almost the same as the ad we read in last week's *Crocus Breeze*, but this one said:

SEE FRONT WINDOW OF MACTAGGART'S TRAD-
ING COMPANY STORE. IT MAY BE YOUR OWN
NEIGHBOUR IN HYPNOTIC TRANCE!

"He said it would be good advertising for both of us, "Mr.
MacTaggart was saying. "Got half a mind to tell him I changed
my . . ."

"Can't back out of it now, Mac. Train's due at 2:10."

"You know, Jake, I don't like this monkeying around with
a person's mind."

"Pretty serious, Mac. Just been talkin' with Repeat. What
he says – this Dr. Suhzee's likely to have a real show for
us."

"That Softly Drowze mattress," Mr. MacTaggart said, "is
an inner spring job I already sold. Harvey Buchanan that just
married Olga Johnston out of the telephone office. They're
due back from their honeymoon any day. Going to start up
their nest in the apartment over the Sanitary Café. It's a double. Only one I've got."

"Looks like a pretty touchy situation, Mac. Way I see it,
this Dr. Suhzee's show must be easy as excitin' as a circus.
Accordin' to Repeat, he's practically got five dangerous an'
death-defyin' rings with untamed tigers, man-eatin' lions,
bloodthirsty leopards, elephants, deadly cobras . . ."

"How's that! How's that?"

"Only he doesn't have to pay any feed bill for lions an'
tigers an' bears. He finds his dangerous animals anywhere he
wants to hang his hat, all caged up in the Sub, uh, sub-some-
thin' of his audiences!"

I saw Mr. MacTaggart's mouth go tight. He slapped his
hand on the counter. "Made up my mind. Only person going
to use that mattress – those newlyweds, Mr. and Mrs. Harve
Buchanan."

"Good decision, Mac," Jake said.

"Jake?"

"Yeah."

"Aah, nearly one now. I was thinking – he's coming in on the 2:10. Why don't you – had your lunch yet?"

"Nope."

"Why don't you have it in town, then drop over here. I could use some moral support. I'd appreciate it when . . ."

"Sure, Mac," Jake said.

Instead of heading home, we stayed in town, ate at the Sanitary Café. Then afterwards we went back to MacTaggart's store.

The Great Suhzee was there ahead of us. He wasn't a big strapping fellow way I thought he'd be. Just about Repeat Golightly's size. He had a beard and he talked kind of fancy like English people do. He did have dark glowy eyes, like Reverend Cameron has when he's up in Knox pulpit telling the congregation how the spirit is so dandy and the flesh is so awful.

As we came in the store Jake grabbed my arm, pulled us over to the men's wear section, and held his finger to his mouth. Where we were we could see the counter and Mr. MacTaggart and Dr. Suhzee pretty good. Hear every word.

"Just didn't seem such a good idea after I got to thinking it over," Mr. MacTaggart was saying to him.

"We have an agreement, Mr. MacTaggart. Mutually satisfactory."

"Yes, but since then I been . . ."

"Once given our word's not to be taken back, is it, Mr. MacTaggart? Can truly be said our word's our bond. Not to be broken."

"Well, I usually try to keep my . . ."

"I knew from our first meeting, Mr. MacTaggart, that you were a man of your word. I see not reason to change that estimate. To do so would insult you."

"Insult me!"

"We shall continue as planned, Mr. MacTaggart, for our mutual benefit. My subject . . ."

"You got one already!"

"Oh yes. Train was fifteen minutes early. I dropped by the hotel and there were a dozen volunteers waiting. I was able to make my selection. She seems a most, ah, receptive – highly sensitive woman."

"Woman! *Woman!* You didn't say anything about sticking a *woman* in the – in the window!"

Jake headed for the counter, me after him.

"The sex of the subject is neither here nor there."

"It sure is! The – it doesn't seem – I don't want a *woman* stretched out on . . ."

"The important thing is the personality of the volunteer. I have made my selection."

"Doctor," Jake said. "Who did you . . ."

"Let me see. Her name – I have it right – ah, Bogart, Miss Bogart."

"Oh, I guess I ain't familiar with . . ."

"Never even heard of her," Mr. MacTaggart said.

"A local woman, I believe. She said she had lived most of her life in the district. Miss Bogart."

"Maybe from Yellow Grass way, or Conception," Jake said.

"Lillian. Miss Lillian Bogart."

"Whaaat!" Mr. MacTaggart said.

"Holy diddle!" Jake said. "Her!"

"Aunt Lil!" I said.

"Then I take it, you *are* familiar with her?" Suhzee said.

"What's wrong with Aunt Lil! Why would she want to . . ."

"I did not inquire into her reasons for offering herself. I'm quite sure she will be an excellent subject. Now, I'm sorry to have to terminate this interesting exchange but – if you have everything readied – the window – I see you have the mattress there."

"But, ah, I can't have Aunt Lil lying there!"

"The sooner the better. Within the next half hour, to be exact."

"Look, we can't . . ."

"Certainly we can. We will, Mr. MacTaggart. I shall put her under."

"But it – it – isn't – What's got into her! She's a sensible woman! What's she want to get hypnotized – bedding down in my front window in front of everybody – letting everybody stare at her in her nightgown!"

"Mr. MacTaggart! Whatever are you saying! She shall be fully clothed. *Fully* and *decently* clothed."

"Oh," Mr. MacTaggart said.

"Oh," Jake said.

"Oh," I said.

"Mine is a *serious* and *scientific* demonstration of mentalism, mesmerism, and hypnotism! Dignity is the keynote, Mr. MacTaggart – educational and *refined*. I am surprised that you could for a moment, however brief, assume otherwise. The international acclaim I have won has been on the highest level – from the intelligent and from those of good taste!"

"I didn't mean . . ."

"Had I known you misunderstood I would not have hesitated to go to, ah, the store I noticed on my way to the hotel – the Bon Ton, I believe."

"It was just that I . . ."

"Your opposition, I imagine. It is still not too late . . ."

"No, ah, I guess it was just that I . . ."

"Miss Bogart could just as well recline in *their* front window. The crowds could just as well gather before the Bon Ton. People could just as well be breathlessly referring to the Bon Ton as to the MacTaggart Trading Company."

"Well, now that you've explained it, Doc – if she's got her clothes on."

"She has. She shall have."

"I did make a deal with you."

"That is correct."

"Seeing it's Aunt Lil, it'd have to be pretty, ah, respect, ah, dignified. I guess we can go right ahead the way we – you go on and put her under, Dr. Suhzee. Lay her on that mattress there between the cream separator and the decoys and shot-gun shell display."

All that time he'd been talking, Dr. Suhzee never took his eyes off Mr. MacTaggart. I wondered if maybe he hadn't used some of his great power to make Mr. MacTaggart cave in. Good warmup for putting Aunt Lil under.

Reason we hadn't realized right away it was Aunt Lil was because nobody ever calls her Miss Bogart. Her folks from England were pretty near the first to homestead in Crocus district and they did well, because when they died they left her a lot. They should have, because she never married and she looked after them right up till they called it quits. She splits her time between Crocus in the summer and fall, and Victoria spring and winter. Everybody's fussy about Aunt Lil. I guess that's why they call her Aunt Lil. She has trouble with her gall bladder.

Maybe he didn't look like I thought he would, but Dr. Suhzee sure could hypnotize. Folks plugged up Main Street in front of MacTaggart's to watch through the front window while he went to work on Aunt Lil, waving his hands in front of her nose. Jake and I were inside so we could see her eyes sort of slide down and open and slide down again, and then she just lay back there on the mattress. Asleep. Dead to the world. You could tell she was in his power. He turned to half of Crocus standing on the street and looking in. He bowed, then he turned and he set down a pail and picked up a fishing rod.

He lifted Aunt Lil to sitting and put the rod in her hand. She started in fishing, and she hooked one right away. Then she baited up and caught another one. And another. And another. Then Dr. Suhzee eased her back down onto the mat-tress and bowed to the audience outside.

I was remembering what Repeat said about a person's sub-conscious, and I was hoping she wouldn't grab a hold of one of those shotguns Mr. MacTaggart had displayed in the window, with those shells all spilled out handy.

When we had supper at the Sanitary Café and Jake and I told Ma about it, she said it was disgusting, but I noticed she came with us to the show at the curling rink.

Jackie Bews was the first one he put under:

"Watch my hands, young man, just watch my hands as they sloooooowly move – keep your eyes upon mine – steady – steady upon my eyes – my hands – my eyes – my hands – my eyes – Ever smoke, young man?"

"No, sir," Jackie said. He was lying, so he couldn't have been all the way under yet.

The Great Suhzee crooned at him and waved his hands some more, then he said, 'I am going to give you a cigarette, young man."

"Make it a cigar," Jackie said.

"Very well, a cigar. You are going to light it with this match . . ."

He didn't have any cigar but Jackie acted like he did have one in his hand. He didn't have any match to give Jackie, either, but Jackie struck a match on his pants, and he smoked that cigar – he puffed and he blew smoke rings – like I've seen him do behind Bews's barn and another time when we went swimming in the Brokenshell.

"I shall now come to the climax of this evening's demonstration with that phenomenon known to psychological science as *mass* hypnotism. I shall ask all of you out in the audience tonight to concentrate on me here.

"I want you all to watch my hands, and as you watch them intently you will feel that your eyes will want to clooooooose – that it's no use struggling against it. Just relax in your seats and keep your gaze upon my hands as they slowllly move – your eyes upon my hands – on my hands – your eyes – my hands – eyes – hands – eyes – hands . . ."

Just like dropping off to sleep. Like lying on your back on the prairie and staring up to the sky on an August day with the grasshoppers clicketing and the wind whispering soft in the grass. He didn't get me, but down the seats I could see Old Man Gatenby's head dropping forward and Mr. Tincher. I guess you might say they were good subjects because they're always doing that in church anyways. Then I saw Mrs. Abercrombie. She was under. Way under.

He invited folks to come to him and they did. At least a dozen of them. He took Mrs. Abercrombie first and that's when she sang for him and talked so funny, said it was an old Ubangi legend.

"... now then, thank you for coming forward. Your name?"

"Golightly – Orville Golightly. Clean tongue and a clean instrument in a clean shop."

"I believe you are a barber."

"Your tonsorial requirements looked after."

"I understand you sing."

"I do. Tenor. I've been told I have a fine voice. Almost perfect sense of pitch. Fine tenor voice."

"Perhaps you would sing for us tonight."

"Certainly. Glad to," Repeat said.

"I suggest something classical," Suhzee said.

"My Girl, She's the Queen of All the Acrobats . . ."

"No. Something a little more app . . ."

" . . . see her perform," Repeat sang, "give you the . . ."

" . . . appropriate for a public . . ."

" . . . big fat one twice size of me. Got hair upon her . . ."

"No! No! Mr. Go . . ."

> Like the branches on a tree.
> She can run, jump, fight . . .

"Enough of that!"

> . . . roll a hoop or push a truck.

"I said knock it off!"

That's the kind of girl
That's going to marry me!

No wonder Ma was disgusted. And a lot of other folks in that audience. I guess there's a lot of dirty songs floating around, but "My Girl, She's the Queen of All the Acrobats" has to be the dirtiest song there is. Dr. Suhzee still hung in with Repeat, but he wouldn't let him sing anymore.

"I have here a bottle – and a glass. You will take them. Fine. You will pour yourself a drink. That's fine. You are feeling a glow – the effect of the drink."

"Aaaaaah. Cuts the top soil right out of your throat!"

"Yes. Another?"

"Don't mind if I do."

"And another?"

"Looking up your address, Doctor. Ha-yah-heee-hah!"

"How do you feel now, sir?"

"No pain, Doctor. No pain worth mentioning."

"Now, you see that chair over there?"

"I do. I see it – matter of fact I see all three of them."

"I would like you to go to it."

"How?" Repeat said. "On foot? By car? By phone? Or simply fly by hand? It makes no difference to me. I'm high as a blue-wing teal and I'm coming in on the evening flight!"

Made the hair stand up on the back my neck. I went cold inside of my elbows. Mr. Golightly passes the collection plate at Knox Presbyterian, sings in the choir, and they don't sing "My Girl, She's the Queen of All the Acrobats". Up to now Repeat was Crocus' leading teetotaller. I took it up with Jake.

"I never knew Mr. Golightly drank . . ."

"Might've at one time, Kid, but he don't now – any more'n Elsie Abercrombie speaks Ubangi or Jackie Bews smokes cigars."

"Weellllll . . ."

"Supports what Repeat told us – den of wild things down

there in, uh, that sub-basement. Can't tell what anybody might stumble over down there."

"Like Aunt Lil wanting to go fishing."

"I guess he runs across some pretty funny things – and scarey – all the places he goes, putting on his hypuhnotical shows. That reminds me," Jake said. "Poor Mac."

"Huh?"

"Havin' aitch of a time findin' out just where Suhzee is. Now he's left town. Right after the show and he got Repeat sobered up, he counted the take and gave the curlin'-rink committee their cut and caught the 10:45 for Minneapolis."

"Uh-huh?"

"That's the tragical part of it. Mac wants to change his window display. Harve an' Olga Buchanan are due back from Carlyle Lake and got a use for that double-size, inner spring Softly Drowze mattress. Before he took off Suhzee plumb forgot about Aunt Lil. She's still layin' there in the fall shootin' stuff. In a deep comma."

OLD FAKERS NEVER DIE

I NEVER BEEN SUPERSTITIOUS MOST OF MY LIFE, THOUGH THE Kid's ma might argue that. She claims water witching is just wishful superstition, says the same thing about the way I can tell change of weather by the lumbago in the small my back. Look at who's talking. She goes by what me and the Kid call "Ma's Law." According to her law, you better not say anything good about the way something might turn out or by the following Thursday it'll all be frizz to rat turds. Ain't exactly the way she'd state her law, but that's the gist of it. Covers almost anything you want to happen good: crop year, weather for a picnic, Kid's marks he'll get at Rabbit Hill school, elections.

I have to own up to *one* superstition. Threes. I noticed that good or bad always comes in threes. You take Professor Noble Winesinger, the way he rolled into Crocus year before last. That was the first time and he got himself into an awful bind. Then the next fall: all over again. If I'd been him, I'd have been bracing myself for the third time. *This* year.

Kid's ma and me, we have a difference of opinion about the Professor and his Lightning Penetration Oil and Tune-Up Tonic.

"I still say he's a quack!"

"You callin' him one don't make him one," I said. It's what she always says about him and it gets under my hide. Each time she says it.

"The bottles of–of–stuff he peddles won't even clear up a stuffy nose!"

"Oh I don't know. How about my bronchitis last winter? Cured a lot of folks with guitar and kidney trouble an' ulcers. There was a fellow had the blind staggers an' . . . ."

"I wouldn't even take it for a . . . ."

"Suit yourself," I said. "You noticed Queenie ain't had a touch of bloat past three months?"

"Because she hasn't got her nose into the grain bin since you covered it."

"She got the bloat *before* she began getting into the grain. An' *after* I covered the bin. It was Professor's stuff cured her. Works for critters just as well as it does for humans. You mentioned colds. There's where the professor really does a lotta good for folks."

"I don't think his medicine does a bit of . . . ."

"Cost of colds gone up. Way up, like everythin' else. Use to be a person could get himself a cold–fix her with mustard–maybe some turpentine, coal oil–swallow a tablespoon–put it on his chest. But not anymore."

"The bottles of–of–stuff that he peddles won't do anything for a cold," she said.

"The price tag on cold medicine these days is somethin' fearful. Why, if it weren't for the Professor's stuff, most of the folks couldn't *afford* to have a cold."

"There are better ways of alleviating cold symptoms than . . . ."

"Goose grease used to be . . . ."

"His stuff won't cure a cold!"

"Look what people have to pay nowadays to have themself a cold. Bottle or a box of pills costs five times as much as one of the Professor's bottles. Dollar fifty-nine. An' into the bargain it's good for your prosperous gland, chill blains, arthurrightus, hot flashes."

She started laughing.

"What's so funny?"

"Jake, I do not have a 'prosperous gland' and I hardly think you're qualified to judge the effectiveness of Mr. Winesinger's remedy for hot flushes. And I still say a quack is a quack."

She's damn near as stubborn as Old Man Gatenby. Wouldn't you know, same morning we had that argument me and the Kid went into Crocus and I run across the Professor. He was just coming out of the Sanitary Café.

"Well, Professor – didn't know you was in town."

"Sir?"

"When did you blow in?"

"I'm afraid you have the advantage of me."

Well, I didn't have. I known him for over two years now, bailed him out twice before he was in Crocus and in trouble. "Trumper, Professor. Sang and played the mandolin for you couple years back and then last year. – How come you can never seem to remember me? My name?"

"Mr. Trumper, one's name is a funny thing. Precious to the one concerned. We have it all our lives. I am a great believer in the rather worn maxim that familiarity breeds contempt. Remembering with ease a face or a name is the shortest cut to familiarity I know."

"But I don't."

"It has become automatic with me to – I am revealing this to you in the strictest confidence . . ."

"Yeah, yeah – sure."

"I'll make a confession to you. It has over the years become automatic with me to show unfamiliarity with the given and surnames of people. Form of self-defence. Also it gives just the touch of professional impersonality and detachment I wish."

"Oh."

"Places the other person at a psychological disadvantage instantly. Places me outside the circle of his associates, whose intelligence, honesty, and talents he knows only too well. Then too, the very nature of my profession – it, uh, it is expedient that I start afresh with a person each time."

"Uh-huh."

"A bit of practical experience gleaned in my travels over this continent from coast to coast – picked up in the fitful flares of earlier times when I looked into the suffering faces of humanity. An unconsciously learned trait." He sort of sighed. "Pity."

"Huh! Somethin' wrong?"

"Indeed. The golden bowl has been broken at the fountain. Finally. You know the hamlet of Tiger Lily?"

"Sure."

"Tiger Lily citizens who listened to my lecture starting out with a general view of the digestive tube, rising to a climax with the excretory ducts of the liver and pancreas – viewed from in front – these citizens who in good faith bought bottles of Professor Winesinger's Lightning Penetration Oil and Tune-up Tonic, uh . . ."

"Yeah?"

"Turned black."

"Huh!"

"Superficial pigment changes extending in somes cases into the nares and in others even the roots of the hair. Pharmaceutical error: formic chloride."

"That's too bad," I said.

"I think that I have come to the end of my days."

"Now look, Professor . . ."

"All the wealth of understanding and sympathy. The keen diagnostic glance that could tell me whether the furrowed brow of a male john – uh, farmer – betokened the grinding ache of a rupture or the the exquisitely keen stab of a jagged kidney stone moving. At an end. At an end, sir."

"Oh, it can't be quite that bad, Professor."

"Sir, I can distinguish between the drops of cold sweat upon the stubble-jumper's forehead at a distance of thirty paces in the fading light of an August evening – between those drops of sweat that have their genesis in the gnawing of a peptic ulcer and those drops on the brow of a hard-tail suffering from a rampant gall bladder. Never again. I have come to the end."

"Now, Professor."

"Not with a bang but a whimper. The end of years of work alleviating the pain and suffering of countless fellow men . . ."

"Hold on, Professor. Can't be all that bad. You'll get rollin' again. Like I always say – bad things come in threes and this is . . ."

"At the very least, Jake. You don't mind if I call you . . ."

" 'Course not."

"We all have to face the facts of life sooner or later – the hard and unfriendly and unco-operative facts. After Tiger Lily there will be no licenses granted me again. There is not the slightest hope. Not with a bang but a whimper."

❧ ☙

I never seen the Professor that low. I never thought of him as an old man before. Not a *beaten* old man. Kind of lost all his spirit. And talking funny that way. Like he'd let a few of his marbles get away on him – hadn't lost them, they just rolled away on him. Rest of the afternoon I couldn't quit worrying about him. More I thought about him, more worried I got. By the time me and the Kid was ready to head back for home I was *real* worried.

"All right, Baldy, Queenie – get your lazy asses movin'!" I slapped them both good with the lines.

"Jake, where you heading for?"

"Just thought we'd take her 'round by the *river* road this time, Kid."

"It's a lot longer by the river."

"No hurry. Nice day. Figured she'd be nice to take the river road."

"But why?"

" 'Mother Nature', as Repeat would say. 'Commune with Mother Nature'." Wasn't my reason for going by the Broken-shell at all. When he'd left me, the Professor had headed towards the CNR depot and that's out of town. Towards the Brokenshell.

"Maybe we might even stop and . . ." Kid slapped at a mos-quito landed on his arm. "Got him! Think we might stop and take a swim, Jake?"

"We ain't got time for" – I swatted at one on the back of my neck. Missed the bugger! – "a swim."

"But you just said we weren't in any hurry."

"And the mosquitoes get worse the closer you get to the Brokenshell, don't they? Worst I ever seen 'em this year."

"Aaaah, Jake. A swim would cool us off real good!"

"What was left of us after the mosquitoes had their dinner. Fellow was to strip off for a swim here, them mosquitoes'd leave him a empty skeleton before he could reach the other side."

"Jake, why did we *really* take the river road? Isn't scenery you been lookin' at. What is it you're looking for?"

"Well, tell you the truth, Kid, I – kind of hate to – hey, what the aitch is that!"

"Where? what?"

"Over there – beyond that willow bush – edge of the cut bank."

"I don't see anything."

"All right there – Baldy – Queenie – leave off now. Cease! Kid, you just jump. No, here, take these lines – I'll go see myself!"

I found his clothes first. They laid there where he stepped out of them: his long black coat, his stripped pants, his bowler hat, they made a limp kind of a ring by the willows, his socks and his boots just to one side. His truss was hung on a branch of the wolf willow. Sun was gleaming off of the gold head of his cane, from the gold chain still spilling out of the vest pocket.

Like the Professor said he'd left us. She was the end of him. Not with a bang but a whimper. You could smell the marsh gas breathing off of the river. Wind was bending the bulrushes. Now and again a frog plopped. Millions and millions mosquitoes whining and landing and lifting.

I heard somebody shout. Then I saw him – naked – slap in the middle of the river.

"Hey! Hey there! Come! Give me a . . ."

"Professor!"

"Get meee out of this – this stinking goddam marsh!"

"Right with you, Professor! Hold on! You all right?"

"Hell no! I'm bogged down in this shit! Mosquitoes eating me alive!"

"Just hold on! I'm comin' for you!"

I peeled down to the buff, and started wading out to him. Right next door to quicksand. He was up to his ass in it, and any moment I was going to be, too. Mosquitoes was holding their annual national convention out there.

I reached him, started pulling at him and then *I* got stuck. I got him loose first and he took a couple steps back towards the bank and hauled and pulled at me. Then we was both of us loose. We made her to shore.

While we was cleaning the mud off and slapping mosquitoes, he said, "Looks as though I can't even do that right." He said it real sad.

"You know, Professor, no matter how black she looks – nothin's bad enough for a fellow to go *killin'* himself."

"Seemed the only answer left to me, Jake. Shuffle off this mortal coil. The end."

"Just *seems* that way. Now if you was to sort of get your breath and take a real good look at her, you wouldn't feel half so . . ."

"Couldn't even do a dignified job of it. Walked and walked

out there – till the water would close over my grey head and I would be washed – "

"Professor, even at spring flood, the Brokenshell ain't – it ain't the Saskatchewan, you know. Highest point, she's never over four foot deep – except there by the CN bridge where they took out the gravel – kids' swimmin' hole."

The both of us was all streaked with our own blood. "Looks like the only way you could've ended it all, she'd of been real slow. Most horrible death of all. Suicide by mosquito bite. Worst year we've ever had to my recollection. Wet spring broke all records. You better let me an' the Kid give you a ride back to the Royal Hotel."

"I am without shelter – asked to leave my room. Held my suitcase, and my Gladstone."

"Then what you . . ."

"Since you stayed my hand – came to my rescue – I suppose I shall have to sleep under the stars."

"You can't do that, Professor! Mosquitoes'll eat you alive!"

He agreed with me. He said he'd bunk down in his trailer. It wasn't till we were halfway back to town, it hit me.

"You got that bad batch of your tonic left? Turned all the Tiger Lily folks black?"

"Yes. At least two hundred bottles of it. Haven't thrown it out yet."

"Can't sell it for human or critter consumption?"

"That's right."

"And it poisoned . . ."

"Not *poisoned*. Some instances of digestive upset, but mostly simple pigmentary change."

"Black."

"Mmmmh."

"They're predictin' a bad year for cutworm an' sawfly grasshopper as well as mosquitoes," I said.

"Yes?"

"Most years out here it's bad. You know, insects is an aitch of a lot smaller'n a human or a cow or a pig or a horse or a chicken."

"Indeed – indeed, indeed! Of course!"

"So what about using that stuff turned folks black . . ."

"Of course!" His face lit up. "Spider, fire-ant, wasp, hornet, bedbug, scorpion, horsefly, *and* mosquito!"

"What about 'em?"

"Formic acid! Base of my remedy is alkaline! Let's head for that general store."

He bought out Mac's entire supply of household ammonia. We headed for his trailer. Kid and me gave him a hand, peeling off the labels and adding ammonia. Chet Lambert set his press up, said he'd go all night so there'd be new labels by late afternoon the next day.

Before we went home the Kid, the Professor, and me dabbed the new stuff onto some of our bites. She was a miracle – the sting and the itch went out of them instant! When we got home, even Kid's ma had to admit that! She even came into Crocus with us.

Professor, he set up his pitch that evening – on the corner betwixt the Hi-Art Theatre and Dingle's Funeral Parlour and Chez Sadie's Beauty Box. Under the streetlight the midges and the mosquitoes and the fish flies hummed and danced and circled. Big moths was out, too, just like the Professor had hatched them for his lecture. One minute he was standing there all alone on his apple box, his hands stretched out – next minute he was surrounded by nearly every person come into Crocus for Saturday night.

"I have no need to introduce myself – you know me well, my friends, as do countless others across this wide Dominion. For half a century now it has been my mission to wander the face of the earth, looking down into the countenances of my fellow humans, their eager or pain-ridden eyes turned up to me in the fitful light of coal-oil flares. I have seen you all in the festive mood you put on for the sawdust and tinsel glitter of the carny ground, and I have diagnosed your body needs in that fleeting moment needed by a Métis buffalo hunter to take a snapshot from the rolling back of his galloping pony."

He wasn't doing all that good. There was some whistles and boos as folks stood in front of him, slapping at mosquitoes. Professor kept right on going.

" . . . as a result of tireless experiment in my laboratories, inspired by the threat to humankind from old, old enemies — enemies that give no quarter in the relentless war they wage, enemies that may one day be victorious over man and wipe him from the face of this green earth. I say again that I bring you tonight a *new* weapon with which to wage our war protecting home and loved ones from the sly and deadly . . ."

"Cut the bullshit, Professor!" That was Jack Bently. Tiger Lily.

". . . bring you a new weapon against, ah, cholera, typhoid, summer complaint, dysentry, tuberculosis, encephalomyelitis, poliomyelitis, Rocky Mountain spotted fever, tularemia, yellow fever, bubonic plague, hook-worm, tape-worm, pin-worm, round-worm, liver flukes."

" . . . and turn folks black, you son ova . . ." That was Bently again, but this time people around him were hissing and telling him to shut up. Crocus folks don't need the Professor to get interrupted to make them do that to Tiger Lily folks.

"Air-borne enemies which come right into your homes, crawling enemies which creep over your floors, destroying enemies which invade your body through the very food you eat! The ordinary housefly!"

Now he really had them by the . . .

" . . . diptera!"

They'd even quit slapping at mosquitoes.

" . . . homoptera!"

Kid's ma had her face turned up to him and she was listening to him just as hard as anybody.

" . . . coleoptera, humenoptera, lepidoptera, and orthoptera, to name only a few. Our insect enemies are twice as many as all *animals* put together! One million, two hundred thousand different species! The wasps and the grasshoppers, the moths, and the beetles, bugs, lice, mosquitoes, gnats, and flies!

"Take the housefly – living in manure and filth, crawling over your food, your face, washing its feet in the milk pitcher, transmitting the germs of deadly diseases, and responsible for the death of more people than all wild beasts and animals, highway accidents and wars put together! Look at the female housefly!"

Kid's ma, she was looking at the housefly – male *or* female. Outside of Wong in the Sanitary Café, nobody hates flies worse than she does.

"She lays hundreds of eggs that hatch in *one* day to maggots passing into the pupal condition and then into the adult stage inside of *one* week. In half her breeding season alone she can produce two million, two hundred thousand million in twelve weeks. Think of it – from one female – over two million million!"

Wasn't a single person out there wasn't thinking about that.

"So I bring you tonight for the first time – Professor Wine-singer's Sure-shot Insect, Bug, and Grasshopper Eradicator, better known throughout the world as Professor Winesinger's I.B.G.E. Formula. It is compounded by myself from an ancient formula entrusted to me by a Cree maiden – Any-etch-ee-ah-ootch-ah-lah, as she was christened in her native tongue. With all her shy wild heart she loved a Cree warrior, Kim-see-nah-wah-nah-gah-soh-key-dray-nee – in the less euphonious sounds of our own tongue, Willie-Wounded-Here-and-There. Her lover was captured by a roving band of Blackfoot.

"They staked him out under a pitiless August sun upon and the prairie sod. Spreadeagled there to die the unspeakable death they called the Pah-noh-gah-fah-lay-moh-ah – the drawn and exquisite torture we would call the death of a billion bites. Death by mosquito!

"Every evening at sunset she pined and she sorrowed and every morning at dawn she stood lined against the prairie sky – calling plaintively for her warrior lover. Only the loons answered her over the lonely waters."

Real heart-rendering!

"She wandered forlorn over the prairie grasses – saw in the distance a black cloud of hovering insects. Drawn there she found her lover – staked out, suffering unbearable agonies, red with the blood – his own blood – drawn by the torturing mosquitoes. Quickly she applied her ancient remedy – the very remedy I bring you tonight – bringing him instant relief and saving his life."

Third time I heard the Professor give his pitch. I don't think before that or after that one, he'll ever do her any better.

"Concocted from the flora of these very plains which nourished the red man and the noble buffalo – deadly poison to all the winged terrors of the insect world. Nature's own weapon against the hungry, killing hordes of *all* insects: culex or common mosquito. Schistocerca americana. Or grasshopper, as it is commonly known. Chicken louse, fleas, cockroaches, chiggers, mites, moths, flies, gnats, potato bugs.

"Professor Winesinger's Sure-Shot Insect, Bug, and Grasshopper Eradicator kills in four ways. It attacks instantly through the insect stomach; it slays them through unfailing paralysis of the insect nervous system; and it congeals and clots the insect blood. In addition to these three, it has a fourth and infallible and magic property unique to Professor Winesinger's I.B.G.E. Formula, possessed by no other insecticide sold in man's unrelenting struggle against the insect hordes."

He stopped and he looked out over that crowd. He held her for a count of ten.

"IT TURNS THE BASTARDS BLACK!"

I guess that's what won him all them Tiger Lily sales. Folks was shoving and pushing and reaching up money to him and

he was taking it and handing them their bottles of Sure-Shot
Insect, Bug, and Grasshopper Eradictor. Sure made a killing
that night. Insect hordes ain't gonna take over Crocus district
in a hurry. Not with them two hundred bottles he sold.

Kid's ma, she bought twelve of them.

GOING TO A FIRE

Out here on the bald-headed prairie we got no maple leafs. We got crocuses, tiger lilies, pigweed, sow thistle, Russian thistle, Canada thistle. Maple leaf just ain't our flower. Got quite a mixture of human beings, too. Pollacks, Galicians, Euchre-anians, Dook-a-boors, Bohemians, Checks, Hungarians – we got 'em all. We got Mennonites and Hooterites. Mustard – I figure mustard would make a real good flower for Saskatchewan, the mixture we got.

Elsie Abercrombie, she can trace her family clear back to the Fenian raids in Huron County. Pure Ontario. Or Aunt Lil from England where she was born – straight English right down from William the Conqueror, and the Twells claim they're more Canadian than the Shivers's. Shivers's is U. E. Loyalists and the Twells claim the U. E. Loyalists come to this country way after the Twells did.

Then you take Steve Kiziw that lives down Government Road from us. Steve, he ain't had no grand-daddy defending the Maple Leaf from the Fenian raids. He didn't come over from merry old England, nor his folks didn't take up no homestead with the U. E. Loyalists. Steve, he's one of these here Central Europeans. So's his wife. So's young Stevie, that goes to Rabbit Hill school with the Kid. Now she'd be nice to say everything's real sweet around our district, Crocus district, but she'd be a little one side of the truth.

Take Pete Botten:

" . . .what I don't like about them foreigners, they're ignerant. Ignerant farmers – you look an' see who's still usin' a thrashin' machine – ain't changed over to a combine. I heard tell in some districts they're so ignerant they'll even harness up their woman and use her to haul the garden plough. An' when they have their weddin' parties – look out!"

Or Hig Wheeler:

"Wolfgang, he had half a pound of fine-cut under his bed in the bunk-house. Boys on the thrashin' crew, they made a joke outa sneakin' their makin's outa his tin. Wolfgang saw that tuhbaccah shrinkin' down in the can an' he got madder an' madder an' he caught one at it. He out with his belt. Ripped that belt outa his overhall pants an' he come in swingin' the buckle enda her. Laid this fellah's face wide open. 'Leven stitches! Them hunkies always pick up somethin' in a fight – rock, knife, piece of a two-be-four. Don't know how to fight like a white man!"

Run across that stuff quite a lot. Not with Steve Kiziw. Folks, they like Steve all right. Have a beer with him. He curls in the winter. Plays snooker in Drew's pool hall. They didn't mean Steve was like that. Nobody had it in for Steve himself. Steve made out all right. First I heard of anything different was while back in Repeat Golightly's barbershop next the Sanitary Café:

"I don't like it. Lot of folks may think I do. I don't. Nobody hates to charge seventy-five cents for a haircut more than I do, Jake. Terrible price. Terrible price."

"Mmmmh."

"Diminishing returns."

"Does it?"

"Reaches the point where folks think twice about getting a haircut. Before they step up to this chair I can see it on their face. Realization bright on their faces – this haircut's going to cost me seventy-five cents. Hair comes in here a little longer. Longer time between haircuts. First thing that drops off – the kids' haircuts. Mother goes out and buys herself clippers. There's tufts of hair all over kitchen floors all over the West these days."

"Is there."

"Diminishing returns. Next step, adult haircuts. Then there's always been a few never did come to me for haircuts. Foreigners. Always had their women do it for them. Like Steve Kiziw."

"Mmh."

"Way they are. Careful. I don't s'pose I ever had Kiziw in this chair once. Not once. Way they live over in those countries – hunk of bread, link of sausage – garlic sausage – do 'em for a week. Whole week. Can't get used to our way. Can't spend. Can't help it. Habit. Got backward habits. Must be awful tough on a barber over there – Ukraine, Poland, Hungary."

"Guess they are."

"Mind you – doesn't make any difference to me. Not a particle. Kiziw could come in here every day for a shave, his wife could be gettin' her hair done over at Chez Sadie's – wouldn't make a particle of difference."

"Uh-huh."

"No. She's just a index you might say – other things."

"What other things?"

"Assimilation."

"What the aitch is that?"

"Take his language."

"Steve gets her across all right. Oh, she's a little twisted up," I admitted, "Like a horse comin' out of the stable backwards."

"Mrs. Kiziw, his wife. Not a word."

"Hmmmh?"

"Just her native tongue. Can't speak a word of English. Assimilation."

"What you drivin' at?"

"Country their adoption. Canada is their new mother. Foster mother. Can't see they've played the game best they could. Tried a little harder to please her. Speak her language."

"Well, that don't mean they oughta be criticized . . ."

"Speak English in their home, couldn't they? Use it there, couldn't they?"

"Well maybe they like to relax when they're settin' aroun' the heater. Must be a awful strain on somebody, usin' a language they ain't used to. When they get home amongst themselves – like to loosen up a bit. Relax. kind of like takin' off their shoes."

"One of the prices they got to pay. Keep her still, Jake. Can't shave a movin' object. Go out of their way to take an interest."

"Who?"

"Good citizens. Fortifications. On guard. Alert. Be alert. Assimilation. Person can't enjoy the benefits of his foster mother country without takin' his turn at the fortification democracy. Battlements democracy. Does his turn up there. Bitter with the sweet."

"Kiziw does all right. Nothin' wrong with his citizenship, is there?"

"Well now . . ."

"Pays his taxes regular, don't he?"

"More than that to it, Jake."

"Hard worker. Clean farmer. Honest."

"Lot more. Look, what every single person does affects this country. Every one. Sum total – country can't be better than her parts. She's riddled through with folks that aren't assimilated, then she's weak. Can't have that. I say that's bad for a country, Jake."

"Mmmh."

"Precious thing. Comes high. Precious thing."

"What is?"

"Citizenship. Canadian citizenship. Precious."

"I guess so, Repeat."

"Price tag on it. There's a price tag marked there. Got to be paid. Ahead now, Jake. Just tilt her forward."

"Now look, Repeat, Steve Kiziw an' his wife an' kid . . ."

"I got nothing against Steve Kiziw."

"You just don't like him cuttin' his own hair."

"Doesn't matter a particle . . ."

"Don't forget them two moles, Repeat."

"Like to see folks, all folks, take a healthy interest in their community . . ."

"Just about the collar line there – one either side – them moles."

"Jake, when that razor slides over your neck . . ."

"Fellow's awful touchy about moles – bleed like the . . ."

"That lather . . ."

" . . . sometimes don't see 'em an' . . ."

"Those moles are standing out like a couple of grain elevators, Jake. Always free 'em of lather first thing. First thing a good barber does with a mole. Bring 'em out in the open."

"Mmh."

"Get those foreign groups people carryin' on. Speakin' their own language – livin' just like when they were peasants in the old country. Why, you take down there in Quebec, there's whole communities where not a soul speaks a word – not a single word of English – from mornin' to night, daybreak to dark. French."

"Maybe most of those folks there is French."

"They aren't the only ones. All over this Dominion of ours – repeats herself. Repeats herself."

"Uh-huh."

"Little islands. Weakenin' islands. Ignorance. Superstition. Awful. Awful thing. Does awful things to a country. Then the church. When the church helps her along, fosters it you might say. Priest – their priest tells 'em right out of the pulpit, tells 'em how to vote."

"Nobody tells Steve Kiziw how to vote."

"I didn't say they did."

"Votes the way he wants," I said.

"Maybe so. Maybe so. But all the same – this affaire Kiziw – he can't blame it all on other folks ..."

"Just a minute – what are you ... ?"

"Feeling – there's a feeling in the district, Jake."

"What?"

"Ricky was in here not two hours ago. Sitting there. Land hog."

"You'r' goddam rights he is!" I meant it.

"What *he* said. Now Albert Rickey and I, we don't usually see eye to eye. But he was muttering there – land greedy, Kiziw. Buying the Hopper half-section."

"Ricky?"

"Kiziw. Rumour going around Kiziw's buying the Hopper place. Albert Ricky's in no position to buy any more land."

"Ricky's got enough for five farmers as it is," I said.

"Like most of the others. Hailed out last year. Got his crop lying there under the snow this year. Won't get it off till spring – if he does then. Not much cash floating around the district this year, Jake. Credit situation's bad."

"So that's why Ricky ..."

"He isn't the only one. Feeling. There's a feeling. Just because Kiziw happens to be the one can pay the price. Jumping right in there and grabbing it off at a time when others are feeling the pinch."

"Well, I don't see ..."

"Sort of a fluke he got his crop off," Repeat said. "Irony."

"Huh?"

"Only farmer in the district hasn't got a combine. Colonel was in here. He says he sold combines or else Hig Wheeler's sold a combine to everybody but Kiziw. Cutting his crop old-fashioned with a binder – got her into stooks – only fellow in the district got his crop off last fall. Got the cash. Folks feel he's taking advantage of his luck."

"Wasn't luck that . . ."

"Didn't say it was. Say that's what folks are saying. Wet or dry. Want her wet or dry?"

"Dry – dry – always have her dry!"

"Lots of 'em say Steve Kiziw's getting too big for his overalls. Feeling. That'll be seventy-five, Jake. There's feeling."

I didn't put too much stock in what Repeat had said. Lot of times he don't get things all that accurate, but that evening I had to change my mind when the Kid told me and his ma what happened at recess that afternoon at Rabbit Hill school.

"Miss Henchbaw sure gets the coal oil on her fire if you get the decimal point out of place," Kid said.

"Does she?"

"Nobody's been doing so good with it. Except Stevie Kiziw. Got every one right up at the board yesterday."

"That's nice." I said, "How's Stevie doin' in school?"

"He isn't first but he's in the first three in grade . . ."

"No, I don't mean that way. I meant, how's he gettin' along with the other kids these days?"

"Oh – well, uh, not too good."

"Uh-huh."

"Haven't you gone up to bed yet, son?"

That was the Kid's ma just come in and takin' off her coat. Tuesday night once a month is her IODE night. Looie Riel Chapter.

"Just finishin' up the decimal point, Ma."

"What you mean 'not too good', Kid?"

"Just finishin' up, Ma. Take last week."

"What about it, Kid?"

"Come on, son – if you're through – morning comes early."

"All right, Ma. At recess this afternoon, there was a fight . . ."

"*You* weren't in a *fight*, son!"

"I wasn't in it. Stevie an' Joe an' Archie an' Alec – a bunch of 'em . . ."

"All onto Stevie?" I said.

"Yeah – five of 'em."

"Oh no!" Ma said. "Five onto one! Did he get hurt?"

"Stevie? He didn't get hurt! He's tough! Joe Sparrow an' Archie Winters quit right away when their nose bled, an' Alec Knowlton got the wind knocked out of him an' . . ."

"How did it start, son?"

"Joe, he called Stevie a damn hunky an' . . ."

"Well, it's no wonder Stevie wanted to fight!" she said.

"An' Archie said they didn't even have their citizen – citizenship – they weren't even Canadians – an' Pete called Stevie a dirty foreign catlicker."

"Miss Henchbaw – where was *she* when all this was happening?" Ma said.

"She came out near the end and they quit. They all got to stay in for a week after four and help Mr. Bollington clean up."

"Stevie too?" I said.

"Nope. An' the other kids say their folks are going to get real hot about it – keepin' *them* in for fightin' an' not keepin' Stevie in. Archie says his dad says the Kiziws are gettin' too big for their overalls – gettin' all that land and buildin' that big barn. I don't get it."

"What, son?" Ma said.

"People don't seem so fussy about the Kiziws any more."

"Perhaps they're doing too well," Ma said.

"Buyin' the Hopper place an' buildin' that barn," I said.

"Jealous?"

"I think maybe, Kid. Steve, he's got his place lookin' real nice, way he painted his house white with a blue roof."

"I – there was some talk at IODE tonight. Mrs. Shivers said something about Mrs. Kiziw getting a new washing-machine. They papered their house this fall."

"Why should that make folks mad?"

"Well, Kid – she ain't been so good for most of us the last couple years . . ."

"But . . ."

"Kind of hard to take – prosperity – when she's your neighbour's prosperity – when the fellow's a little different from the rest of us."

"You mean his moustache?" the Kid said. "And the way he talks, an' him bein' a – a foreigner?"

"That's it, son," Ma said.

"Repeat says there's lot of feelin' around town over him buyin' the Hopper place," I told her.

"Well isn't that just too bad!" Ma said. "What are they . . ."

"Claims he's a land hog."

"Like Mr. Ricky! Son, if anything starts again in Rabbit Hill schoolyard – if you ever hear anybody calling Stevie a – hunky – or anything else – I hope you *know* which side I expect *you* to be on!"

"Sure. Stevie's still my best friend."

Folks, they didn't mind Steve while he was working as a hired man for Herb Baird, nor when he was farming Lizzie Baird on shares after Herb died. Nor they weren't hot under the collar when he got the mortgage from Mert Abercrombie so he could buy the Baird place. But now he was buying the Hopper place – really had the world by the tail on a downhill pull – they weren't fussy. They weren't fussy about him at all.

She got an aitch of a lot worse. Wherever you went the Kiziws was all folks could find to talk about: them old fellows in the leather chairs in the lobby of the Royal Hotel, or in Malleable Brown's blacksmith shop, or setting on the platform rail at the CNR depot, just like old crows except crows don't chew tobacco and spit their cuds all over CNR property. Repeat's barbershop. Of course.

Take the Maple Leaf Beer Parlour:

"Four here, Taffy. Taffy – get off your ass an' up on them roller skates!"

"She told me 'good riddance – never set foot in this house again.' "

"Beat their wimmen an' live like pigs." That was Archie Tait. "Don't cost them nothin' to live, so no wonder they can buy up alla the good land."

"Happenin' all over the country – everywhere," Don Whitaker said.

"I got to admit they're real workers," Archie said. "Look at all them vegetables Kiziw grows. He's got turnips an' beets an' tuhmatuhs an' lettuce clear to the c'rrection line – acres of 'em. In town here peddlin' 'em to folks – Wong's Sanitary Café."

"Oughta be a law," Sam Donaldson said.

" . . . so what's the CCF ever done for me? . . ."

"How he got all the cash was by livin' like a pig. Stickin' his nickels in a sock, waitin' till he's got a flour sack full so's he kin buy out the fellas that didn't even have hired help durin' the war because their sons was overseas fightin' Kiziw's relatives!"

"Happenin' all over the country – oughta be a law," Don said.

"Take my boy," Archie said. "He ain't got that kinda money. Him an' his wife ain't got that kinda cash. They could use that Hopper place."

"You seen her lately? Anybody seen my wife lately . . . ?"

"My boy was fightin' overseas whilst Kiziw made hay right here . . ."

"She think she's punishin' me? I don't *wanta* set foot in that house again . . . !"

"Oughta be a law. Protect our own kind," Fred Spicer said.

"There sure oughta," Archie said. "Right kinda gover'ment put in a law keepin' 'em from buyin' land unless they got assimilated."

"Yep."

"Yep."

"Yep."

" . . . everybody thinks a bricklayer just slaps em' up there. Well, I got news for them – a bricklayer's gotta plumb three ways . . ."

" . . . hell, my wife ain't plumb *one* way! . . ."

"Don't see 'em lettin' them Hooterites swarm out in Alberta," Pete Botten said. "Hooterites can't buy no more land for no more of their colonies whenever they feel like it."

I was with Gate, liftin' a couple before we left town. We was off to one corner and we just set there and listened to them fellows goin' on an' on an' on. Gate nudged me an' pointed to the entrance.

It was Steve. He stood in the doorway.

"Hallo – hallo – hallo this place." Steve, he don't whisper when he talks. "What you fallas do? You Indians plot against us whites? Taffy – hey, Taffy, I buy round for house."

"Not for me, you ain't." That was Archie Tait.

"Er me."

"Er me."

"Er me."

"Er me."

Didn't stop Steve. He went from table to table to table.

"Leave me out."

"I still got a couple."

"Nope."

Steve, he stood there in the centre of the Maple Leaf, looked for a minute like he was going to take off, then changed his mind.

"Fonny thing happen me last week." It was like he was up

on a platform deliverin' a speech to everybody. "Stevie and me comin' in Govermand Road. Fast. Dad, Stevie says to me – what's horry? No horry, I say, no horry, Stevie. Goin' to a fire, he say. No fire, I say, no fire, Stevie."

"I gotta push off."

"Then we smell somethin' bornin'. Was bornin' somethin'. Cigarette ash drop down. Car seat on fire. Was bornin'. Was at fire. Wasn't goin' to fire – was *at* fire. An' Stevie askin' what's horry – goin' to a fire? *At* fire ollraddy."

"See you later, boys."

"*At* fire – not horry *to* fire."

"Herb, you goin' to have one – with me?"

"Nah, I got to bugger off."

Steve got the message. He stood there a minute, then he turned and went out. I guess he didn't see me and Gate over in the corner. I hope he didn't.

I guess he got the same cold shoulder wherever he went: Drew's pool hall, the curlin' rink . . . . And she got worse. By the time he'd *bought* the Hopper place folks was really up in arms. Women, too. Kid's ma, she come home from her Atheniums Flower and Vegetable Gardening, Book and Discussion Club meetin':

"Jake, I didn't realize how far it had gone!"

"She's been rollin' right along."

"But it's not like them! I – they don't talk like the women I know."

"They're the women you know, all right," I said.

"Sometimes men – I think *men* have *real* intolerance."

"You ladies got no right to go 'round pattin' yourself on the back. Mrs. Kiziw – she belong to your Atheniums?"

"Well, no . . ."

"It's you women had the chance to do the most good! The men – fellows like Steve, they get out an' get around, they don't need a helpin' hand so much. But the woman – the ma, mother – she's stuck home an' she's the one that's got the say with the kids, the second generation!"

"I'm not saying she hasn't . . ."

"So it's the women of the community can do the most good with the wife an' through her the kids – whole family. There's your chance to work this here assimilation everybody's yappin' about."

So the Kid's ma – just like me – was beginnin' to wonder what kind of folks we'd been living alongside all these years. Week or so later our phone rung. Two longs an' a short.

"That's ours, Jake."

"I'll get her, Kid, I'll get her." I lifted her off the hook. It was Gate.

I guess the Kid's ma must've seen from my face something was wrong as soon as I hung up.

"What is it, Jake!"

"Kiziws' – fire."

"Their barn!" That's what the Kid hoped it was.

"House. That was Old Man Gatenby – gettin' everybody over there. Gotta dangle!"

"Me too," the Kid said.

"Me too," his ma said.

When we made her over to Kiziws' the chemical truck from town was there. Half the folks from Crocus district was there all lit up in all that orange light from the Kiziw house. Time we got there, the flames was coming out the roof. They hadn't got nothing out the house and there was women with their arms around Mrs. Kiziw. They had already formed a bucket brigade. Heard kind of different talk about Steve Kiziw than what was floating around the last few weeks:

"Shame. Damn Shame!"

"He got insurance on her? He got any . . . ?"

"Not a cent. All his furniture – that new washin'-machine . . ."

"Didn't get a chance – oil furnace blew up. Went up like a straw stack . . ."

"Well, what we waitin' for? Get them buckets goin'!"

"Yeah!"

"Sure!"

"Get in line, boys!"

Fellow kind of realized all the talk hadn't gone so deep as he thought. Now Steve's house was going up in flame. Made a fellow feel kind of good to see all them neighbours ready to pitch in and help. But I guess – things don't come that easy. Steve come around the corner the house. He had an axe hanging out his hand. He stood there all lighted up against his burning house. He was facin' Archie Tait.

"No, you don't!"

"Steve – we're – she looks like she ain't gonna do much good," Archie said. "But we got buckets an' . . ."

"Sure. Sure. First falla step forward wit' bocket – I brain him wit' axe!"

"Now hold on," Archie said. "We're sorry to see your . . ."

"Sure – sorry – all good fallas now! Fine – you halp when my house goin' up! Then you halp when isn't any good for halp person then! Thanks! Oh thanks you very much! Grateful! You from the bottom my heart. Dandy – oh sure. Stevie, you go halp your mother, go on. You ain't gonna halp before with kind word – well, you ain't gonna halp now. You don't – you feel sorry my house! Yeah. Awful sorry my house! Go right on be sorry my house! When you raddy be sorry my wife – me – my kid – come back. All right come back again! Not before. Ain't gonna work like before no more. No sir. You take my business – my vegetables. Alavaytor take my grain. Sure, that's all right. You take hunky grain. You take hunyack vegetable. An' you take dorty foreigner money too! But we ain't like you. Oh no. Different, Kiziw, his wife, his kid! Not British. Who the hall British – who they by God! I tall you. British people savage when my people culture – when my folk beat shit out of Roman! Why they so spacial – Angle-oh-Saxon! Jus' human bein'. Me too. I got muscle – human muscle. I got human heart – same British! I work. Hard! Golden Rule. Use Golden Rule. Golden Rule belong you Angle-oh-Saxons! In-went Golden Rule! Yours! How you like to be alone sometime! Only one different whole place! How you like that! Everything think one way – say another! I tell you. Terrible! So terrible I don't wish to happen even you. Even you!"

Nobody emptied a bucket. Not a bucket. That was the end of her. I guess Steve Kiziw made his point that night – standin' there in front of his burnin' house. Kinda late for most of us in Crocus district. But he made it.

WILL OF THE PEOPLE

I DON'T DO ALL THAT GOOD IN ARITHMETIC WITH ALL THAT stuff about Mr. A. and Mr. B. and Mr. A. is running north across the top of a freight going south at fifty-one miles per hour while Mr. B. is running from the front end of the thirty-two-car freight with each boxcar a hundred foot long and when they going to meet? But I do pretty good in Hygiene that teaches you all about the human body and the way your heart and lungs and gizzard work. Miss Henchbaw, that cracks the whip over us kids at Rabbit Hill school, doesn't spend so much time on the intestines or the urination system.

She has a skeleton in the corner behind her desk. Not a real one. It's only about three foot high. Wasn't me tucked the black horse hair up between its legs one recess. Stevie Kiziw, but nobody squealed on him. All the boys had to stay in after school for a whole week. Ma said Miss Henchbaw is one of the finest teachers around and Crocus district is lucky to have her. Ma used to be a schoolteacher. Down in Ontario before she came out west and married my dad, who got killed in the war when I was young.

I guess my best subject is Composition. I actually like doing paragraphs and essays and standing up front and reading them out to the whole class. Miss Henchbaw picks three of us to do that each time. The one I did on King Midas she picked for first.

"King Midas was a King who lived in the Olden Days long

ago in this fairy story we just took up. He already had a lot of gold . . ."

"Put that down, Stevie!"

Stevie lowered his ruler with a spitball on the end of it, aimed right at Muriel Abercrombie, that always gets to be Mother Mary in our school Christmas play. Stevie Kiziw and Rob Totecole and I generally end up as the Three Wise Hired Men. That's what Jake calls them.

"Continue," Miss Henchbaw said to me.

I did:

> Some folks are still like this today. Some farmers in Crocus District that never had a crop failure or got hailed out or dried out and always got a good price for their grain after the war was over but they still complain about no freight cars to haul their crop East and there isn't ever going to be free trade and the cost of machinery is going to go sky high with the tariffs Ottawa keeps sticking on so they are not happy like King Midas wasn't happy with all his gold . . .

"I'm afraid that's a pretty long run-on sentence."

"Sorry," I said.

> And when King Midas made that wish of his that every thing would turn to gold when he touched it and he touched it and he found out it was awful. Like his grub turning to . . .

"Food," Miss Henchbaw said.

> Food turning to gold and his children when he kissed them turning to gold when he tried to kiss them. I think this story proves you can pile up an awful lot of money and then you get so much it doesn't do you any good. It can hurt you. Like Mr.

Ricky in Crocus District. Mr. Ricky's like King Midas if King Midas went wheat farming . . .

"Just a moment!" Miss Henchbaw interrupted me and all
the kids quit giggling. "That will be enough of that!"

"I was just . . ."

"Young man! How dare you! How dare you compare our
school board chairman to King Midas?"

"Well, he sure watches his nickels . . . ."

"What Mr. Ricky does with his – nickels," Miss Henchbaw
said, "is no concern of yours. You have no right to pass judgement on your elders. I will not tolerate it in my classroom!"

"Gee, Miss Henchbaw, I didn't mean to be – I was just tryin'
to explain about the story . . . ."

"Next time," she said, "you'd better find a better way to
illustrate what you mean!" She looked down at her watch and
her mouth looked like she'd been eating horseradish through
a wove wire fence. "All right, school dismissed. Leave your
compositions on my desk as you go out."

The desk tops started in banging and the kids lined up to
drop off their compositions at Miss Henchbaw's desk. Miss
Henchbaw had taken off her glasses that she always wears
kind of pinched up on her nose, and she was rubbing them
with her handkerchief. I was almost the last one to leave, and
when I did I forgot my lunchbucket. I went back for it and
she was still working with that handkerchief, but it wasn't at
her glasses. She was dabbing her eyes.

I kept thinking about it, riding Auction Fever home. He's
my buckskin pony we got at Colonel Hepner's Auction, and
Jake taught me how to halter-break him and sack him and
saddle-break him and top him off. By myself. By the time I'd
watered him and unsaddled him, and thrown down some oat
bundles for him, I knew I was going to have to tell Ma what
had happened.

"Miss Henchbaw really got the coal oil into her fire – took

me right by the face right in front of the class. When I went back for my lunchbucket she was at her desk – bawlin'."

"Oh no, son!"

"Ain't all that bad, Kid," Jake said. Jake, he isn't all that fussy about Miss Henchbaw.

"You'll have to apologize!" Ma said.

"Why should he? Albert's tightest fellow in the district. King Midas an' Albert – two of a kind – like the Kid said in this . . ."

"The point is Albert Ricky's the chairman of the school board and he's been sniping and snipping at her at all our meetings. He has it in for her. I don't know why."

"Easy enough to guess. He's got a schoolteacher daughter."

"Nonsense, Lizzie Ricky has a school of her own," Ma said.

"That's right." Jake said. "Couple hundred miles away. Blood's thicker 'n water – Albert'd like to have her home."

Ma turned to me. "Well, he's not going to get any assistance from you. Tomorrow's Saturday. You're coming into town to apologize."

"Now hold on," Jake said.

"That's final, son!" She headed out of the kitchen. Even from her back I could tell she was upset.

"Gee, Jake, I didn't know. I didn't mean to . . ."

"You weren't too far off the mark on Ricky, Kid."

"Well, nobody is all that fussy about him – are they?"

"He gives a lot of folks the ragin' heartburn. All the same a lot of 'em laugh at his jokes. They voted him three times chairman of the school board. He nearly defeated MacTaggart last time round for mayor. That school board – every one of 'em except for your Ma – they just jump every time he hiccups. 'Specially Herb Dotty."

Our farm is two miles down Government Road from Crocus and we get into town quite a lot, for one reason or another. If I'm not in school after I've helped Jake hitch up Baldy and Queenie, he generally lets me come in with him. Keeps us well informed about goings-on. You might say Jake has a sort of a town-talk trapline: Repeat Golightly's barbershop, Chet Lambert's *Crocus Breeze*; Drew's pool hall, Malleable Brown's blacksmith shop, MacTaggart's Trading Company store, Maple Leaf Beer Parlour. Jake checks them out regular. He says you can get even more dirt that way than listening in on a party line.

Jake was in the Maple Leaf when he first hit pay dirt. He said everybody in there was laughing, but it wasn't at some joke of Albert Ricky's this time. Soon as Ricky stepped through the door, they were calling out to him from all over the place:

"Well, well – if it ain't Midas!"

"The King hisself!"

Jake said Ricky's face turned red as he headed for Dotty's table.

"Hold on, Albert! Set down an' have one on me! Get alla that gold dust outa your throat!"

"Hear your crop's gonna run sixty carats to the acre, Albert!"

I was with Jake later in MacTaggart's store and Mr. Ricky came in. Ma said she'd meet us after she was through at Chez Sadie's Beauty Box. Mr. MacTaggart was behind the counter and just finished doing up our order when Mr. Ricky came through the door. He pushed right past me and Jake, straight for Mr. MacTaggart.

"Day, Albert – what can I do for you?" Mr. MacTaggart said.

"I'm havin' a special school board meetin' tonight. I want you there."

"School board meeting? What for?" Mr. MacTaggart, he knew what it was for, all right.

"Miss Henchbaw! Those kids just run all over her!"

"Oh now, Albert. Not Miss Henchbaw . . ."

"Wilder than hooty owls. Moral decay has set in. Next thing

you know they'll be ruining desks, smashing windows, ripping up the taxpayers' property!"

"I haven't heard of anything like that going on, Albert," Mr. MacTaggart said.

"You haven't, eh? You heard the language those kids is usin' on the school grounds?"

"Little bit of language outside the school – recess time, after hours – got to expect that."

"I don't expect nothin' of the sort. Way I been insulted . . ."

Ma had just come in. Mr. Ricky didn't let her get half a dozen steps inside the store.

"I been lookin' for you . . ."

"And I've been looking for *you*," Ma said.

"The insults and the – this mornin' – everybody, it's all over town – that rotten raised kid of yours . . ."

"Hold up there, Ricky," Jake said.

"Now, now, Albert," Mr. MacTaggart said.

"Mr. Ricky, please don't make it more difficult than it is. My son . . ."

"Your son could do with a good – if you'd a thinned his hide a little more often. Lettin' kids get away with murder. I'd've warmed my Lizzie good if she ever done a thing like that. She had good discipline."

"I'm sure she did! My son did an unpardonable thing . . ."

"It's Henchbaw I blame the most, encouragin' a kid to . . ."

"She did *not* encourage him. She bawled him out . . ."

"That woman's gotta be fired – her discipline . . ."

"Mabel Henchbaw is an excellent disciplinarian. I know!"

"We'll decide that tonight at the school board meetin'!"

"Now, just a *moment*. I'm not attending any school board meeting until Miss Henchbaw knows what's going on!"

"She's right, Albert," Mr. MacTaggart said.

"Of course I'm right," Ma said. "Mr. MacTaggart, before you go to any meeting I think you should hear her side of it."

"Yes, I think I should," Mr. MacTaggart said.

"We're not hearin' nothing outa her. No point in . . ."

"Now look, Albert," Mr. MacTaggart said, "there's a decent way of doing things, and I think she has the right."

"She's a teacher! She's got no rights!"

"Suit yourself," Mr. MacTaggart said, "but I'm going over to Rabbit Hill school and hear *her* side of the matter!"

"Good luck," Mr. Ricky said. "Today's Saturday. Generally there's no school on Sat . . ."

"She's at the school," Ma said. "I talked with her this morning."

"Great." Mr. Taggart had come round the corner of the counter, and you could tell he meant business. So did Ma. So did Mr. Ricky, because he headed for the school with us.

There were a few kids on the swings and teeter-totter and some more with agates playing poison. They all quit to watch us going into the school. The girls' door.

"Miss Henchbaw!" Mr. Ricky yelled from the back of the room. She didn't look up right away, finished writing first, then looked up. Later Jake said she knew it was Albert's voice, and she did that deliberate.

"Sorry to bother you without notice, Miss Henchbaw," Mr. MacTaggart said.

"That's all right, Mr. MacTaggart."

"What we called about . . ." Mr. Ricky started to say.

"Miss Henchbaw, we have a little matter to discuss," Mr. MacTaggart said.

"Mabel," Ma said, "we think we ought to clarify . . ."

"Let's not beat around the bush! It's about that composition that impudent and undisciplined kid wrote . . . about me!"

"Mr. Ricky, that was most unfortunate . . ."

"That's puttin' it mild!"

"I'm so sorry the child . . ."

"Don't go tryin' to shove it off onto the kid! You're his teacher an' you're responsible for him!"

"Now just a moment, Albert," Mr. MacTaggart said. "Mabel, could we see the composition, please? Let's see what he actually wrote."

"Certainly." She hauled up my composition.

Mr. MacTaggart looked at the top of the first page that Miss Henchbaw had written on. "Well, well – listen to this, Albert: 'You should be ashamed of yourself. It is disgraceful to ridicule your elders. See that it never happens again.' That doesn't sound to me like *encouragement*, Albert."

Mr. Ricky reached for the paper but Mr. MacTaggart pulled back on it. "She – they – they – " He pointed at Miss Henchbaw and then at Ma. "They got their heads together this mornin'. Let me see that there paper!"

Miss Henchbaw reached up and took it from Mr. MacTaggart. "I am not quite through with that composition, Mr. Ricky." She picked up her pen and she wrote on the top of the first page and then handed the paper to Mr. Ricky.

"Eighty-five percent!" Mr. Ricky yelled.

"That's right. Hadn't been for comma splice and run-on sentence fault, ninety-five percent."

I never got eighty-five, let alone ninety-five, percent out of Miss Henchbaw ever before. She's a real hard marker.

"For a composition such as this one, which has shown me that the young writer has learned to think and to express himself so colourfully, well, eighty-five percent is a just and accurate mark."

"You see! She does encourage 'em. Encourages 'em to run wild! Eighty-five percent! Wait till the school board hears about this . . ."

"Don't bother, Mr. Ricky!"

"I certainly will bother!"

"I've taught a great number of years! I've had all sorts of school board chairmen in my time! And I've had just about enough of you!"

"Huh!"

"For over a year now you've interfered with my work. It's given me a great deal of distress – hampered my efficiency as a teacher . . ."

"I ain't . . ."

" 'I have not'," Miss Henchbaw corrected him.

"I ain't har'ly . . ."

"Your use of 'har'ly' signifies a double negative, Mr. Ricky."

All Mr. Ricky could manage was a couple of swallows.

"Don't bother with your school board meeting, Mr. Ricky." She stood up and shoved her chair back. "I resign! As of now!"

Mr. Ricky should have been grinning from ear to ear, but he wasn't. He just stood there with his mouth open.

"King Midas!" She headed for the door.

Like I said, Jake isn't all that fussy about Miss Henchbaw. He's had some run-ins with her. She all the time keeps saying History's got to be accurate, and she doesn't like the way Jake embroideries the truth now and again. I can understand how Jake feels about her. She sure does correct folks all the time.

But that day in the Rabbit Hill school room when she resigned and took Mr. Ricky by the face, I guess Jake changed his mind about her.

"I ain't ever been one of her great admirers," he admitted to me. "Bossy, but she's sure as hell got a lot of starch in her. For a woman. Never found a fellow would marry her. No kids of her own. All her life teachin' other folks' kids. Now she's really gonna be alone. I know a bit how she must be feelin' right now – lot like I felt before I come to work for you and your ma."

Miss Henchbaw didn't waste any time. Friday the next week we had the party to say goodbye to her. She said she was going down to California to visit her sister in Long Beach, make up her mind about her future. Most of the girls cried. Last thing she did was pick up the blackboard eraser and wipe out:

FOR TOMORROW:
EMPIRES OF THE FERTILE CRESCENT
HIGHROADS TO ARITHMETIC – PERCENT
QUESTIONS – EXERCISE 53
EXPRESSING YOURSELF – EXERCISE 21

Only good thing about it, the school board were having a hard time finding a substitute in the middle of spring term. Looked like we were getting a two-week holiday. Miss Hench-baw loaded us up with a lot of stuff to do at home till the new teacher would show up. Jake suggested that Ma could maybe take over, but she didn't think much of that idea. I was just as glad she felt that way about it.

"What upsets me about it all, Jake," she said, "is the way everybody just sits back and lets it happen."

"What can they do?" Jake said, "except maybe try talkin' the school board out of accepting . . ."

"But look who's on the school board with me! Mr. Dotty . . ."

"Yeah – yeah."

"Pete Harrison. He's had it in for Mabel ever since she suspended his son for a week last year. And Merle Thomas. Mr. Ricky took over the mortgage and bailed Merle out last year."

"Looks like Ricky's holdin' a pretty good hand. Royal flush."

"Jake, surely there's something can be done!"

Jake thought about that for a minute. "Ah, now – when anybody leaves the district, uh, retires – you *usually* give 'em a party, don't you?"

"Why, yes . . ."

"Well that's one thing you *could* do. Take some of the sting out of it – give her a party."

"That's a marvellous . . ."

"All right – you phone every ratepayer in Crocus district. Tell 'em you're organizin' a party for Miss Henchbaw. You get

Ben Tincher, Sam Gatenby, Mr. Totecole – make it real official."

"At least we can do that, Jake."

"Call it Henchbaw Night. Tell all the folks comin' to this party you're gonna get up a present for Miss Henchbaw. I mean if she's retirin', why not get her a gold watch?"

"Yes! Yes! Wonderful! Now, where will I start? Martha Tincher – Mabel taught all six of her boys." Ma headed for the phone, lifted the receiver and started to crank the handle.

᰿ ᰿

That was the beginning of the Henchbaw prairie fire. Chet Lambert at the *Crocus Breeze* printed up a hundred posters for nothing:

> "Henchbaw Night"
> All Parents
> All Grandparents
> All Uncles
> All Aunts
> All Ratepayers
> Pupils – Ex-Pupils
> Young And Old
> Come To The Party
> April 27th
> Credit Union Hall

Jake and I nailed them up all over Crocus and on telephone and fenceposts within five miles of town. Mr. Lambert printed up form letters asking for donations, and Ma was licking and stamping envelope two nights in a row. In Crocus folks kept coming up to Jake and me. In Drew's pool hall, Dan Mc-Cullough said:

> "She gave me hell lots of times I was a kid – but so'd
> my old man. Used to whale me every day the week.

An' when I run away on the freight that time, and they brought me back, it was her told my old man she'd have the law on him if he ever laid a finger on me again. Sure, deal me in for twenty dollars."

In the Royal Bank, we got contributions from Mr. Abercrombie, and Homer Plante in his cage said:

"Put me down for ten. First day in school, I climbed under the desk and bawled and I stayed under there until noon. She got me out. I had her right through to Grade Nine. Never was much for books and school, but by Judas there isn't another teacher could have knocked as much into my head as she did! And there's lots of folks here in Crocus feel the same way. They don't like what Ricky did to her – they don't like it at all."

Homer was waiting on Loretta Tregillis, who said:

"It's a dirty rotten thing for Ricky to do to her! Forcing her to resign. I wouldn't be in public health if it hadn't been for Miss Henchbaw. She told my mother and father they'd better forget the new barn and send me into training – of course I'll contribute to your fund."

Just about down to our last poster, Jake and I were nailing up by the door to Repeat Golightly's barbershop when Albert Ricky came down the walk. Like always, Herb Dotty was tripping along with him. They stopped and Jake looked back over his shoulder with a couple tacks in his mouth. They dropped out when he said, "Hey, Albert – lookin' forward to seein' you Thursday night in the credit union hall. Natcherly you're gonna be there with bells on. *Gold* bells."

"Not me, you won't!"

"Then I better take your contribution right here an' now . . ."

"Not a cent!" He took off.

Herb Dotty started to follow him, turned back to Jake. He had his hand in his pants pocket and he brought it out and slipped Jake something.

"Thanks, Herb," Jake said.

Herb scuttled off after Mr. Ricky.

"How much, Jake?"

"Just a dollar," Jake said, "but for Dotty that's considerable."

⋅⋅⋅

The whole district turned out. There were cars and trucks parked clear to the correction line. Mr. Tucker and the Crocus town band played while folks filed in. Except for Mr. Ricky and Merle Thomas and Pete Harrison, the Crocus school board were up on stage with Miss Henchbaw. Ma, too. Jake was in the front row with Old Man Gatenby. I was backstage because I was in Miss Henchbaw's Sixth Grade chorus. We were opening the show and after we'd sung "We Gather Together" I'd go down and sit with Jake and Gate.

Everybody clapped when we finished and Mayor Mac-Taggart got to do his opening speech:

> "Fellow ratepayers – and friends of Miss Henchbaw – this is a party given in testimony of our very sincere gratitude for thirty-five years of service. She has taught our children and our children's children. First on our program tonight: Stevie Kiziw, who will fiddle with his – play with his fiddle, 'When the Work's All Done This Fall'."

After Stevie came Cora Swengle and she played "The Robin's Return" on the piano. I heard her play that one so often

I wished that robin had lost his way back home. Then it was Rob Duncan reciting "Bruce and The Spider". I was hearing that for the twentieth time. Jake leaned across me to Gate and said, "Too bad they didn't have black widow ones them olden days."

"And now we come to the piece dee resistance – the main event of our Miss Henchbaw Night Party." Mr. MacTaggart stuck his right hand in his coat pocket.

"Miss Henchbaw, you have just heard from your children of today . . . ." He stuck his left hand into his lefthand coat pocket.

"Your children of yesterday wish to show you their heartfelt gratitude for all you have done for them."

He quit fumbling and took his hand out of his pocket and held it up high.

"This is a key, which they have asked me, as Mayor of Crocus, to give to you. It is the key to a brand new Dee-Luxe See-dan automobile from Crocus Central Motors, bought by the grateful students and their parents. It was going to be a gold watch, but the collection got out of hand."

Out of the left wing of the stage came the nose of the car, dragging pink streamers. It was a red one with Homer Plante at the steering wheel. It stopped halfway out and all aitch broke loose in the audience. Folks were all standing, a lot of them up on their chairs. Not just kids. When Mr. MacTaggart could get them settled down, he bowed to Miss Henchbaw and held out his hand to her, and she got up and he took her to the front of the stage and then he stepped back. She looked at the key in her hand and then out to the audience and then over to the car and then down at the key again.

"Thank you – oh – thank . . ." She was having a hard time getting it out. She swallowed a couple of times and she took another try at it, but she couldn't get out a word. She started crying.

Mr. MacTaggart put his arm around her shoulders and led her back to her seat next to Ma. He came back to the centre of the stage.

"Miss Henchbaw, what we have given to you cannot begin to make up for what you have given to us over thirty-five years. But some people are never satisfied. There is more to come. This gathering just happens to constitute a legally posted meeting of ninety-seven percent of the ratepayers of Crocus school district. In the lobby there are two tables set up for the purpose of giving everyone an opportunity to vote on the issue of whether or not you wish to *accept* Miss Henchbaw's resignation."

Even before folks started out into the lobby to cast their votes, Jake said he saw Herb Dotty skin out, not to vote but probably to find the nearest phone and tell Mr. Ricky what had developed. When I asked Jake if kids could vote, too, he said, "Nope."

"Why not?"

"You ain't registered bonny-fried ratepayers. Don't really matter, Kid. The result's a fore – ah, gonna be a wipe-out."

He was right. There were only three that were against. Everybody cut loose again when Mayor MacTaggart announced the results. That was when Albert Ricky showed up. Right on the stage.

"You can't do this!" he yelled. "It's the school board hires an' fires teachers. We have accepted Henchbaw's resignation! I am calling a meeting of the school board . . ."

"I don't think that'll do you any good, Albert," Mayor MacTaggart said. "Beginning the week the Deputy Minister of Education comes to Crocus personally to take certain steps . . ."

"What steps?"

"Why – in the event that your board does *not* reinstate Miss Henchbaw – instantly – he will have to dissolve your board and take over as chairman himself to carry out the will of the people. Section Three, the Revised Provincial Education Act of 1923 – Paragraph Seven."

It was a real bombshell. Not for Ma, though. She told me and Jake afterwards that she and Mayor MacTaggart had cooked it up together. She hadn't said a word to Jake and me about it.

"Until we knew the percentage of ratepayer turnout, and the Deputy Minister of Education's response to our request, we didn't want to raise false hopes," she said.

Jake, he figured that was a pretty feeble excuse for holding out on us the way she did.

We had a substitute teacher till summer holidays because Miss Henchbaw didn't withdraw her resignation right away. Said she wanted to drive down to Long Beach, California, in her new red car to visit with her sister and to think the matter over.

"Come fall," Jake said, "you watch. You'll see her back at Rabbit Hill school giving you kids aitch again."

Like always, he was right again.

LOVE'S WILD MAGIC

I NEVER KNOWN ANYBODY MORE STUBBORN THAN OLD MAN Gatenby is. Once he gets an idea into his head, stumping powder won't blow her out of there. Hard to say what gets Gate into more of his mix-ups: being stubborn or that temper of his.

Last winter we come close to losing Gate. Had Doc Fotheringham stymied. And after Violet Bowdry moved in to look after Gate, it turned *real* serious. Violet, she's a widow – four times. She all the time tells folks how them four fellows of hers went west:

". . . and Albert felt that bundle fork go. Caught one of the tines in the feeder and ripped it right out of his hands and he leapt up onto the feeder track to get the fork before it would go through the thrashing machine. Poor Herb didn't make it. I mean *Albert* didn't make it. And the fork went right through the – aaah . . . !"

She never did say how many bushels the wheat and Albert went to the acre that crop year.

". . . year after Albert passed away I married Herb and he got to feeling peaked – turned yellow as a buttercup, and Dr. Fotheringham said to me, 'Violet,' he said. 'I got to operate.' Herb never got down off that table. Gald stones. Nine of them. I still have them in that Mason jar on my bedroom dresser.

"I lost two to the knife, one to the thrashing machine. Harold – my last – kicked to death by a mule . . ."

Violet has to be about the most un-cheerful woman in all Crocus district. Or the province of Saskatchewan. Or Canada. She was the one damn near put the finishing touch on Gate.

First I knew something was the matter with him was the night last January he came over for an evening of rummy. Just me and Gate at the kitchen table. Kid and his ma visiting Tinchers'.

"What's eatin' you, Gate? You let the five of spades go by for a run of three an' it would've put you out."

"Was it."

"And that hand before – you end up with a whole slew of face cards and aces – they count high, you know. Can't get caught with face cards and not suffer."

"Ah-huh."

Gate sure loves to win. At anything. Something must've been eating him real bad. "What's botherin' you, Gate?"

"Nothin'. Nothin'."

"You ain't buildin' up for – haven't had your lumbago both-erin' you?"

"No." He sighed a long one. "Uh-uh."

"Started up another them crazy diets? What is it this time – alfalfa and pigweed porridge?"

That should've got a rise out of him. It didn't. He just grunted. "Reminds me of a fellow I knew out Hairy Hills way. Name of Clifton. Arley Clifton," I said.

"Mmmh."

"Arley Clifton – always tormented – always bothered with trouble. Women trouble."

"Ah-huh . . ."

"Worst I ever seen him he got tangled up with a woman nickname of 'Scatter-Piss Annie'. He spent whole month flat on his back with a beaver pelt on his – and a rock he kept on the window sill, to keep it froze cold so he could put it on the end of – no, serious, Gate – what is the matter with you? Puttin' you off your rummy game."

"Jake, Jake – she's been an awful year for me."

"I never noticed that."

"Every way you look at her."

"Oh, I don't know, Gate."

"Late, cold spring, no summer to speak of at all. Humid – more like Ontario – kind of smothery. Then winter set right in. You know, Jake – this year there's been snow every month but July."

"That's what's gettin' you down – weather, Gate?"

"Not just the weather. She's been a bad year – for humans and for critters. Look at Old Candy Sangster."

"Well now, Gate."

"Went west."

"He was to go any time, Gate. The weather didn't have nothin' to do with . . ."

"Candy Sangster an' me homesteaded together – way back when the West was in knee-britches."

"Sure, sure," I said.

"Mort Dewdney. He got it, too."

"Yep."

"Then there was . . ."

"Now look, Gate. Ain't good to let your mind brood over depressin' stuff like . . ."

"I had a birthday – last week – Tuesday."

"Did you now! That's real nice. Happy – happy returns, Gate."

"Thank you, Jake. Ain't likely to be."

"Ain't likely to be what?" I said.

"Many happy returns. Jake – seventy-three. Seventy-three long years I been leavin' an' breathin' an' eatin' an' workin' an' sleepin'."

"Don't have to lick all over her like a all-day sucker! Other folks done alla that with their eyes shut an' one hand tied behind their back."

"Ain't gonna be with you much longer," he said.

"Takin' a little trip?"

"Takin' a *long* one, Jake. One-way ticket, an' she ain't CNR. I got death settin' on my wishbone."

"The hell you have!"

"Oh, I may hold out till next spring, but not till much after. Seventy-three . . ."

"That ain't old!"

"Runs in our family – always run in the Gatenbys."

"Dyin' runs in just about everybody's family!"

"Put the rummy deck away at seventy-three. My father. Died at seventy-three. My grandfather, he went west at seventy-three. My mother – no Gatenby ever got past seventy-three. I am *now* seventy-three."

"I never thought you was superstitious, Gate."

"I ain't. In our blood an' in our bones. Feel it in my bones all year. What they call a fore-boddin'. She's comin' one way or the other. Don't matter how. She's comin' for Samuel Titchener Gatenby."

"Who's comin'?"

"Death."

"Aw shee . . ."

"Like an old lady in spring to get this old horse outa the pasture. 'Come on, Sam,' she'll holler, sweet an' coaxin'. 'Come on, Boy. We ain't gonna bother Doc Fotherin'ham – just you an' me an' away we go.'"

It ain't easy, but I'm fussy about Old Gate. About *Gate*. I didn't argue when he cut off the rummy early and headed home. When the Kid and his ma showed up, I told her how worried I was about Gate. She was too. *And* the Kid. He's all the time listening in.

Just before we turned in he said, to me, "How old are *you*, Jake?"

"Kid, I quit countin' before I come to work for you an' your ma."

"How long do you figure you've got . . ."

" 'Bout as long as Old Man Sherry. Had lotsa sleep alla my life – good hard back-breakin' work from daylight to dark – out in the open from time I kicked the doo off the stubble till the springs creaked at night. Same as Gate."

"Well, if Gate's going west this spring . . ."

"He ain't. He ain't. Don't pay no attention to him. He's healthier'n I am. Gate's never had nothin' ailin' him in his whole life a couple tablespoons of Professor Noble Winesinger's Lightnin' Penetration Oil and Tune-up Tonic wouldn't fix up."

"But the way you said he was talking tonight . . ."

"Just talk. Just talk. Worst he ever had was a cold in the head."

"What about rheumatism – lumbago?" Kid said.

"Hell – them ain't bein' sick. Not *bad*. Just sort of a pest attackin' folks. Like horseflies or – Sam, he's too stubborn to die!"

Ma and me talked quite a bit about Gate the next week.

"I don't understand what's gotten into him," she said. "At first I rather liked the change in him. Gentler – quieter. But now I'm not so sure. He's lost weight, Jake."

"Nah. Always was a prune type, Gate. Tough – elastic – kind that bounces right back."

"Several people have noticed a change in him," she said.

"Just ain't arguin' with folks so much or screechin' his head off, that's all. Gate's all right."

"Well, he is getting on. It isn't just lately, but I've often wondered why he didn't have himself a housekeeper. To cook regular meals for him. *Proper* meals. Or if something did happen . . ."

"Nothin's gonna happen to that old . . ."

". . . an accident. He sleeps soundly, you know – he ought to have somebody there to take care of – just in case."

"Ain't ever had a hired girl – ain't likely to. An' nobody could do it to suit him anyways. Wouldn't last one minute.

You can't find a soul in this here district would be willin' to put up with Gate long enough to boil him an egg an' butter a slice o' toast."

"You may be right. But all the same – all the same."

"I know I'm right!"

⊷§ §⊷

Whenever Gate goes off half-cocked on some whim of his, it's too bad that folks got to get pulled into her. All the time false smoke signals and a fellow runs to help him out an' it's like runnin' into a buzzsaw. Or Violet Bowdry's Albert through that thrashing machine. Wasn't just us an' the neighbours worried about Gate. Folks in town was concerned about him, too. I found that out in Repeat Golightly's shop.

"Autumn of his days. I say Old Man Gatenby has reached the long shadows of the fall of his life."

"Mm-mmmmh."

"The wick is turned low in the lamp chimney. All it needs – puff of wind – out – goes – the – lamp. Gatenby's lamp."

"He's got a lot of coal oil left in his lamp yet," I said.

"Those are the ones that fool you, Jake. Never tell. Never tell. Been a bad year. Lost a lot of our beloved ones this year. Take Candy Sangster . . ."

"Now look here, Repeat. I heard all this bull – !"

"This was Candy Sangster's year."

"Candy Sangster might just as well've got it any year since Ought-Four. He's been drivin' straight from the Maple Leaf over the CNR tracks with a hide-full of beer long as I knew him. Just a matter time till him an' the mules an' the wagon an' the Sooline 4:10 would hit her the same moment."

"Thing is, Jake, this year, they did. And Mort Dewdney – another old friend of Gate's – Mort Dewdney."

"Been sick for over five years."

"Helga Petersen."

"You sound more an' more like Violet Bowdry every . . ."

"Wonderful woman, isn't she," Repeat said. "Seasoned."

"With what!"

"There is one who had gone down into the valley the shadow . . ."

"She didn't. Just her husbands did – four of 'em."

"Sensitive – sensitive to the darker side of life. Serious. There is a woman."

". . . to give a gopher's ass the heartburn!"

". . . a woman has brought solace and understanding and comfort to countless folks – on their bed of pain – in their time deepest sorrow."

"All I ask, if I ever get laid out – one way or the other, sick or dead – keep her away from me!"

"Gentle ministrations – healing and soothing. Tell me she did twenty-four-hour duty with Mrs. Petersen. There to the very last."

"Mmmmh."

"Can't get specials down from Regina. Dr. Fotheringham been leaning heavy on Violet the past couple years. Doesn't know what he'd do without her. They say she read to Helga Petersen right up to the very last."

"That's be better'n listenin' to her."

"No formal training, but she's what you might call an *instinctive* nurse. No formal training – sympathetic heart tells her what to do next. Nightingale – Florence Nightingale."

"I heard of her," I said, "but I didn't know she was a Crocus district girl."

"And when Sam Gatenby's time comes – as he feels it will, this year – it'll be Violet Bowdry that'll smooth his fevered brow. Be her sweet voice and tender care will soften Gate's last hours pain before he . . ."

"Repeat, for the love of – what the hell did Sam Gatenby ever do to you!"

"Jake, I count Samuel Titchener Gatenby one of my best

friends. And when he goes it'll be a great shock to me – to the community he's served so well. Wet or dry?"

If there is a hell like the preacher says – and I got no reason to figure there ain't – there's something that'd be pretty close to her right here on this earth: a fellow laying flat on his back – with Violet breathing down his neck.

She's a great reader, Violet. All them glossy magazines in Pill Brown's drugstore – the ones with the woman's head on the front cover with real nice teeth – *True Story, I Confess, Revealin' Love Stories, Appallin' Love*. She don't read them just to herself. She reads them to them poor sick women she's – indecent!

Wouldn't you know, after a bellyful out of Repeat, when I get home there she is, in the parlour with the Kid's ma. Having tea. Kid's ma invited me to join them. I said there was chores I had to do.

"Oh, chores can always wait, Jake," Violet said. "Set a minute. Cup of tea'll revive you. Nothing like the lift a cup of tea *or* coffee gives a person when he's feeling all draggy and done in."

"I'm feelin' fine. Just fine. Never felt better – I don't need no lift."

"Just like Carl," Violet said.

"Carl?" Ma said.

". . . Binestettner, my husband – was – third. Carl was always protestin' – nothin' wrong with him, he was all right, right as could be – an' all the time that growth in there in his . . ."

"I gotta go out to them chores."

"Always on the go, never let up. I said to him when he was just slipping off: 'Carl', I said, 'it ain't the sarcoma, Carl, it's the top speed you always went at. You've depleted your reserve energy. Worked your fingers to the bone, never time to take the load off your feet.' I'm the same way. You take those varicose ulcers. That's just because a woman's on her feet twenty-four hours the day – on the go."

"Well, I got to go out an' finish them . . ."

"Breathless rush – overworked body can only take so much, I always say. Or rather Herb used to say. Now Herb . . ."

"Your cup's empty, Mrs. Bowdry," Ma said. "Another . . . ?"

"Thank you. If folks could only learn to ease off on their oars – relax."

"I relax all right," I said.

"Readin'. I always say readin' has been the savin' of me. Read all the time, whenever I can. Broadens a person, deepens their understanding of human nature. Why, I always – thank you, no cream, thanks, half the usual sugar, kidneys – I guess I'm no different from a hundred other women. Have their problems, make mistakes, tryin' to enrich one's life. Set – set, Jake."

I did. I needed to!

"Happy as a lark makin' a home for a loved one – all four times – and it was true-to-life stories of other women which helped me the most, all through the bitter and all through the sweet. Lots of lessons to be learned from these stories – on lovelier livin'. I've enriched *my* life, an' my husbands' . . . ."

"All four," I said.

"Physically – spiritually – morally – emotionally whilst we made a life together. I think *I Confess* . . ."

"To what?" I said.

Kid's ma glared at me.

"*I Confess* has given me more comfort and help. I have the January copy with me now. I – here . . ."

"I guess I could use a cuppa tea now," I said.

"Titled 'The Unmarried Bride' . . ."

"Usual – four spoons."

"Yes, Jake. I know," Ma said.

"Ah, here. Just listen to this: 'After the bright rapture of the honeymoon comes the dawn of understanding. The grey dawn of the betrayed. Kirk had *forged* the wedding certificate and Veronica knew finally . . .' "

"Slurp," I said.

" '. . . that she was *the unmarried bride*'."

"Rather unusual situation," Ma said.

"Oh, it's the way it's written – it's so true to life . . . ." She went back to the goddam magazine.

I had another cup of tea.

" 'With a snide little laugh Sabra turned to Veronica. "So you two have been playing at marriage, have you?" she said.' "

I had two more cups of tea while she finished 'The Unmarried Bride'. She started in on another one.

" 'My trousseau was modest, but in one fling of extravagance I had bought a dramatic negligée of pale rose-dawn coloured lace and chiffon – delicate but daring. I fastened it about me.' "

In this one a fellow name of Raymond turned out to have two other wives he hadn't told Kimberly about.

" 'I sat shivering until the pale fingers of morning lightened the room. My anguish deepened with each passing hour. After a long time I stripped off the negligée and groped my way, blinded by tears – to my clothes – young, vulnerable, bewildered. I stood frozen for an eternity.' "

I knew exactly how Kimberly felt!

" '. . . then I collapsed on the sobbing bed – I collapsed sobbing on the bed. I saw now that Raymond's love for me was not on a higher, more spiritual plane. He had done his best to drag it down to the level of . . .' "

She closed up *I Confess*.

"You see what I mean," she said. "I'm not the weepy type but I think all of us – women – are happiest when we're having a good cry or worryin' over somebody else's problems. I've been told so many times I have a sympathetic ear, and I must admit I enjoy sort of ponderin' over other people's problems. Now, you take Old Mr. Gatenby down the road from you."

"No!" That really shook me!

"Oh, I don't think Sam Gatenby has any *real* health problem," Kid's ma said.

"I hear he's been failing," Violet said, "just in the last year – the last few weeks as a matter . . ."

"Sam's all right!" I said.

"I know he's been in to see Dr. Fotheringham several times now," Violet said. "They say he's spent several afternoons with Title Brown."

"What the – what's Title Brown got to do with . . ."

"Affairs – affairs," Violet said. "Getting them in order. So many of us leave our wills to the last minute. Till it's too late."

I skinned out of there to do them chores I didn't really have to do. I headed for Gate's. Found him in his rocker. Afghan throwed over his shoulders. All hunched up and staring at the mica belly-button of his Quebec heater.

"Pull out a chair for yourself, Jake." Didn't even *sound* like Gate. All breathy.

"Sure. Sure, Gate – dropped over – few han's of rummy."

"No – no . . ."

"Euchre?"

"No – I no . . ."

"Five hundred? Say, look Gate . . ."

"Sorry, Jake. Ain't got the strength to pick up the cards an' lay 'em down."

"Now look here, you gotta get a grip on yourself! You been lettin' this foolishness go too far . . . !"

"Foolishness? Foolishness? Jake – Jake – for your own peace of mind – so you won't be kickin' yourself after she's happened, watch yourself . . ."

"What are you tryin' to tell . . ."

"Nothin' hurts more than the unthinkin' harsh word spoke in thoughtlessness – remembered, when it's too late."

"You ain't ready for no shiny box with handles yet!"

"I'm more'n ready. All square with the world. Will's made out."

"Look, you're gonna carry this thing too far . . . !"

"Borrowed time. Livin' on borrowed time . . ."

"The hell you are – any more'n I am!"

"An' I want to – now you're here – I want to ask you a favour."

"Why sure – ask away, Gate."

"I'd like it real well if you was one of my polar bearers. Active. Or if you ain't up to it – honorary."

"We'll bury you – we'll bury you in a banana crate out by the slaughterhouse the way we did with Chuck Swengle in Ought-Eight when he passed out at the old Arlington – only turned out he wasn't dead. Just passed out."

"No laughin' matter, Jake. Another thing – my favourite hymn is 'There's a Beautiful Land on High'."

"Gate, I always knew you was the stubbornest fellow I ever run across, but this one time it ain't gonna do you no harm nor no good. You ain't gonna die this year not the next – nor the next – and it don't matter a whoop how hard you try to do it, you – ain't – gonna – die!"

Even back then, I wasn't all that sure about that. Got worse. Each time I dropped in on him he seemed to've sunk lower. I come to a conclusion. Me visiting him wasn't doing him one goddam bit of good. Matter of fact, just the opposite. Only helped him to feel sorrier and sorrier for himself. Maybe if I stayed away and he got to wondering why I wasn't visiting him, might upset him enough to make him perk up.

Even though I wasn't checking him out regular all that week, didn't mean I didn't know how he was doing. Kid's ma, she answers a lot of rings on our party lines that ain't our ring. She picked up more about Gate's condition than I wanted to hear about.

"Martha Tincher's seen Dr. Fotheringham's car go past their windbreak three times since Tuesday."

"Maybe he wasn't headed for Gate's."

"Oh, he was. Shirley Totecole saw him turn in there."

Totecoles are right next to Gate's place.

"She dropped in after Dr. Fotheringham left the last time. She says he's staying in bed. Isn't eating. Cheeks all caved in . . ."

"Probably had his dentures out," I said.

"Jake, maybe you ought to go over and – why don't you . . . ?"

"Because I am tryin' to get him stubborn in the opp'site direction!"

"Evidently it's not working."

I was afraid she was right, but what the hell could a fellow do? I decided to drop in on him next morning. I changed my mind when the Kid got home from Rabbit Hill school.

"He's got a housekeeper now, Jake."

Well at least that was something good for a change.

"Stevie Kiziw's dad drove her out there this morning. She's going to cook and clean for Mr. Gatenby."

"Thank goodness!" Kid's ma said. "Just what I've been saying all al . . ."

"Mrs. Bowdry," the Kid said.

"Shee-yit!" I said.

For the first time since I ever said that word in front of the Kid, his ma didn't take me by the face. I didn't wait till *morning* to go over to Gate's.

She was there all right.

She stopped me before I could get into his bedroom.

"I just don't know what we're going to do. He won't eat. Even soup or tapioca." I happen to know that Gate hates both of them equal. "Not enough to keep a sparrow alive."

I noticed sparrows eat a lot of what Baldy and Queenie drop our there. For their size. The sparrows.

"That's probably all what's wrong with him," I suggested. "A couple of rare steaks an' . . ."

"Oh no, it's much worse than that, I'm afraid – goes deeper.

I have a feeling – though I'm no doctor, goodness knows, but I've seen enough of them – I have feeling there's a growth – malignant . . ."

"That's for Doc Fotherin'ham to . . ."

"Yes, but sometimes even the doctors are helpless. I'm afraid it's so with Mr. Gatenby. I'm doing my best. And tomorrow Martha Tincher's dropping in to relieve me so I can get into town."

"Mmmh," I said.

"I can tell when the end is near. He's lost all interest in this life, Mr. Trumper – " she sighed. "Too bad he isn't a woman."

Now what the hell did she mean by that? "What the hell do you mean by that!"

"Ssssh! Lower your voice! He can still *hear*! My reading to them – women – works wonders for them, but the appeal is only to women. I did try it with Harold, hoping he would rally, but he didn't. Too far gone – seemed to sink even faster. If only Sam were a woman patient of mine, I'd be right in that bedroom beside him, reading aloud to him these wonderful and inspirin' stories . . ."

"Yeah! Yeah!"

"I read to Helga Petersen – near the last – for twelve straight hours."

"You thought of tryin' it out on Gate?"

"Oh no – he's a *man*."

"Yeah. Noticed that. All the same, even though it didn't work when you tried it on Herb . . ."

"Harold."

". . . just the once with a fellow."

"You think so?"

"Can't tell if you don't try it, can you?"

"I suppose not," she said.

"Gate, he'd never ask you to read to him. Never did read

much himself – *Crocus Breeze, Nor'west Prairie Farm Review,*
like of that. Might not be so bad a idea for you to read to him
some of them wonderful stories out of *Appallin' Love* . . ."

"*Appealing Love.*"

"If you really want to do your best for Gate . . ."

"I do! Oh, I do!"

"All right, then. You said Martha Tincher's drivin' you into
Crocus . . ."

"First thing tomorrow morning."

"So – you go into Pill Brown's an' get a pile of them shiny
magazines an' you take an' read 'em to Gate. No matter what
he says – or does. I got a notion that's just what he needs.
Might just turn the corner . . ."

"You really think . . . ?"

"Sure do. You read to him. Like you did with Helga an' all
them other women. Here. This oughta cover it." I handed her
the ten-dollar bill. "You read to him till your voice gives out."

We didn't wait for Martha Tincher to pick her up. I got on
the phone to her and said *I'd* take Violet in. Then I phoned
Pill Brown an' he agreed to come to the store and open her
up for us. Ten dollars bought one hell of a lot of them
magazines – enough to fill a bundle rack. After we got back to
Gate's I took as much as I could of it the rest of the evening:

" '. . . didn't know marriage could be like this. She had
thought it would be all love and kisses and tenderness. When
Darryl kissed her brutally, then revelation dawned in her hith-
erto blinded heart . . .' "

Gate, he just laid there with his eyes closed the way he'd
been doing the past week, not saying a word.

" '. . . life had been one long and carefree flirt. Little did
Sandra care for the lives she had wrecked. Until debonair
Lindsay came along. Here was a conquest that really mat-
tered . . . !' "

By the next story, Gate had started to make kind of grunting
sounds.

" '. . . had Darby been deceiving her all along through those tempestuous three years they'd been together? Only Willa Lynne herself could answer that searing question! How could she ever be sure of his love for her? How could she find the answer her parched heart thirsted for?' "

I'd known Gate a long time and I seen that squeezed-up look around his mouth whenever he had them gas pains an' trots you get out of catching Looie Riel's Revenge from a bad water supply in summer. Salmon Nellie, Doc Fotheringham calls it.

I guess it was the morning of the second day Gate quit grunting and groaning. He'd opened his eyes to curse, but she kept her promise to me, went on reading to him. Only quit if he dropped off to sleep.

When I come by in the afternoon, she said, "He still won't eat a thing, but you were right. It does seem to be working. He threw the urinal at me this morning."

"Good sign," I said. If it was full.

I went in with her while she read to Gate some more.

" '. . . his lips on Carla's were sheer magic . . . ' "

"Jake — Jake, for God's sakes . . . !"

" '. . . he was hers. Yet why did he draw back? Why was he keeping the check-rein on the untamed passion that coursed so wildly through his veins? Only time would . . . ' "

"Stop it! Stop it!"

" '. . . what strange force stronger even than his love for her was holding him back . . .' "

Me, I was wondering what strange force was still holding Gate back.

" '. . . she knew then the idea of marriage had never even entered his head. Or his heart. What a mockery it would have been if . . .' "

"Turn it off, woman!" Gate had made it up to sitting.

"Now just you lay back, Sam."

"Chuck them magazines!" At least that's what it sounded like he said. He didn't have his teeth in.

I nodded for her to go on.

" '. . . what a mockery it would have been had I brought him round to it. Anything outside of marriage was unthinkable, of course, and yet I knew we both came from two different . . .' "

"My pants! My goddam pants!"

" '. . . worlds. There was no overlapping of those two different worlds really, except for this exquisitely torturing *physical* attraction . . .' Mr. Gatenby!"

Gate had flang back the covers and most of his nightshirt with them. "Pants or no pants!" he yelled, "I'm runnin' you outa here! An' after her I'm takin' care of you, Trumper!"

He did, barefoot, his nightshirt flying, out the bedroom through the kitchen, the back stoop and into the backyard and past the chicken coops beyond, but it wasn't no physical attraction or untamed passion driving him on after her.

I skinned out of there before he got back inside to keep the rest of his promise.

Doc Fotheringham had to come out to him again, and the Kid's ma moved in to take care of Gate with the kettle steaming and a blanket over his head. Pneumonia from chasing Violet over the snow in twenty-below weather. He's just about over that now.

Same old Gate again.

THE FACE IS FAMILIAR

I GUESS SHE'S KIND OF LIKE THEM ICEBERGS. FOUR-FIFTHS OF her under water. Me and the Kid and his ma live on the farm couple miles out of town, so we only get to see the one-fifth. But what we do see of what happens in Crocus gives us enough to go on. Gives us plenty to go on.

I suppose to most people what happens in Crocus don't matter much, unless they happen to live in Crocus. But when you're right up on her an' you know the folks she's happening to, it seems like all aitch is breaking loose. That's the sort of stuff they make news out of. We got a newspaper for that, *Crocus Breeze*. Chet Lambert runs it. Four pages. Thursdays. You can tell when she's paper day if you go by the *Breeze* building next to Dingle's Funeral Parlour. Shakes and shimmies like a popular on a summer day in a high wind. So you wonder if something's gone wrong with your eyes.

Something in the *Crocus Breeze* for everybody. In the advertising section stuff like:

"Weaner pigs. Good milk cow and MacDougall seven-foot mower almost like new. Phone R125." ". . . Unwanted hair permanently eradicated from any part of the . . ."

Then there's this column, "Newsy Notes From Round About":

> Ray Thurlow is down with his old complaint, quinzy. We hope he will have a speedy recovery.

The Ladies' Auxiliary of the Burning Fundamental Church of Nazareth in Gladys Ridge have bought new cream blinds for the windows. Any contributions will be appreciated.

Merton Abercrombie, our genial bank manager, and his charming wife Elsie have returned from a two-week sojourn at Banff.

Can't say I'd've called Mert "genial", or any other bank managers I've ever run across. Chet runs a lot of educational stuff too. "Fillers", he calls them. Like this one under the obituary column here:

A five-year plan has been recommended for India to include birth control in an effort to cut down India's vast population increase.

Chet's a nice fellow. He's editor, typesetter, bookkeeper, janitor. Got an awful lot to do. So he gets stuff mixed up once in a while. You take this piece on the Solway wedding:

The bride given in marriage by her father, George Solway, was dressed in a gown of gleaming white satin, which was styled with long lily-point sleeves five blue grouse, three cock pheasants, five prairie chickens.

Helen Solway, the bride's mother, was in powder blue crepe with picture hat. The bridesmaids wore daffodil yellow taffeta, and pastel toned gladioli graced the wedding table swathed in tulle.

The groom was attended by his older cousin, Marvin MacLeod of Fort McMurray, Alberta, as well as one male mountain sheep, one male mountain goat, one male elk, mule deer, antelope, one male grizzly, black, brown or cinnamon bear.

The bride's brother, Ben Solway, was the usher

and may be shot October 3 to November 12 in all areas except the Eastern Irrigation District.

The happy newlyweds left for their honeymoon in Regina, the bride travelling in a dove grey suit with white accessories.

Now, George Solway's a prickly fellow, last person in the Crocus district for Chet to have his printing-machine mix up the wedding report with the opening of the shotgun season and the big game regulations. George is what we call a prairie lawyer, and there's lots of them around Crocus district. Our winters are long and folks get to talking, turns into arguing. Stuff like: what year was the driest year we ever had, how far can you walk into the bush, how do porcupines mate, does a whale give milk? Sooner or later one of them gets real hot, loses his temper. He stews over it and gets to wondering if the fellow that got him mad really owns all that lower pasture where they got a quarter-mile common fence. So he heads for the land titles office and he figures out the fence is fifteen foot over onto his property. He sends a hot letter to the other fellow telling him to get his fence the aitch over onto his own land. Other fellow tells him to go jump into the Brokenshell River.

He says he'll take her into court. The other fellow says just fine with him, because he's a prairie lawyer too, read all of those law books big enough to prop open a barn door. Then they stand up on their hind legs before the judge.

"Your Worship, this here defendant has got his barb wire fence a good twenty-five foot over onto my land!"

Other fellah he jumps to his feet an' he yells, "I object! Uh, that fence – that line was run by Pete Dewdney when he homesteaded back in Ought-Four!"

"I raise you," other fellow yells, or "Uh, I raise a objection! Pete Dewdney tied a bandana on to his wagon wheel an' measured by turns, but that there wagon wheel had a loose rim so in a mile she's out almost thirty foot an' the fence has got to be moved back, uh, Your Worship, and I claim alla the money from alla the crop on that same strip fer the past forty-eight years!"

Judge, he weighs her, weighs all the evidence pro an' con-dom, then he throws the whole thing out of court. Clear out. Both has to split the court costs and the fence stays where she is.

Soon as I read the Solway wedding story, I figured George wouldn't let that one slip by. When you print something makes folks laugh at other folks, that's libellous. Chet printed an apology next issue.

I kept waiting and wondering when George would let Chet have it. One night after supper, Kid doing his homework at the kitchen table, his ma darning socks, I brought the matter up.

"I guess Solway ain't takin' Chet into court over that wed-ding story."

Kid's ma was looking down hard at one of my socks and shaking her head. "He did print an apology the next week."

"I know he did, but with George bein' like he is . . ."

"I feel sorry for him," she said.

"Chet?"

"George Solway. His only daughter's wedding." She was still looking at that sock. "I'm sure he suffers from an inferiority complex."

"Solway just suffers from being touchy and mean," I said, and I meant it.

"No, Jake. There's an explanation for everything." Now she was holding up my sock with her fingers stuck out of the hole in the toe, three of them. "Tell me something – when did you last cut your toenails?"

"I'm still waiting for that explanation everything's got," I said.

"His physical appearance," she said.

"What about it?"

"Oh come on, Jake. He's probably very sensitive about it – The way he looks . . . ."

"Oh yeah – that goatee of his."

"Red." That was the Kid looked up from his homework.

"Ain't red," I said. "Roan."

"Just like Malleable Brown's goat he's always got tied up by the blacksmith shop," the Kid said. "Always chewin' – way Mr. Solway does, only it isn't a cud, it's a wad of chewing tobacco so his goatee's always waggling too . . ."

"All right, son."

"Just like Malleable Brown's . . ."

"Son, that'll do!"

"Still think he'll take Chet into court," I said. "You were wrong, Kid."

"What about?"

"Goatee colour. Roan. Both of 'em."

Next time I was into Crocus I went by Malleable's blacksmith shop. Deliberate. Just to get another look at that goat of his. Real shaganappy, like he had a ragged blanket throwed over him. His head had a lopsided look to it same as George, the way he always looks at a person sideways only. The goat looked like that because he was missing one horn and there was just a stump in that roan hair of his. The ears hanging down and ahead of him made a person think of George's big ones. Goat was chewing just like George does most the time. Also I'd forgot. He was wall-eyed. Same as George. Maybe the Kid's ma was right.

I went to Repeat Golightly's barbershop and, wouldn't you know, both Chet and George Solway was in there. Repeat had George in the chair. Chet and Old Man Gatenby were waiting their turn. I took the chair next to Gate.

"Now look, George, I've told you that wedding piece was a regrettable mistake and I'm sorry for it. I've apologized in print for it . . . ."

"Yellah journalism!"

"Oh," Repeat said, "I would say we are very lucky with the fifth estate we have in Crocus."

"Quit changin' the goddam subject," George said. "I'm talkin' about that yellah rag Chet . . ."

"Same thing, George," Repeat said. "Fifth estate – Press – *Crocus Breeze*."

"And I say all we got in this town is yellah journalism!"

"I've done everything I can do to make amends, George," Chet said.

"Awful difference between yellow journalism and the type journalism we get from Chet." Repeat had quit snipping at the back of George's neck, come round and was waving his scissors at the goatee. "Chet's the articulate voice of our community. Speaks for all of us. Our own voice. Strong, clear voice. Healthy press is important. Important, like my father used to say. Speak out clear and loud and strong . . . ."

". . . but get her right before he bellows her out!"

"I do my best, George."

"Which ain't worth a pinch of gopher . . ."

"Take it easy, George," Gate said.

Me, I decided to stay out of it.

"Platform," Repeat said.

"Huh?" Gate said.

"Platform of the people. Air their convictions. Letters to the editor colyum. My father used to write letters to the editor every evening of his life. Every evening. I remember once he sent in a letter to the editor the *Nor'west Prairie Farm Review*. All about church attendance falling off in rural communities. He signed it 'Father of Seven'."

"Was you one of seven, Repeat?" Gate said, "I thought you was a only child."

"I had one brother. On the sides, George?"

"Right round. If there was just two of you, then why'd your pa sign . . ."

"Yeah. Why'd he say 'Father of Seven'?" Gate said.

"Manner of speaking – or writing – or signing. Uh, one about stray dogs in town in fall – steamin' letter. He signed that one 'Arcturus'."

"His given name?" Gate said.

"No, no. Pen name. Letter-to-the-editor name," Repeat explained.

"Don't seem right. Father claimin' he has seven kids, changin' his name," Gate said.

"He wasn't – he didn't. Poetic license, you might call it. Poetic."

"Was he a poet?" Gate asked.

"No, he wasn't. But it was all right for him to sign his letters 'Father of Seven'. 'Arcturus'. 'Just A Dirt Farmer'. Sometimes he used to sign them 'Fairplay' or 'Justice', and when they cut down the populars in front of the CNR depot he wrote a steamin' letter an' signed it 'Sylvaticus'."

Now Gate was looking real confused. "Was your pa a Greek?"

"No!"

"Changed his family name to Golightly?"

"No!"

"Then how come . . ."

"It's a pen name, Gate," Chet explained. "Not unusual with letters to the editor."

"Like getting stuff all mixed up," George said, "and making a laughing-stock out of folks in public!"

"Look, George – I'm gettin' just a little tired of hearing about that wedding story. Do you think you could quit harping on it?"

"I'll harp on it as long as I goddam please!"

"All right, boys," Repeat said, "let's not get bitter. I say my shop isn't the place to . . ."

"I'll get bitter whenever I like. I'll . . ."

"Talk can cause trouble." Repeat was snipping at the goatee now.

"It sure can!"

"Trouble with you, George, you think everybody has it in for you personally," Chet said.

"Clean and civil tongue in a clean mouth in a clean shop is my motto," Repeat said.

"You keep outa this!"

"Now look, George, this is my shop, my rules. Goes for everybody. There's no sense you fellahs . . ."

"Don't you tell me I got no sense!" George yelled up at Repeat.

"I didn't say you didn't have no sense . . ."

"See what I mean, reading into what people say," Chet said.

"You attend to printin' alla them lies, you . . ."

"I try to print . . ."

". . . shaganappiest rag from here to Hudson's Bay! I wouldn't hang your paper up in my backhouse!"

"You've always got Eatons or the Hudson Bay catalogue for that," I said. Figured it was time somebody did something before it was too late. "You know, you don't have to read his paper, George."

"Just for people who can read anyway," Chet said.

"Aha! Your head all stuffed with words an' education an' schoolin', pokin' fun at them which never went past – which – arrh! I can read! I can read!"

"He's not illegimate," I said.

"Illiterate," Repeat said.

"You can't call me illiterate! You an' your old man . . ."

"I'll ask you not to . . ."

"Runnin' a two-bit slander shop, runnin' off at the yap twenty-four hours a day . . ."

"Look here – I say, you look here . . ."

"I never knew your old man . . ."

"My father . . ."

". . . but if he was anythin' like you I'm sure glad I never run acrosst his trail! I had a belly-full listenin' to you yappin' on about your father! All of them false names he used . . ."

"He did not!"

"Callin' me a liar, are you?"

"Liar is a word I never lay my tongue . . ."

"I heard you . . ."

"Well, you didn't hear right – you old goat!"

George jumped out of the barber chair, ripped the sheet from round his neck. For a minute I thought he was going to strangle Repeat with it. Them wall-eyes of his was blazing. "What did you call me!"

Repeat didn't answer him – just swallowed and backed up a couple of steps.

George shoved that roan goatee in Repeat's face. "You just called me a . . ."

"Goat," Repeat said. "Old goat! Meant it! Fits you! I say there isn't a fellow in all Crocus district – maybe Saskatchewan – North America – looks more like a goat than you do!"

"You asked for it, George," Gate said.

"Only a goat'd have more decency than to come in a man's shop and start running down a man's father. In front of other fellows."

"I'm going to nail your hide to a fencepost!"

"Shaved you for twenty years. Trimmed that goatee – trimmed her – every time I put the scissors to her, reminded me of Malleable Brown's goat!"

"When I get through with you . . ."

"Pass Malleable's shop four times a day – four time a day – see that goat four times a day. Goatee wagglin' back an' forth, back an' forth . . ."

"All right, Repeat," I said, "that's enough."

"Same colour – texture. I say they're both coarse. Blindfold me and put a pair of scissors in my hand, I couldn't tell the difference."

"Ridicule an' contempt an' blame . . ." George sputtered.

"That's right! That's what you were doing to the memory of my father . . ."

"In front of three witnesses! Slander! Slander! Callin' me a goat!"

"I don't imagine Malleable's goat could hear him," Gate whispered to me.

"Clear case. An' you're not gettin' away with it! No, sir! You're going' to hear more about this. Percy."

"Who's he?" I said.

"Slanderous Percy – goat – contempt – ridicule – I got an open'-an'-shut case agin' you! I'm gonna lay a charge agin' you! I'll take you through every court in the land!"

Poor old Repeat. Last fellow in the world to lose his temper and say somethin' foolish. Why, all he was trying to do was sort of keep the peace between Chet an' George. Innocent bystander, as Repeat would say. Innocent bystander.

George kept his promise to Repeat about laying that slander charge. Wasn't a week later I dropped by Repeat's barbershop. Nobody there but Repeat, sitting in his barber chair. He looked kind of gloomy.

"Dropped by, Repeat. See how you was doin'."

"Not so good, Jake. I say, I'm feeling little peakid."

"That's too bad, Repeat – what seems to be the . . ."

"Just before you came in. Corporal MacBride – corporal dropped in."

"Oh?"

"Summons."

"Summons?"

Repeat held up the long piece of paper he had in his hand. "Stood right where you're standing now. Stood there for a minute kind of embarrassed-looking, then he hands me this paper. Folded paper."

I could see it was folded all right.

"Slander."

"Which one?"

"What's that, Jake?"

"George or the goat?"

"George. Week Friday, got to appear before T.W. All the times I shaved T.W., an' now I got to go before him—criminal—like a common criminal."

I should explain: T.W. is Crocus district magistrate, Tom Wilson.

"Hold on, Repeat, you ain't any common . . ."

"Might as well be. Might as well. If I'd kept my mouth shut . . ."

"All you was tryin' to do was keep the peace between him an' Chet."

"That's right. That's right. Just doin' my best. Keep the peace."

"Mainly he was interested in gettin' at Chet. Too bad."

"Bad for business. Shop gets a bad name . . ."

"You'd better see a lawyer. Talk to Charlie. He'll take care of you. You oughta have somebody to take care of you, Repeat."

Repeat took my advice, headed for Charlie Pickersgill's office. Couple of days later when I went into town with the cream cans Repeat told me all about it. Repeat don't hold much back.

"Charlie says it doesn't look so good—you fellows there hearing me going on and on comparing him to Malleable's goat."

"Uh-huh."

" 'Buy some space in the *Breeze*—buy some space in the *Breeze*, Orville,' he said, 'and print an apology—public apology—saying you didn't intend saying what you did.' "

"Uh-huh."

" 'Eat crow in public in the pages of the *Crocus Breeze*,' he said, 'and make him feel mean till he gets to feelin' a little sorry for you, an' after a while he might drop the action. Might be a good chance of that.' "

"Yeah."

" 'More'n a fifty-fifty chance,' he said."

"Yeah, yeah, that was real good advice, Repeat. When you gonna . . ."

"Trouble was, I got to thinking what my father would have done. Got to thinking that – and seemed like I could hear his voice – real dry voice he had – advising against it."

"Well, if I was you I'd take Charlie's advice, Repeat."

"That's what I figured. Figured that way at first. Only trouble was . . ."

"Yeah?"

"Went on home to lunch. Passed Malleable's."

"Yeah?"

"Saw that roan goat. Just like him! Spitting – chewing image – I am not eating any crow in front of the readers of the *Crocus Breeze* – not to the man that resembles Malleable Brown's goat and said what he said about my father – in my own shop!"

Repeat, he can surprise a fellow sometimes. I chewed over what he said about not eating crow in the *Crocus Breeze* – she didn't taste so good. Figured I better take a dangle over to the *Breeze* building, have a chat with Chet. Fellow been in the paper business long as he has oughta have some ideas about slander.

"Well, I imagine any judge would understand," Chet said after I explained about Repeat. "Mostly costs. They won't hurt him too much."

"Trouble is she's the principle of the thing with Repeat," I said.

"Mm-hmmh. George too. Only thing would make him let go of Repeat – that'd be bigger game."

"Huh?"

"George has really got his sights trained on me. I, uh, think I have an idea that might help out Repeat."

"Yeah?"

"I got the space. Isn't every week I have the space. Yep. That's it."

"What you got in mind, Chet?"

"Oh, I – think it might work – might work out. We'll wait and see. Hate to make you an accessory before the fact, Jake."

I didn't push him. Figured he had something up his sleeve. Have to wait. Till Thursday, when his paper come out. Kid, he picked up the mail an' brought it in the kitchen.

I grabbed the *Crocus Breeze* and started looking through it. I didn't have to look for long: second page, first paragraph in "Newsy Notes from Round About".

A deplorable case of mistaken identity occurred yesterday when a visitor in town dropped by Malleable Brown's place and endeavoured to engage Malleable's roan goat in conversation. Not until he had wasted fifteen minutes of his time, did he realize that it was a goat and *not* our town's bon vivant, George Solway. We find it hard to believe this report, for we fail to see how any man, in his right senses, could credit George Solway with either the intelligence or the appearance of a self-respecting goat!

Now that there is real libellous. For the life of me I couldn't see how Chet figured doing that would help out Repeat. Like throwing coal oil on a fire to put it out. When I run across him in front of MacTaggart's store I told him that.

"In a way you're right," he said, "but have you ever got caught in the middle of a good fire – prairie fire?"

"Yeah."

"What's the best way of fighting it, Jake?"

"Oh sackin' it, ploughin' – sometimes a fellow can – Oh, I got it."

"That's right. *Back* fire. Start another fire. Burn it over so there's nothing for it to feed on."

"Yeah, but . . ."

"The story is a back fire. George really wants to get at me. Now he's got a good chance. Very good chance. Libel. Lot easier to prove than slander."

"One thing you could do, Jake, to help things. Drop by the barbershop – now's the right time for Repeat to get in touch with George – tell him he's sorry he flew off the handle."

"Sure."

"Oh – Corporal."

It was Corporal MacBride had come up to us. He had a long folded paper in his hand – just like the one Repeat got.

"You've got something for me," Chet said.

"I have."

"Civil – criminal?"

"Civil. Damages."

"Uh-huh."

"Two weeks. Courthouse isn't – won't be finished redecorating – we'll be using the school."

"I'll be there," Chet said. "I'll be there."

"You people interested in a cup of coffee?"

"Thanks, later," Chet said. "I have to get to the office." He waved the paper. "Put this in a special file-folder I have. Libel section. With all the others. Under 'L'."

I headed for Repeat's the way Chet suggested, to get him to apologize to George.

"But you gotta, Repeat. Way Chet's got him all steamed up

about this here libel action, why, George, he'll be willin' to listen to reason. He'll be so tickled to toss out your . . ."

"I meant what I said to him. Can't do it. Wouldn't be . . ."

"Now look here, Repeat, don't carry her too far."

"Nothing's been changed, Jake. Nothing changed."

"She sure has. Chet, he's put himself out on a limb to help you. Making a sacrifice of himself . . ."

"Owe it to the memory of my father."

"You paid off your pa when you told off George Solway the first place."

"That's the way I see it. Way I look at it, Jake."

"An' now you owe a debt to Chet."

"How's that?"

"Chet asked me to ask you to go see George. Wants the decks cleared for this libel suit of his."

"Does he?"

"Sort of threw himself in to save you, Repeat. Least you could do is appreciate it."

"Well – I – when you . . ."

"It'll help him, Repeat. You wanta help Chet, don't you?"

"Why, sure. I certainly do, Jake."

"You keep right on doin' the noble thing, Repeat. You hightail it over to George's right now."

"Well, maybe after lunch . . ."

"Right now, Repeat – don't you waste a moment. Chet, he didn't think twice when he stepped in for you."

"I will. Certainly will. Yeah – I will. You come with me?"

"Sure, Repeat. Sure."

Chet sure had her figured out right. Repeat kind of tithered and tothered around, but George didn't even give him a chance to say he was sorry. He just bust in and said he already withdrawed the charge – the day the *Crocus Breeze* hit the street. Said he didn't want to cloud the main issue: nailing Chet's hide to a fencepost.

❧ ❧

Lot of folks made it into town the day of the trial. I never seen so many outside of Crocus Fair an' Little Britches Rodeo Day. Seen them standing in front of the post office, the Royal Bank corner – in front of the Sanitary Café – nearly every one of 'em talkin' about Chet Lambert's case with George Solway.

Desks in the schoolroom Judge Wilson was usin' for his court was full. I only got a chance to stand at the back the room. Mayor MacTaggart, Malleable Brown – I could see them in the front row.

Then Judge Wilson come in and set down at the desk, Corporal MacBride standing right beside him. Corporal had moved over a chalk-box filled with sawdust for George Solway to spit his tobacco juice into.

Chet pleaded not guilty for himself. Then George Solway got to his feet, stuck his hands under his coat-tails.

"An' I say to this court the defendant has a wicked and depraved heart. His course in publishin' in the *Crocus Breeze* false an' defamatory an' malicious writin' has injured my reputation to the extend of fifteen hundred dollars. He has injured it to this extend by imputin' to my appearance the qualities of Malleable Brown's goat. I want to point out emphatically that the defendant cannot claim justification nor privilege . . ."

Real prairie lawyer. Then she come Chet's turn. He got up an' he walked to the front of the room . . .

"The complainant has said that my comparison of him to Mall'able Brown's goat has exposed him to contempt and ridicule, but milord, I fail to see that this is so. Any contempt or ridicule to which he feels I have exposed him by comparison could have little or no effect. I have little to say in my defense, but I would like the permission of this court to bring in – a, well, not a witness, rather another complainant."

"Another complainant!" Judge Wilson said.

"The goat, milord."

George Solway jumped up. "I object!"

"From what I have been able to find out there have been animals in courts before," Chet said. "There was . . ."

"Presence of that critter in this court would make a – farce outa this court," George Solway interrupted.

". . . The case of a dog in *Bodely versus Collins*, a cow in the – in *McConecky versus the Grand Trunk Railway*."

"It is customary for the court to adjourn to view the animal or vehicle in the case of an accident," Judge Wilson said. "In the interests of expediency I see no reason that the goat should not be brought to the court. It is mobile?"

"Extremely so," Chet said.

Chet, he must of had Malleable's goat tethered just outside. Didn't take him five minutes to get it inside. Door opened an' he backed in. Goat wasn't so fussy about getting mixed up in a court case – had his four feet braced against the pull of the rope. Just inside the doorway he quit hanging back, run forward, spilled Chet, and with the rope trailing, he leapt over a desk top, then headed down the aisle. Met Corporal MacBride. Dropped his head, bleated, and charged. Corporal kind of doubled forward with the goat's head in his stomach, his arms beatin' the air in front of him before he went down.

The goat cleared the corporal. He rose, kind of sailed lazy through the air, lit on the window shelf. No sooner lighted than he flew to the top of a cupboard behind the judge. Then he got right up on his hind feet, right on the tips his hoofs, lookin' over the court – real sad with that there roan goatee drooping, his wall-eyes wicked looking and mean.

"Let – let the livestock remain. Perhaps the Corporal would like to retire for a moment." That was Judge Wilson.

"Ugh-mmmh." That was MacBride. I think he meant "Yes – thank you, Judge."

"Defense continue, please."

"Thank you, milord. Now, I would like to point out that

this man is George Solway – this, up there, is the goat with which the comparison was made."

"Hey, what you . . . !"

"I point this out because of the striking similarity between the two. Perhaps I can help the court in distinguishing by pointing out that the goatee of the *goat* – like that of the complainant, red, or roanish in colour, straight, and of the same coarse tecture – is not set *quite* so far forward under the chin – the chin, that is, of the complainant, George Solway."

"IIIIIIIIIIII ooobject!"

The rest of us in that court didn't.

"Take the mouth," Chet went on, "of the goat. It curves up at the corners like that of an insensitively pious woman seated in church, or a gambler holding four aces at the poker table. Now, if you will look at the complainant – the same thin lips, the head held up and back as though Mr. Solway – and the goat – both smelled something not pleasant."

That one made the goat bleat.

"The eyes of the complainant have the same uneven pupil, and upon close examination prove to be almost colourless. The goat, too, is wall-eyed."

That one made George bleat.

"The goat – at the base of its one horn and the stump of the other – has a beetling conformation covered with ragged red hair which reminds one of the hair and brows of the complainant. Combined with the bland and colourless eyes, the goatee wagging in chewing movement, and the mouth, this bony structure over the brow completes a startling resemblance!"

Now the whole room was bleating, except for Judge Wilson. He was banging his gavel.

Corporal MacBride, who was coming back through the door, was just in time to yell, "Order!"

Folks toned down and Chet started up again.

"I admit that the complainant has not got horns. A horn.

The comparison drawn referred only to facial characteristics, but I maintain that there – that no man can claim that a false statement has been made."

"I object!" George yelled. "How long you gonna let him go . . . !"

Judge Wilson banged his gavel again. "Mr. Solway, I intend that in this action you have initiated, every latitude shall be given to opinion and prejudice. The question is whether a reasonable man, however prejudiced or however strong his opinion may be, could say that comparison of the plaintiff to this, uh . . ."

From up on top of the school supply cupboard the goat bleated again. Almost like he agreed with the Judge.

"The defendant is obviously relying on the truth of the comparison as an answer to the action."

"Thank you, milord," Chet said, "I plead that matter specifically. Not because it negatives the charge of libel but because it shows the plaintiff is not entitled to recover damages. If the statements complained of are true in fact, then I have made no false statement. That George Solway looks like a goat – is true. That the goat looks like him – is true. That he has always looked like that goat – is true. As sure as the truth is absolute defense in this civil action for damages – as sure as there are only four aces in an honest deck of cards – THAT MAN LOOKS EXACTLY LIKE THAT GOAT!"

"He sure as hell does!" Being at the back I couldn't see who it was, but it sounded like Old Man Gatenby.

"Escort that man from the court!"

Corporal MacBride headed for the windows with all the little chicks and crocuses and tiger lilies pasted on them. I'd been wrong. It was Hig Wheeler runs the lumberyard the Corporal was escorting.

She was all over. I don't think anybody in that schoolroom was surprised when Judge Wilson come down with his decision.

"I'll make it short. The defendant has relied on the truth of comparison as an answer to the action. I find for the defendant. Dismiss the plaintiff's claim for damages—with costs—to the plaintiff."

He banged his gavel. "This court is adjourned. Mr. Brown."

In the front row Malleable stood up. "Yes, Your Worship."

"I would like you to escort your goat out of this courtroom."

"Yes, Your Worship," Malleable said.

"With all expedience unless you wish to appear before me at the next session, on charges of trespass."

I ain't had all that much to do with lawyers and judges any more than I could help, but I guess they like to think they're the real witty profession.

Week or so later on, I told the Kid's ma all about the case. She hadn't been able to go, because that afternoon she had a meeting of the Atheniums Flower and Vegetable Gardening, Book and Discussion Club. She said, "I feel a little sorry for George Solway."

"He brought it all onto himself."

"Perhaps—you may be right—taught him a lesson."

"Nope."

"What?"

"*Nor'west Prairie Farm Review, Regina-Leader Post*, Saskatoon *Star-Phoenix*."

"What about them?"

"Talk around town—they covered the story. He's suin' them."

"No!"

"Once he gets the bit in his teeth, it's pretty hard to pull up on a prairie lawyer."

POLITICAL DYNAMITE

I seen good times and i seen bad. i seen flood – i seen drought. Now she's one way – now she's another. But there's one thing a fellow knows ain't going to change out here in the West. Governments can come and go – folks can leave the farm and head for the city – but there'll always be curling.

All kind of different curlers. I seen what you might call social curlers – game now and again, take her or leave her. Then there's your binge curler – leave her alone all through December and into January, promisin' his wife he'll get the stuff done around the house, eyeing his broom now and again. Then about the middle of the month away he goes. Morning, noon, and night. Going without meals – all out for a month. Gets it out of his system, tapers off, and by April when the gophers is running over the prairie sod and the crocuses is out, he's all right for another eight months.

Then I seen the chronic curlers. Only one cure for them. Take them clear outa the country – south, where there ain't any ice nor brooms nor rocks. I'd say round our district ninety percent of our curlers is *chronic* curlers. Mac MacTaggart of MacTaggart's store, and Old Man MacLachlan, they're the worst of the worst. Mac takes her real serious – curling.

"I been in the political life now almost thirty years – counting the school board."

"That's nice, Mac."

"And it's funny how things go. No reason at all the machine

will hum along smooth – not a miss in it. Then it turns personal, and when it does, there is where your trouble comes in. Closer you are to the voter, more personal it gets, and the stickier it is."

"Not much different from runnin' a business is it, Mac? Or on a farm. Just going' to council meetings once in a while."

"Twenty-four-hour job, Jake. Takes up more time and energy than this store of mine."

"Well, Mac, it can't be hurting *too* bad or you'd 've dropped her by . . ."

"Council's big business, Jake. We got a pay-roll twice the size of the creamery. Same for the fire department. Why, in the street sprinkler and the road grader we got five times what the average farmer's got invested in machinery. Weighty responsibility – things to decide. Try to do the right thing. Takes a lot of judgement. Careful judgement."

"I guess she does, Mac."

"I can't take all the credit. I got a good council. Pipe-fitting Brown, Malleable Brown, Cross-Cut Brown – I can depend on them when something serious comes up – money by-law, water, uh, sewerage, roads, school . . . ."

"Well, Mac, I'm glad to hear she's hummin' right along fine."

"She isn't."

"Uh?"

"Active."

"That's good, ain't it?"

"Atheniums Book Club meeting at Elsie Abercrombie's last week. Four nights . . ."

"Yeah I know, Kid's ma, she . . ."

"Running."

"How's that, Mac?"

"Heralds. Storms do not blow up without warning. When did the Burning Bush Booth Knox Presbyterian Church have three meetings in one week? Before?"

"Search me," I said.

"Years ago when the Provincial Government was considering beer by the glass. Where there's smoke there's fire."

"Like the kiyoot said when he pissed on the snow."

"Being mayor of Crocus would be a nice clean job – if it wasn't for the women."

"They're human. They're human," I said.

"Four meetings of the South Crocus Homemakers!"

"Oh."

"IODE."

"What about it?" I said. Kid's ma belongs to that one too.

"I happen to know now what these meetings are about."

"What?"

"Curling."

"Mac, now hold on. That's ridiculous. Curlin'? Why, ah, curlin' ain't their – they got no . . ."

"There is a movement on foot – agitation – powerful agitation by certain factions in this town in re curling."

"Who? What?"

"Female factions – every single one of them," he said.

"But I don't see how they can – I mean, a woman curlin' is a sort of a onnatural thing," I said.

"Just what I been telling Hattie now for over twenty years. 'A woman is a graceful thing, Hattie.' I've told her, 'Certain sports and games are for women – certain one *aren't*.' "

"Yeah – yeah."

"Intrinsic in the – the – I mean – now nobody thinks anything of a woman playing bridge or golf or tennis."

"Nope."

"Riding."

"Sidesaddle," I said. I didn't really mean that. Kid's ma ain't too bad forking a saddle.

"Lot of things don't detract one single bit from the natural grace of a woman. Natural for a woman to do. She can play bingo, whist – I've told Hattie that. Smoking – I don't mind seeing a woman smoke. Was a time when I *did*, but they're all doing it now. Cigarette in a woman's mouth looks quite natural to me now. Hattie and all those other women at the Athenians Club – they all smoke, Jake."

"Not the Kid's ma. She don't."

"Just one exception. I've said to Hattie a hundred times, 'You've got to face up to it – can't go hog wild over this thing. Got to be reasonable about it. Don't let this new emancipation go to your head. You women are all emancipated. . . .' "

"NO!" That was a real shocker to me. "Did Doc Fotheringham . . ."

"There simply have to be sensible and reasonable limits to it: cigarettes, yes; pipe, no . . ."

"Chewin' tobacco . . ."

"No! Bridge, whist, yes!"

Till Mac brought that up, I'd never give it much thought. He was dead right. "Stud, Five Card Draw, Spit-in-the-Ocean, Deuces Wild . . ."

"Certain pastimes are *un*womanly. Goose hunting . . ."

"No argument with you there, Mac."

"I like curling as much as anybody." Mac said, "But I'm the first to admit that a man sliding sideways down the ice, sweeping that broom ahead of a fast rock – is a – it's a comical and a ridiculous-looking sight."

"Maybe."

"But a woman – in pants, or slacks – or a woman with her – with – all hunched up with her – when she's leaning into the broom and her head pointing south and her, uh, rest of her bobbing north . . ."

"That's right, Mac."

"I'm surprised the women of our community – good women, mothers of families – I'm surprised they can't see the inherent – the – Jake, curling is *not* for the female sex!"

"That's right, Mac."

"I think the Crocus Caledonian Society of Knock-Out Curlers has been more than generous in their attitude towards the women of the greater Crocus district in permitting them to curl – as they have – unselfishly giving over to them the two afternoons a week they have, uh, given them. Turning over the entire rink for the use of wives and sweethearts and daughters for their own bonspiel during the first week of April! More than generous! And now, in thanks and appreciation, the Athenians, Burning Bush, IODE are mounting a formal petition."

"What kind of pet . . . ?"

"Political dynamite!"

"Yeah, but what's the pet . . ."

"Council can't tell precisely. We've wondered about it. We've discussed it. Pushed aside everything else: wing on the school, new garbage dump, snow removal . . ."

"All on account of them women's pet . . . ?"

"That's right. There's a municipal election coming up and the deciding factor is going to be the women's vote."

"That so."

"The female block. They all curl now, so it's the female curling block. Dilemma!"

"Come again, Mac?"

"What they call a political dilemma, Jake. Like when a fellow's caught on both horns of a steer. Either one of them's going to hurt just as bad if it punctures you."

"I guess she would."

"Jake, I have had a bellyful of Crocus womanhood!"

I still didn't know what that goddam petition was about. Sure had Mac worried. I felt kind of sorry for him. He gets jittery pretty easy. Always worrying about something, and he could've been building the thing up a lot more than he should've. One place I knew where I could sure find out. Repeat Golightly's barbershop.

"Heard a lot of talk around the shop. Lot of talk. Snippets. Bits here and bits there. Snippets. Mind you, it doesn't go out of this shop."

"The aitch it don't."

"Stops right at that door. Threshold. I say it's confidential. Not like over at Chez Sadie's where the women get their marcels."

"What do you hear lately, Repeat?"

"Just bits. Here and there. Just a little to the right, Jake. Hair to the right."

"Mmmh."

"Snippets."

"This talk going around, Repeat – any of it about the council? Comin' 'lection?"

"Always political talk, Jake. My shop's a public forum when it comes to political talk."

"Ah-hah. And what's the talk in this public form of yours?"

"Curling."

I already knew *that*. Even though he said council wasn't certain, Mac had mentioned curling quite a bit while he wasn't telling me what that petition was about.

"What *about* curlin', Repeat?"

"Without representation," he said.

"Come on! I asked you what about curlin'?"

"Bulwark of our democracy."

"Maybe it is!"

"Our forefathers fought for it. Both sides the Forty-ninth. Voice in the administration – democratic right. Womanhood Crocus want it. Their slogan – 'No Curling Without Representation!' "

"I don't get it."

"On the curling-rink board," he said.

"No!"

"Proportional representation."

So that was why MacTaggart and his council was worried. Election coming up – women's vote.

"Women curlers pretty near equal the men nowadays," Repeat was saying. "On a board of six they figure they should have three members."

"You're kiddin'!"

"No. And I have to admit, it does make sense, Jake. Seems to make . . ."

"Repeat, tell me somethin' . . ."

"Yes, Jake?"

"You – you ever curl at all?"

"Time or two, Jake, just a time or two. Never could see it – not my dish, Jake."

"I thought so."

No wonder Mayor MacTaggart and his council was worried. If that petition of those women ended up in a plebishit and the women won it, they'd lose all the male curling vote. If it got defeated, they'd lose all of the female votes. Some steer! Some horns!

I had to drop by Malleable Brown's and pick up a set of shoes for Queenie and Baldy. I always trim and nail them on myself. Generally closer on to spring seeding, but Malleable's on town council, and I wanted to know more about what the Crocus women was up to.

CLANG – CLANG – DUH-DUH – CLANG – CLANG!

"Malleable."

"Jake."

"Nice curlin' weather," I said.

"Yep."

SSSSSSSSSSH-SISSSSSSSSS – SUSPIT!

"*Real* nice curlin' weather, Malleable."

"Fast ice," he said. "Nice."

"Hear you fellows took Doc Fotherin'ham last night."

"Yep. Sweeter'n income-tax rebate."

"Malleable, I just heard over at Mac's an' then at Re-peat's . . ."

"Down to the last rock. Doc had the hammer but he hogged the rock. Ours went straight an' true as a revival-meetin' fart through a brass curtain rod." He sighed. "Got a chew? I'm out."

I give him one.

"Tell me, Malleable. What's all this talk goin' round – women curlers trying to grab the hammer?"

"That's right, Jake."

"Wanta be on the board."

"Uh-huh." He spit.

"Accordin' to Mac and to Repeat, you've got political com-plications. Election comin' up soon."

"Not for me there ain't. Politics, political fame – aaah! She comes to a sacrifice between a man's curlin' an' his political life – curlin', that's for the men, Jake. *Politics*, that's for the boys. Votes of women curlers for councillors or no votes of women curlers, far as I'm concerned the board of the Crocus Caledonian Society Knock-Out Curlers remains as she's been since her foundation in nineteen-six – plumb male!"

As soon as I got home, I took it up with the Kid's ma. She's charter member all four of them women's clubs: Atheniums, Burning Bush, IODE, South Crocus Homemakers. I figured she'd have an opinion about it. She did. Strong one.

"I don't curl myself," she said. "Don't suppose I ever will. I find it boring."

"That's nice," I said.

"But I know exactly how those other women feel about it. The principle involved is just as important to me as though I curled myself."

"Ah-hah."

"This has been a man's world for a long time. This – this question of women being represented on the curling board is

256

a minor thing, in a way – but the principle is not minor. Those men intend to remedy the matter, of course."

"Well, they . . ."

"They'll have to!" she said.

"Oh, I don't know as they'll *have* to."

"Yes!"

"Depends on how a person looks at it."

"No."

"You, uh, you girls figure you, uh, got her all figured out, do you?"

"We have," she said.

"Got the council in the spot where they – where they're, uh, they're in a die – lem-nah?"

"The council and the curling board are faced simply with a question of what's right and what's wrong. When half the Crocus curlers are women, and those women have not one representative on that board, that is wrong."

"The board's been doin' a good job of runnin' the . . ."

"I didn't say they hadn't," she said.

"All right then, why do the women got to . . . ?"

"Doesn't change it. In the slightest."

"But it *does*!" I said.

"No! If the men were running the affairs of the curling club in the finest way it – as wonderfully as it – it still wouldn't right the undemocratic wrong."

"Look, I'm talkin' about curlin' – not electin' a new prime minister! Men got the right to run their curlin' the way they . . ."

"They have not! If they think they have, they're wrong!"

"*Your* opinion. What I say is some things is for women to do, and some things is for men to do, and . . ."

"Cream can's full."

". . . women don't play poker and they don't chew and they don't stand up to . . ."

"And *this* time I am coming into town with you!"

"You don't hafta . . ."

"Oh, yes I do!"

"What the aitch for?"

I really didn't have to ask her that.

Once she was in there she'd be plotting with them other women how to sweep to victory in *this* political bonspiel. I dropped in to see how Mac was doing. He was looking pretty glum.

"You know, Jake, it isn't just a matter of the curling board, or the coming election. It goes much deeper than that. It's a changing world, Jake."

"Yeah," I said. "I noticed that."

He shook his head kind of sad. "Battle of the sexes. It has heated up terribly. Not just the cities now."

"Uh-huh."

"Women into bars – wrestling matches – they play baseball. Hockey's next. Look at Ottawa. They've been creeping into politics for years! Just a matter of time."

"For what?"

"Woman prime minister. President United States." He shook his head again. "Then there's that American fellow – soldier, a while back. Changed his – mind."

"What about?"

"Went to Denmark. Changed his sex. Hers."

"Whaaaat!"

"Don't you read the papers – listen to the CBC?"

"Why, sure, but I didn't – I must've missed . . ."

"Blonde."

"Was he?"

"*She*. Now. Science. Seems it can do anything these days, Jake."

"If it can switch a person's priva . . ."

"*Except* – teach a *woman* – how to run a goddam curling club!"

Kid's ma didn't come back out to the farm with me, said she was bunking in with Elsie Abercrombie, didn't know for how long. Said she was sure I could dust and mop and crank the cream separator and cook and wash and dry dishes and do laundry and change sheets and clean lamp chimmeys till after they'd gone to the people to get a democratic fee-at. That American solder made a bad decision when he went to Denmark for that operation of his! Hers!

Those women had a real head of steam up. Public meetings every night. Big turn-outs. You'd think it was a federal election. I took in the South Crocus Homemakers' one. Packed to the ceiling the credit union hall. Both sexes.

"Herschel contributed one hundred and fifty dollars to that curling rink!" That was Ruth Tait. "It was a bad crop year and I had that egg-and-cream hundred-and-fifty dollars earmarked for a new Pride of the Prairies kitchen range! I didn't get it! I am *still* cooking on the same old stove I cooked on for twenty-five years. If I can't have the – if I have anything to say about it I'm going to have some voice in the running of the rink I helped pay for – with my Pride of the Prairies kitchen range I did not get."

Then it was Merna Plunket's turn:

"Who says it's a man's sport!? Seems to me I seen brooms bein' used in any curlin' game I've ever saw. An' I guess I been sweepin' with a broom for men for goin' on thirty years of my life now. Curlin's the first time I ever had a broom in my hand an' swep' my gizzard out an' got fun outa doin' it! I wanta see women on that curlin' board! Gaw-dammit! I'm gonna!"

Even in church, Merna wears overalls. I heard tell she chews now and again, but I always figured that was just idle humour. When I heard her using language in public like that, I wasn't so sure anymore.

Hattie MacTaggart – looked like she was the skip of the whole meeting. She spoke last:

"My husband keeps telling me that curling's a *man's* game. But I curled before I ever met him or married him and I intend to go right on curling for a long time after–I intend to go right on curling! And I don't mean just on those days when it suits the men to let us have the rink for curling. I'm sick and I'm tired of curling on sloppy slow ice–puddles! As long as I can remember we've had to hold our women's bonspiel in early spring when the *weather* won't hold. *They* use that rink for themselves all during the best part of the year, then throw it over to us when it suits them, and there isn't much curling ice left!"

•§ §•

Wasn't no draw–only a few fellows put a foot in the hack. They hogged every rock. Wipe-out. I don't know whether any of the Crocus municipal budget was used to do it, but they brought in Fergus MacGillvray. All the way from Aberdeen, Scotland. Regina *Leader-Post* and the *Moose Jaw Herald* and the *Nor'west Prairie Farm Review* wrote up *that* meeting. He was a redheaded fellow:

"As travelling secretary of the International Caledonian Society of Knock-Out Curlers–of which univairsal organization ye are a local chapter–I have made this special trip. The eyes of the world are on your sma' toon today. And I may say that we wait with one foot in the hack, ready to support your fight to the last rock.

"There shall be no petticoat rule of any chapter of our great organization! I must speak frankly to you. The parlous state you have now reached here could never have happened in the Old Country. Had you been wary and careful you would have seen this thing at its very first beginning–when the first woman curled a rock down the ice.

"We must keep the game clean and shining–the game that was perhaps Scotland's greatest gift to the rest of the world.

A gift from the same people who generously gave you out of their culture the bagpipes, haggis, oatmeal, free trade, the steam engine, the bicycle, the Bank of England."

They give him a standing ovation. The *men*. I fought in two wars: the Boor one and the Great one. Too old for the last one, where the Kid's dad got it. I was only twelve when Looie Riel come up from Montana to–but I was with General Middleton at the seige of Batoche, and I hauled up hard tack and chewing tobacco for these fellows in them pits on their stomachs.

This was civil war, too. Worst kind. Husband against wife. Brother against sister. She cut across all party lines: Liberal against Liberal, CCF in the same stall with Conservatives. When you got that, you're just down the road from anarchery!

I don't know how many folks signed the petition. Must've been a lot because the women was out on the street every day for over a week getting signatures. But they didn't present it to Mac and his councillors right away. They waited another week till the Crocus Annual Ratepayers Meeting, then they all met at Elsie Abercrombie's house and struck out in a body–on foot, wearing tams, with their brooms up an' over their shoulders. They marched right down Main Street, past Chez Sadie's Beauty Box, Royal Hotel, Dingle's Funeral Parlour, MacTaggart's Trading Company Store–to the council chambers over the town firehall.

For years now, ever since he took over as mayor, Mac's been complaining how only a handful of Crocus citizens ever show up to exercise their democratic privilege of attending the annual ratepayers meeting. He didn't have to worry about that this time.

They filled the council chambers, spilled out into the hallway. It was Hattie, Mac's own wife, at the head of the parade.

"As spokeswoman for the *feminine* members of the Crocus

Chapter of the Caledonian Society of Knock-Out Curlers, we present a petition that there shall cease to be – in our community – curling without representation . . ."

She had to quit till the cheering died down.

". . . that this unjust, inequitable, undemocratic, intolerable state shall *not* persist! That it shall be put to a plebiscite vote to determine whether or not the majority favour that . . ."

They wiped her out again.

". . . three of the six members of the board shall be women!"

And again!

". . . with us tonight marches the spirit of those women who marched with their men in the French Revolution – the spirit of Laura Secord when she drove her cow through the Revolutionist lines – the spirit of all those who took up the fight for feminine suffrage and marched with Mrs. Emmeline Pankhurst!"

Whoever the aitch *she* was.

Mac and his councillors just sat there and looked helpless at all them women clapping and cheering, then Mac leaned forward and he rapped with his gavel. "Now – if . . ."

He banged again. "Ladies, ladies – may we have . . ."

This time the handle on that gavel snapped off, but they did shut up for him.

"I shall now invite each member of Crocus town council to reply to this petition. Mr. Jack Brown, blacksmith?"

"I resign."

"Mr. Jack Brown, plumber?"

"I resign."

"Mr. Jack Brown, carpenter?"

"I resign."

"Mr. Title, ah, Mr. Jack Brown, lawyer?"

"I resign."

"Mr. Jack Brown, CNR Station Agent?"

"I resign."

"Dr. Fotheringham?"

"I resign."

"As mayor of Crocus, I resign."

One slice: no mayor – no council – no curling board. Mac, he's mayor now, after the snap election he called. Malleable didn't run again. Isn't going to be any new two-way bridge built over the Brokenshell River this spring, though, or a few more springs down the road. I guess nowheres in the West you can find a town the size of Crocus that's got *two* curling rinks: the old one – that's the Crocus Caledonian Society of Knock-Out Curlers – an' the brand new one over behind Chez Sadie's Beauty Box. That's the one that's got an all-female executive board. Feminine Auxiliary the Crocus Caledonian Society of Knock-Out Curlers.

Don't build yourself a eight-sheet curling rink for nickels these days. But she'd be awful good insurance at double the price!

THE YOUNG AND THE OLD OF IT

Not much happens around Crocus where we live; we don't get earthquakes or murderers or the like of that. Once there was a two-headed calf born out at Magnus Petersen's that farms down Government Road from us, but that kind of stuff doesn't get a town spread all over Regina and Winnipeg and Toronto papers. It doesn't put you clear across the country on the CBC, and it doesn't make people in England sit up and take notice while they're listening to *their* radios.

Except for Brokenshell River and maybe a couple extra grain elevators Crocus isn't any different from Tiger Lily down the line or Conception or Broomhead, so a person gets to taking her natural – like breathing. You would, too, until the morning you're listening to your radio kind of husky and hoarse and all wavy the way it is coming across the ocean from the Old Country. You'd be listening to the bagpipes and the bands and all those people yelling – even the ones that got titles – and Her getting Her crown and Him beside Her and everybody swallowing and blinking the way Jake was doing because you don't pick up a new Queen for an Empire every day of the week. Then bang. You wouldn't take her natural any more after what happened. Not after Crocus was on the map – the world map – not after Crocus, Saskatchewan, was on the whole world wide map with a bang!

On the Royal Bank corner, in MacTaggart's Trading Company and the Maple Leaf Beer Parlour, most of the Crocus district people talk about crops. Not last summer. They even forgot to squint up to the sky for hail clouds every once in a while, the way they do in August. When she was an open fall and the combines were rolling, you'd hear them in Repeat Golightly's barbershop, wondering where the aitch the CNR were going to get more boxcars for grain. In Malleable Brown's blacksmith shop, Chez Sadie's Beauty Box, it was hoof-and-mouth and when were the northern geese coming down. They talked about that kind of stuff all right, but they always came back to the same thing – the *real* important thing. The coronation!

Like when the straw stacks were burning and we were stacking green feed and it was one of those yellow days you get on prairie at harvest time. Mr. Gatenby was helping us, and Stevie Kiziw and Old Steve. Ma brought us out lunch and a pitcher of lemonade and we were sitting in the stubble alongside Steve's loaded rack. Mr. Kiziw has a very wide moustache, spikey if it isn't raining. At first it makes him very fierce looking, but he has a deep gentle voice and laughs a lot and there is this look in his eyes. Even when he is laughing it is like his eyes are asking you a question. When he talks it is like a horse backing out of a stall and then turning around.

Old Steve had just taken a drink of lemonade and he wiped his moustache with the back of his hand. "Over there," he said, "next spring she'll be hummin', eh?"

"Where?" That was Old Man Gatenby. He puts you in mind of a banty rooster. Little, always on the fight – talks sort of suspicious like he expects an argument all the time.

"Anglich," said Mr. Kiziw. "Dukes and Dukesses – that Anglich party for the queen."

"Oh," said Old Man Gatenby. "Yeah – coronation."

"That's right," said Jake. "Gettin' their crowns all polished up – buffin' 'em, shinin' 'em. Hear they're addin' a new wing onto the Abbey. Weasel pelts."

"What's that got to do with the coronation, Jake?" I said.

Jake turned to Stevie. "You runnin' your trapline again this winter, Stevie?"

"Uh-huh."

"I seen weasel pelts sell as low as ten cents a hide." Jake bit into his ham sandwich. "They'll go high this year – higher'n a cat's back. You watch. Better hope the weasels is runnin' good this year. Wouldn't be surprised to see 'em hit seven dollars a hide. Coronation year. Snow white – them black tips to their tails. Ermine. Yes, sir, when they strike up 'God Save the Queen' over there next spring, they'll all be decked out in prime ermine weasel pelts in Westminister Abbey at seven dollars a hide. Guess we better roll, boys. She's nighttime in the swamp an' we got half a stack to do before the end of the day."

Now there's not many people would think of that, like Jake did. Jake, he's smart, and that's something you're born with; it doesn't rub off on you as you go along.

By the time curling season rolled round, like Mr. Kiziw said, she was really humming over there – in Crocus too. Mrs. Allerdyce bought the first ticket to go, then Mr. and Mrs. Abercrombie, then the Shackertons. Mayor MacTaggart and the town council sent coronation year greetings over to the mayor and town council of Crocus, Sussex, our sister town in England. Louie Riel Chapter IODE took their Preservation Shrines in Defense of British Unity Fund, turning it over lock, stock and peep sights to the town council to use the best way they saw fit to help the coronation along.

Along about the middle of February Jake and I took the cream can into town, dropped in on Way-freight Brown, who runs the depot for the CNR in Crocus. Mr. Brown looked up with the green eye-shade on and the telegraph going ticky-tick – ticky-tick.

"Banner year," Way-freight said. "She's shapin' up for a banner year for this railroad right now."

"Freight rates goin' up again, Way-freight?" Jake said.

"No."

"Outa the red are you?"

"Oh, we been out of the red for number of years now, Jake. No – coronation year, Jake. This railroad from Atlantic to Pacific piercing our wild land of rocks an' rills, evergreens an' lakes an' rushin' rivers . . ."

"Yeah, yeah, Way-freight . . ."

". . . with its terminal at the Great Lakes. Life line to the mighty industries – minin' pulp an' paper, gold an' copper, coal. Girdlin' the continent by rail an' the world by water an' stratosphere – gonna carry a new an' greater cargo to the Old Land. First an' second an' third class they'll go to the Old Land – visitin' friends an' relatives on the other side – watchin' the breath-takin' splendour an' pomp an' awe of the coronation . . ."

"That's nice," Jake said when Mr. Brown stopped for a breath.

"Plan now to make your dream come true, Jake."

"Huh!"

"Make your reservation now."

"Hell, I ain't intendin' . . ."

"They're all goin' over – Mrs. Beeton-Cross, Allerdyces – bedroom – compartment – stateroom. Fly high above the blue Atlantic with comfort to keynote your transatlantic flight."

"Not today, Way-freight."

"World beneath your feet with hot full-course meals, bar service, champagne suppers, foam rubber seats soft as a royal bed . . ."

"Way-freight – that's a little outa my line . . ."

"Everybody's goin', Jake. It's an exodus."

"Yeah," Jake said. "I guess it will. But I don't think you'll be makin' out schedules for an aitch of a lot of hired men. You know, Way-freight, lookin' over the list of folks takin' off from Crocus district, I'm a little worried."

"How's that?"

"Look at 'em – wrong folks goin'. Over there in England they're gonna get the wrong idea about us."

"I don't see that, Jake."

"Yep. She's the crust, you might say. Ones that's got wheat in the bin."

"Nothing wrong with that," said Way-freight. "Like we're puttin' our best foot forward."

"That's right," Jake said.

"Well?"

"They need to sort of lighten her up. Tone down all that purple blood of the Allerdyces an' the Abercrombies an' the Shackertons an' the Clifton-Wells's, I'd say. They oughta have a handful of section hands – sprinklin' of hired girls – maybe Malleable Brown outa his blacksmith shop, an' Pipe-fittin' Brown, an' Aunt Lil." Jake turned away from Way-freight's wicket. "Some of those folks goin' over to the coronation, I'd say Crocus'd be real well, ah, represented."

We dropped into MacTaggart's Trading Company, and after Jake gave Mac our grocery order, he told us what the council was doing for the coronation.

"Council's matching Looie Riel chapter dollar for dollar, Jake. Last meeting we figured out fine way to use the money – at least the Committee did."

"What Committee?" Jake said.

"Special Coronation Committee under Repeat Golightly – Committee for Ways and Means Stimulating and Expressing Sentiment of Patriotism Binding Men, Women, and Children Round the Throne and Empire. Same Committee gave the pictures to district schools last year."

Mr. MacTaggart was talking about the ones we got out at Rabbit Hill school: "Canada's Answer to the Mother Country". Right at the front we got the one where these soldiers got blood-stained bandages around their heads and their hats over top and there's this wounded horse lying on his side.

That one's called: "Somewhere With a Veterinary Unit in France". Horse looks like he's got the bloat. Then all around the room there's pictures of Kitchener of Khartoum and Clive of India and Louis St. Laurent of Canada.

". . . decided last meeting," Mayor MacTaggart was saying. "Use that money to send some deserving person over to the coronation."

"That's real nice," Jake said.

"Of course we haven't got all the wrinkles ironed out of it yet, but that's what the council's doing. All the way to England – all expenses – with the finest available seat . . ."

"Seat!"

"Bought and paid for. Right on the royal procession route." Mr. MacTaggart put both his hands on the counter and leaned over to Jake. "That item alone, Jake, is going to cost us – one – hundred – dollars!"

Repeat Golightly's shop is right next to Barney's Vulcanizing, and on the other side you got Len's Harness. Jake headed for there, and I had my haircut first while Jake sat in one of the chairs along the wall. Repeat started right in before he even pumped me up.

"Too hot for us to handle, Jake," he said. "Person takes a clear cool look at it, he realizes that – just hold her there, Kid – too hot to handle, told 'em when the matter first came up."

"How's that, Repeat?" I could see Jake getting out a plug. In the mirror where Repeat has all his bottles hair tonic and instrument shelf, the clock over Jake's head had all her numbers backwards.

Repeat started up the clippers. "Too hot to handle. Can't send everybody – everybody wants to go over to the coronation. Whoever you pick there's going to be a hundred – be a thousand people – every soul in Crocus district didn't make it. Bad feelings."

"Uh-huh." Jake was chewing and staring down at the tufts of hair all over the floor; every once in a while they'd lift and sort of breathe along then settle down again.

"My committee got the idea," Repeat said. "Our idea in the first place. Good idea. Had a meeting at my place last night. Tilt her a little to the south, Kid. First we thought might be a good idea to send a dignitary – official. Somebody elected by the town – people. Elected representative."

"Ah-hah."

Repeat turned off the clippers. He went to the shelf and stood there a minute with the comb and scissors. "Member of council – mayor maybe."

"Might be all right," Jake said.

"We thought so – we thought so." Repeat lifted his elbows, snipped a couple of times at the air with the scissors, blew on the comb, then he lowered his knees and started on the back of my neck. "Couldn't agree – which one? Human nature. I say human nature reared her ugly head. Exception me and Mert Abercrombie, they all wanted to be the delegate – coronation delegate."

"How come you two . . . ?" Jake started.

"Can't get away, Jake. Couldn't leave the shop that long. And Mert – he an' Mrs. Abercrombie already made their arrangements, they're already going."

"I see." Jake spit.

"Spittoon right by your left heel, Jake." Repeat spun the chair around and looked at the mirror a minute. "We got her licked – we think."

"That's nice."

"We think it'll work out better than we figured. Hold a draw. Going to hold a draw. Then nobody can kick. Lucky person goes. Nobody's feelings are hurt. Sell tickets."

"Wait a minute." Jake sat up. "You said you already got the money for the . . ."

"Folks expect to pay for draw tickets, Jake. No reason we shouldn't charge for them. Raise more money. Good cause."

"You mean the coronation trip . . ."

"Oh, we got another cause as well – another cause." Repeat cleared his throat. "Need a new roof on the curling rink."

"Well." Jake said it that surprised way a person has when he finds a dime on the street when he's walking along not even looking for a dime. "That ought to tickle the curlers . . ." He leaned forward to spit.

"Right by your heel, Jake."

Jake settled back without spitting. "All you fellows curl on the council, don't you?"

Repeat whipped the cloth from around my neck, brushed off my shoulders. "That's right, Jake. That's right. But, ah, there – couldn't say there was any selfish undercurrents – none of that. Self-interest played no part in our decision. New roof on the curling rink. Good cause. Whole town uses the curling rink – Rotarians hold their carnival there every year. Women's Atheniums hold their flower show. Sort of a community centre."

Jake got up and reached in his pocket for the price of my haircut. "I don't know, Repeat. Don't seem right."

"How's that, Jake? How's that?"

"Lot of folks get to talkin'. I can just hear 'em. Wrong for the finger chance to pick the person have the honour goin' over to the coronation."

"Maybe. That may be. Lesser of two evils. Only fair way, Jake. Justice is blind. She's blind."

"Is she?" said Jake.

"And that's the way she's going to be," Repeat said real firm. "Two dollars seventy-five cents."

"Hey wait a minute – the Kid's haircut . . ."

"That's right – seventy-five cents and . . ." Repeat held out two tickets. "Got them printed this morning at the *Crocus*

Breeze office. One for you and one for the Kid's ma. Royal draw tickets. Dollar each. Cost a dollar apiece. Going like hotcakes, Jake. Two dollars and seventy-five, unless you want one for the Kid here as well – *three* dollars an' seventy-five cents."

Jake looked down at me. "Better make it the three, Repeat."

When the summer fallow starts to steam and they find the first gopher of spring or the first crocus or a butterfly out on Gladys Ridge, a funny thing happens to folks. Like a fever – seeding fever. Jake says it's the same thing hits them at an auction so they buy table lamps for their parlour before they stop to figure they haven't got the power line in. This year a sort of double fever hit Crocus folks from two sides at once; spring seeding and the Royal Coronation Trip Draw.

They sold out the first printing of tickets within a week. End of the next week they had enough money to build the curling-rink roof. Mr. MacTaggart sold three hundred by himself to grocery and hardware and dry-goods travellers coming through. *Crocus Breeze* couldn't print them fast enough so there'd be a supply handy at the cash register of the Sanitary Café or the General Delivery wicket at the post office, let alone to send out to Macoun and Tiger Lily and Conception where they were yelling for them. Everybody wanted them.

Take Old Man Sherry that lives with Mrs. Southey. Every Saturday he puts a shawl over his shoulders, takes his cane and goes downtown with careful slow steps. He always get a shave from Repeat. That was where he bought his first ticket, and afterwards Repeat said he didn't know whether he ought to have sold the old man a ticket, him being so old and shaky he'd never be able to make it to the coronation if he did win. Old Man Sherry's stubborn, and he heard about the draw. Repeat said it was one of his good days. He has his good days and he has his bad days – clear as a bell Monday, and Tuesday he's way back in the Fenian raids or marching with Middleton to the Riel Rebellion. If a person could get himself inside Old Man Sherry's hide and head I guess it would be like on the prairie when the sky is clouded and melting shadows over the grass – light, then dark, then light again.

He bought another one in the Sanitary Café when he picked up his House of Sentate cigar he smokes every Saturday, and Taffy sold him another when he dangled over to the Maple Leaf Beer Parlour.

But it was Stevie Kiziw really went overboard. He ran his trapline all right that winter – never missed an after-four, and the weasels were running good. Two, the Saturday I went out with him, and he got a badger and a skunk and one of Tinchers' chickens. I asked him what he was going to do with all his money, and he just looked at me and he slipped off his mitt and reached into his pocket, and then he reached into his other pocket. When Stevie wants something, he really goes after it.

"I didn't buy 'em all in one batch," he said.

"Gee, Stevie. How many you . . ."

"Eighty-nine so far. They're all spread out – every other day." He stuck them back in his pocket. "All my hide money's gone into tickets." He snuffed and he leaned down and he picked up the weasels by their tails and the badger he'd just taken out of the trap. " 'Nother month yet an' when the trapline isn't payin' off I'm selling my .22 to Willis – I figger I'll have nearly two hundred."

After that I didn't even bother to take out the ticket Jake bought me – wasn't much point in looking at it when Stevie had two hundred of them! She'd have to be a miracle for them to draw my ticket, and she'd have to be another miracle if they didn't pick one of Stevie's two hundred.

I figure it was smart of them to hold the draw the twenty-fourth of May and patriotic the way it's Queen Victoria's birthday. Getting a lump in your throat is patriotic and that happened to me four times, first when the Crocus Millionaires beat the Conception Beavers, then when they played "The Maple Leaf Forever" and later on during the harness races with those drivers' silks brighter than poppies and them holding their heads sideways out of the way of the horses' tails and *their* feet flipping out fancy and delicate and prancy and tilting while they rounded the corners. Jake says horse racing is the royal sport and all the royalty go in for it – only not harness-racing so much as staple-chasing.

But the main thing was the draw just before dark and the fireworks. Mayor MacTaggart got up on the platform and grabbed the microphone they had for speaking over. He said a lot of folks didn't approve of drawing for the coronation because it was gambling, but he said it was the only democratic way and fair way to do it, and the Queen wouldn't mind, seeing she ran horses herself. He said the coronation was a solemn spectacle and they would be putting the crown on a queen and a thousand years of history. He said they would crown triumphs and defeats on that June day.

He ended up. "She's a human same as anybody else but she's something else besides. She's a symbol – a living symbol joining all the future of the British Empire with its history. When they crown her it'll be the self-same way they crowned kings and queens ever since there's been kings and queens. That coronation hasn't been changed one iota in a thousand years just so's it can remind us of our hopes and prides and our ideals we had in common for a thousand years and are going to for another thousand years!"

Me, I was watching the sun setting over towards Hig Wheeler's lumberyard and just touching the top of the grain elevators beyond. What Mr. MacTaggart was saying made a person feel real noble; I felt so noble all I wanted was for Stevie to win that draw and not me, because I knew right then Stevie Kiziw didn't have to have Mr. MacTaggart tell him what a coronation meant. He knew when he put all his hide money into draw tickets!

"The fireworks display you are about to see – after the draw – has been paid for by part of the money as well. And after you have seen them I think you'll agree with me they're the finest outside maybe what you'd see at the Toronto Exhibition."

He turned away towards this big drum they had all decorated with tissue paper. Elsie Abercrombie was standing there all dressed in red, white, and blue, and after Mr. MacTaggart turned the drum like you would a butter-churn, she stuck in her arm and she pulled out a ticket. Mr. MacTaggart looked at it a long time. I could see Stevie ahead of us and he was holding his tickets all fanned out like playing cards; next to him Old Steve had a bunch, and Stevie's mother, and Mr. and Mrs. Tincher, and Old Man Gatenby that had brought them into town. They were all the tickets Stevie had bought.

Mr. MacTaggart stepped up to the microphone. "The winner – is number..." He looked down at the ticket again. "Number two thousand, nine hundred and seventeen. Two-nine-one-seven." He waited a minute. "Will the holder of ticket number two-nine-one-seven please come up to the platform."

It was like everybody was holding their breath. A kid cried; a dog barked; somewhere somebody in a parked car leaned on their horn by mistake. I could see Stevie and his dad and his ma and Mr. and Mrs. Tincher and Old Man Gatenby looking over Stevie's tickets.

Then she cut loose – to the south and down near the front – long and shrill and curdly.

"Ha – YAH-HAH-YIPEEEEEEEEEEEEEEE! Hold her, boys! The fife an' drum is out!"

Everybody's head turned and their jaws dropped open.

"When you hear the bugle blow assembly – come a-runnin'!"

Even in the dusk you could tell it was Old Man Sherry dangling across the tracks. I never saw him move so spry – cane and shawl flying, waving his ticket, and then doing a sort of a jig on the platform.

When he spoke over the loudspeaker Mr. MacTaggart's voice sounded kind of numb. "Mr., uh, the winner . . ." He looked down at the ticket Old Man Sherry held out to him. He shook his head and brushed at his face like he had a spider web tickling across it. "I'm afraid, ah, the holder of the winnin' ticket is – Mr. Andrew Sherry. Would . . ."

But Mr. Sherry had grabbed the microphone so it sputtered like a lynx with the heartburn. He cleared his throat into her and she whistled wheezy and hoarse like the Brokenshell going out in the spring.

Right then over behind the platform they lit off the first of the fireworks – the cannon ones. Old Man Sherry leapt three feet, lifted his cane like it was a sabre. "Hold her! Hold her, boys! If they come – they come! She's no use whangin' at 'em till they're in range!"

"Just a minute," Mr. MacTaggart's voice came over the microphone, but Mr. Sherry slashed him back with his cane just as a skyrocket cracked and went railing its fire tail to blossom out against the sky.

"Fire away now, boys! Don't matter if you don't see 'em! Let 'em have it! She's the York and Simcoe Rangers every time!"

The excitement of winning and those fireworks had rammed Old Man Sherry right into one of his bad days, right there in front of the whole town of Crocus.

⤚⧐ ⧐⤙

After they got over the surprise of it, Crocus folks were kind of upset about Mr. Sherry winning. Mrs. Abercrombie said it was a shame. Even if he could make it, she said, he was hardly the one they'd pick to represent Crocus at the coronation. Jake told Ma he'd pick Old Man Sherry a damn sight sooner than Mrs. Abercrombie. Ma said Mrs. Abercrombie was right; even if the old man made it over there, they couldn't tell what would happen to him if he hit one of his bad days. Then Jake said if Mr. and Mrs. Abercrombie were going, then maybe they could look after Old Man Sherry, and Ma said don't be ridiculous.

I wasn't so fussy how the draw turned out. Like I said to Jake, "Stevie feels bad."

"Yeah."

"Over two hundred tickets."

"Can't win every time, Kid."

"Yeah but – with all those tickets, Jake! You'd think he'd – you'd think Elsie would've picked *one* of his."

Jake just sort of shrugged.

"Every bit of his hide money and seven dollars he got off Willis Tincher for his .22."

"Yeah – yeah," said Jake.

"Lot of weasel pelts, Jake."

"Uh-huh." Jake spit. "I guess he just about done the works of 'em."

"Huh?"

"Pelts. I guess Stevie dressed damn near a hundred percent the House of Lords this coronation."

But it was Mayor MacTaggart and Repeat Golightly were the most upset. We hit MacTaggart's store afternoon after the twenty-fourth. Mr. MacTaggart was just on his way out.

"Come with me, Jake. Got a nasty – got a ticklish job to do."

"What's that?" Jake said.

"Headed for Old Man Sherry's."

"Why, sure," Jake said. "Me an' the Kid got nothin' pressin'."

" . . . an' hoping it's one of his good days," Mr. MacTaggart said as he went through the door. "I'm gonna need your help, Jake. You got a way with him."

Old Man Sherry was sitting in his black walnut rocker on the porch. Mr. MacTaggart pitched right in.

"Mr. Sherry, I've come as a – spokesman for – I been sent as a – by the Royal Coronation Draw Committee to . . ."

"Out with her, out with her – tie her off and be done with it!" His eyes were sparkling in that caved and wrinkled old face; his voice was breathy like a husky whisper, but she was strong all the same.

"You won the draw on the coronation trip."

"That's right!"

"We – we didn't plan – it's rather embarrassing. I've been sent to ask if you'd, uh, care to, ah, have the trip put up to the draw again."

"What for!" He was starting to breathe hard so it whistled through his nose.

"So we can – so that somebody else . . ."

"So's you'll have more money fer yer curlin' rink!"

Mr. MacTaggart had his handkerchief out and he was wiping his face. "No, no – it's just that – why, it's obvious to anyone that you're too – that you – at your age, uh, better if – you weren't making a long – hard – tiring trip to the Old Country."

"That's so! That's so! Wouldn't miss her for the world. Not for the world!"

"But," Mr. MacTaggart's voice cracked, "you're nearing a hundred and – you can't . . ."

"Hell I can't!" He had his cane and he was standing now. He faded back and his voice got real tight. "Fenian Raids I helped save – kep' the colony from the U.S. an' the Pope, didn't I!" He lifted the cane so she was sloped over one shoulder. "An' again – fi' dollars a day an' rum an' feed fer my horse – service of the Queen! I won her fair! I won her fair!"

"Hold on," Jake said, gentle. "Set. Set. Take her easy."

Mr. Sherry sank back into his rocker.

"Nobody's tryin' to take her from you. She's yours. It's just that folks were a little worried. You can't go all the way over there – alone."

"Alone! I ain't goin' alone! I'll find somebody go along with me."

"Mrs. Southey," Jake said.

"She ain't – she can't. I ain't askin' charity. I can pay. I'll find somebody."

"You ain't yet?" Jake said.

"Not yet."

"You ain't got much time left."

"I know it. I know it!"

"All right." Jake turned to Mr. MacTaggart. "Mac, I think you an' your committee can forget about him puttin' that ticket up to another draw."

"But, Jake – he . . ."

"Can't see any reason he can't make it – all he needs is somebody to kind of look after him." Jake kept looking down at Mr. Sherry. "An' I got a good notion of the fellow for the job. Just the fellow."

⌁

So there's how Crocus got in all the papers and on the CBC and the English BBC and the world map. Every time you looked you saw pictures of Old Man Sherry and Stevie Kiziw. "Colourful Visitors to the Coronation," it said underneath – and then the one where they were shaking hands with Churchill: "The Oldest and the Youngest From the Farthest Meet Prime Minister."

But it was the day of the coronation while we were listening to our radio that it happened. First there was this announcer talking to people and then he said he had an old man and a boy and then he said their names and they were from Crocus, Saskatchewan, Canada. He asked Old Man Sherry what he

279

thought of being over in England and Mr. Sherry said fine, fine, and then he mumbled a bit and that was bad, because when he mumbles that's a sign he's not having one of his good days, but the announcer didn't know that. He went right on and asked Old Man Sherry for some of his impressions. Mr. Sherry mumbled some more and the announcer asked him would he please speak up and tell the folks back home what he thought about the Queen. That did it.

"The Queen – the Queen." Just a whisper. Then he ripped her out. "The Queen – yes, sir! I fought for her in the Fenian Raids – shouldered a musket for her in sixty-nine an' again in eighty-five. Long live QU-EEEEEN VICK-TOR-IAAAAAAAAAAAAAH!"

It was Jake really tied her all up for me. "Kid," he said later, "you'll hear a lotta different ideas on Old Man Sherry and Stevie goin' over to that coronation, but I figger we did all right."

"What you mean, Jake?"

"We done her deliberate, we couldn't sent over two better fellows." For a minute Jake stared at the Wine-dot picked along by the windmill, her legs going jerky. "Like Mac said, 'Queen, she's a symbol.' We sent our own symbols over there. Old Man Sherry – why, when we sent him over there we sent 'em Confederation. We sent 'em the Riel Rebellion – we sent 'em the history of the Dominion Canada all wrapped up in his old hide."

"Where does Stevie . . . ?"

"Stevie, you might say he was the other end of the stick. Canada's new too, Kid. Pollacks and G'llicians, Euchre-anians, Dook-a-boors, Checks, Mennonites, an' Hooterites – they're the new ones, Kid. With them two we sent the old symbol and the new symbol. The old and the young of it."